Readers love *Friends Like These*

'I couldn't put this book down and read it in one sitting.'
5★ Amazon review

'Full of surprises and very engaging. I loved the writing style. Highly recommended.'
5★ Goodreads review

'This was a brilliantly written book that held my attention throughout and I can't wait to read more from the author.'
5★ Amazon review

'The great character development and the way that the story unfolds feels fresh and exciting.'
5★ NetGalley review

'Absolutely loved every second of it and didn't want it to end.'
5★ Amazon review

'I absolutely love a creepy, crazy, twisted character and *Friends Like These* has two of them. This book was RIGHT up my street.'
5★ Goodreads review

'You can't trust any of the characters in this book. Nothing is as it seems. Just hold on to your hats, and hope to finish it unscathed!'
5★ Amazon review

'WOW! I did NOT see that twist coming. Such a fast paced, very clever, modern psychological thriller!'
5★ Amazon review

'Terrifying and action packed this book kept me on tenterhooks from start to finish.'
5★ NetGalley review

'Excellent book, gripping story. Very well written and fantastic twists and turns.'
5★ Amazon review

'I could not wait to finish – I had to know how it was going to end! I did not see it coming.'
5★ Goodreads review

'Kept me guessing right to the end and even then I was shocked.'
5★ Amazon review

'FABULOUS. Best psychological thriller I've read. And I read a lot. Not often I don't guess the ending.'
5★ Amazon review

'If I was in marketing I would be offering a money back guarantee if you didn't thoroughly enjoy every word!
10/10'
5★ Goodreads review

'A must read for anyone who likes an edge of your seat page turner.'
5★ Amazon review

SARAH ALDERSON

Friends Like These

MULHOLLAND
BOOKS
HODDER

First published in Great Britain in 2018 by Mulholland Books
An imprint of Hodder & Stoughton
An Hachette UK company

This paperback edition first published in 2019

1

Copyright © Sarah Alderson 2018

The right of Sarah Alderson to be identified as the
Author of the Work has been asserted by her in accordance
with the Copyright, Designs and Patents Act 1988.

A CIP catalogue record for this title is available from the British Library

Paperback ISBN 978 1 473 68182 8
eBook ISBN 978 1 473 68183 5

Typeset in Plantin Light by Hewer Text UK Ltd, Edinburgh
Printed and bound in Great Britain by Clays Ltd, Elcograf S.p.A.

Hodder & Stoughton policy is to use papers that are natural, renewable
and recyclable products and made from wood grown in sustainable
forests. The logging and manufacturing processes are expected to
conform to the environmental regulations of the country of origin.

Hodder & Stoughton Ltd
Carmelite House
50 Victoria Embankment
London EC4Y 0DZ

www.hodder.co.uk

For Rachel

Transcript of 999 call

Sunday, 10 December, 11.23 p.m.

Female Caller: She's got a knife. Please hurry.
Operator: The police are on their way. Can you get out of the house?
Female Caller: No.
Operator: Is there somewhere you can hide, somewhere with a door that locks?
Female Caller: I'm in the bathroom . . . Downstairs. Please hurry. I can hear her coming.
Operator: Stay on the line with me.

[0:31:44 – unclear – indistinct crying]

Female Caller: *[whispered]* I think she's outside the door . . . I can hear her. Oh god, please, hurry up.
Operator: The police will be there any minute. Stay on the line with me. Can you tell me what's happening? Who is it that's got the knife?

[0:44:16 – unclear – series of bangs – followed by a crash]

Female Caller: No!
Operator: Hello? Are you there?

[0:53:33 – screams]

Female Caller: No! Get off me . . . She's going to kill me!

[1:05:33 – unclear – sounds of a struggle]

Operator: Hello? Are you there? Hello?
Female Caller: Hello?
Operator: Are you OK? What happened? The police are pulling up outside now.
Female Caller: She's dead. I think she might be dead. Oh god. Oh god . . . please . . . oh my god. She's not moving. There's blood. A lot of blood.
Operator: Is she breathing?
Female Caller: I don't know.

[2:04:16 – whimpering – panting]

Operator: Can you check for a pulse?
Female Caller: I . . . oh god . . . I don't know. Please can you send an ambulance?
Operator: It's on its way. You need to stay calm. Can you do that for me?
Female Caller: Yes. Yes, I think so . . . Oh my god.
Operator: What's your name? Can you give me your name?
Female Caller: She came at me . . . with a knife. She just came out of nowhere. I think she's dead . . . I think I've killed her.

Part One

Partial transcript of police interview with Miss Elizabeth Crawley, subsequent to filing of Missing Persons Report

PC Kandiah – Sunday, 10 December

Have you ever had one of those Facebook friends – more of an acquaintance really, like a colleague or an old school friend – who you accept a friendship request from and then wish to god you bloody hadn't? We all have, right? You don't want to unfriend them just in case they realise, even though they've got like seven hundred friends so the chances are they'd never know. But if you're honest, you're also a little bit intrigued by their life and sometimes, maybe after a couple of glasses of wine, when you're tired of trawling through Netflix to find something to watch, you find yourself randomly Facebook-stalking them. Admit it, you've done it.

Next thing you know, you're falling down a rabbit hole and feeling like a bit of a voyeur. It's funny, isn't it? The whole time you're scouring their feed, you're waiting for someone to tap you on the shoulder and shout *Ha! Caught you!* Even though you haven't done anything wrong. I mean, they wouldn't put it all out there unless they *wanted* you to read it.

You want an example of Becca's social media posts? OK. She was one of those people who hashtagged *every* post with something like #gratitude or #blessed or #yolo. Oh, and also,

#bestboyfriendever. That was her favourite. You know the kind of person I'm talking about. You're smiling. You know someone just like it.

She was forever posting selfies of herself at the gym, you know the kind, complaining about having eaten too many pies and needing to work off the extra pounds, while at the same time showing off her abs. Or posting a thousand photos of herself on holiday in Ibiza – and every shot was taken from a lounger, framing the setting sun through her thigh gap. Or she'd take pictures of herself with a full face of make-up, hair blow-dried, and hashtag it #wokeuplikethis because yeah, sure you did, don't we all? I know I do. *Not.*

Listen, I swear, you can ask anyone, almost every other post was about her boyfriend, James. About how amazing he was, how he'd arranged yet another romantic getaway to New York or the Cotswolds or Paris, how he was hashtag best boyfriend ever. Or she'd take a picture of him asleep, head under the pillows, stick a black and white filter on it and tag it #hotboyfriend and #luckiestgirlalive.

I guess, for want of another word, it came across as smug. I can see you laughing. You totally get it. And let's face it, there's something kind of suspicious about someone who's always posting gushing updates about their other half. Think about it. All those celebrities who make huge public declarations of love, they all end up divorcing three weeks later.

A couple of people at work unfriended her, or at least unfollowed her because they found her so annoying. Not me though.

Were we jealous of her? No. *Honestly.* I can tell you don't believe me but it's true. I mean she was pretty, yes, sure, but we weren't jealous. I think some people were a bit put out that she'd got the job of assistant to the CEO. There were others who'd been there longer and who thought they deserved it more, but that's just how this industry is. And, besides, I work in the finance department, so it didn't bother me in the same way as it did those who were trying to make the jump from assistants to agents.

If you met her by the water cooler and tried to make polite conversation, she'd just look at you like you were a lesser being and then walk off, like you weren't worthy of her time or something. She was only really friendly to people she thought could help her get where she wanted to be. Where was that? At the top of the ladder, of course. She was . . . ambitious. And don't get me wrong, there's nothing bad about that. I'm all for women climbing the ladder and shattering the glass ceiling. It's past time, isn't it? What's that quote? *There's a special place in hell for women who don't support other women?* Something like that. Well, I agree. And the rest of us women in the office, we stuck together, we had each other's backs – you have to in this industry – you have no idea . . . but Becca, she definitely didn't get the memo on that one.

God, I sound like a bitch. And I'm not. I really am not. I hate talking ill of people. Especially people who are . . . Look, I don't want to make it sound like I hated her. I didn't hate her. I didn't *know* her. I *don't* know her. That's my point.

Oh wait, I remembered something else. For Claire's birthday a few years ago Flora made her a chocolate cake. She put it in the fridge at work. Well, when the time came to bring it out someone had helped themselves to a massive slice. I mean, these things happen at work all the time. People are always nicking bread or helping themselves to your cream cheese, even if you stick a Post-it note on it. I know some people who spit in their food and warn people that that's what they've done to ward them off. Like holy water with vampires.

But this . . . this felt deliberate. Whoever it was hadn't used a knife and cut a slice of cake. They'd gouged it with what looked like their hands. A huge chunk of cake. It was completely ruined. Who does that? We had no idea. But as I'm comforting Flora in the kitchen, in walks Becca with a plate covered in chocolate crumbs. She saw us, froze, and then she just smiled and stuck her plate in the sink. We knew. She knew we knew. But what are you going to do? Of course, we didn't confront her about it. She would only have denied it.

It was things like that. She lied a lot too. God, I feel awful, and I don't even know if this is helpful in any way. Is it? Shouldn't you be out there, looking for her or something? How is this helping find her? You want a picture of her, I get that, but I'm not the best person. I haven't seen her in years. And I never really knew her to begin with. That's my point. I keep telling you. No one knew her. Not the *real* her.

How did she lie? OK. Here's an example: she'd always name-drop famous people she knew. Or that she *said* she knew. She told people she once dated Prince Harry after meeting him at Boujis, that nightclub in Kensington. Oh, and that her father invented LED lights. Ridiculous things. Unbelievable things. I mean . . . come on, if you're going to lie, at least make the lies believable. It's almost like she was playing a game, like she wanted us to call her out on it. But no one ever did.

Even some of the guys found her too much. A little too . . . into herself, I guess you could say. She was always really well dressed, that's another thing. She had great taste but she'd wear clothes to the office that were more suitable for a night out. Always really high heels too. Manolo Blahniks and Louboutin. We used to wonder how she got the money because she wasn't earning much more than us and we were all pretty broke. We were shopping at ASOS and she was turning up to work in Stella McCartney and Chloé. She told people her family were dead

– her parents and her siblings had all burned to death in a fire
– god knows if that's even true – and that she'd inherited a lot of
money. An LED light fortune.

But now we know the truth. Everything she told us about
herself was a lie.

So if you ask me why I think she's gone missing, I'd have to
tell you that I don't know.

I'm just giving you some background about who she was. *Is.*

Tuesday, 5 December
Evening

'Night, Lizzie,' Flora shouts.

I wave with the tips of my fingers. My hands are full with my jacket, scarf, bag, phone and five coffee cups containing dregs that I don't want to spill down my tights. I wrangle the cups into the dishwasher, noting that as usual I'm the only person in this office who seems to know what a dishwasher is, and give a cursory glance at the contents of the refrigerator, checking I don't need to buy more almond milk. Damn it. Someone has been at it! It was brand new this morning, unopened, and someone's gone and helped themselves. The nerve of it.

Tim from IT has written his name in black Sharpie all over his stash of Vitaminwater. Maybe I should do the same. Not that it seems to make any difference. The thieving in this building is out of control. Maybe we need to put a nanny cam in the fridge, hidden inside that jar of gherkins that's been lurking there since 2016.

I walk out past the breakout areas, double-checking that no one has left any confidential documents lying around on any of the coffee tables. We wouldn't want the cleaners getting hold of a contract deal for a big name actor and leaking it to the *Daily Mail*, though sometimes when I've seen how much more a male actor is getting than his female co-star I have been tempted to leak the news myself.

Once, someone from HR left out an internal report on one of the board members, who had been accused of sexual harassment by a junior agent. It didn't end well for the HR assistant, or the junior agent for that matter. The board member is still a board member. No surprise there.

It's not my job to check for confidential papers that have been left lying about, just like it's not my job to clear all the used coffee cups from the finance department's desks, but like my mum taught me, you can waste energy on being angry or you can use that energy to get on with life.

And there's a manuscript on the printer. Someone must have forgotten about it. I take a quick peep at the title page, recognising the name as a new writer the head of the agency just signed. I flick through it, interested to see how good she is after all the hoo-ha over signing her. She's only twenty-two. How good can she possibly be? Word is that they think her book will net a seven-figure fee from the publishing and film rights. Can you even imagine what you would do with that much money?

I'd buy a house on Hampstead Heath, one of those classic Georgian mansions with a carriage driveway – just like the ones you see in all the Jane Austen movies. I'd have a writing room with a view over the heath, a sauna and gym in the basement, marble countertops and a breakfast room with French doors leading out onto a lawn that's flat enough for croquet and Pimm's in the summer. That's my dream. Oh, and a walk-in wardrobe and a bathroom with one of those stand-alone tubs. And a personal trainer and chef.

To think that a two-inch-thick pile of paper like the one I'm holding in my hand could be the key to getting all that.

It's miraculous. Magical. Like winning the lottery. I weigh the manuscript in my hand, then, glancing around to make sure no one sees, slip it into my bag for safe-keeping. I'll return it tomorrow.

'You off out?'

I almost jump out of my skin. It's Flora. She's snuck up behind me like a ninja, which is quite surprising as Flora is the very opposite of a ninja. She's a size 18 and has flat feet that necessitate wearing white Scholl shoes that, as she likes to joke, make her look like a nurse on a psychiatric ward. She's my best friend at work, though recently I've been feeling like she's avoiding me. I think she might be annoyed that I don't go out for lunch with her any more.

I shake my head and pull on my coat. 'No, just going home, why?'

Flora shrugs. 'You just look nice, that's all. Like you're going on a date or something.'

'Not tonight,' I tell her, feeling pleased with the compliment. 'What about you? You're working late.'

Flora nods. 'Yeah, we're putting the finishing touches to the pitch for that new manuscript. We're sending it out tomorrow.'

She's talking about the manuscript I've just slipped in my bag. 'I heard,' I tell her. 'Seven figures, huh?'

Flora lights up. 'Yes, isn't it amazing? We've already had interest from all the major studios. It could end up being the biggest deal we've ever done. And she's only twenty-two!'

I force a smile.

Flora glances over my shoulder and her face puckers into a frown. 'Oh,' she says. 'You didn't see anything on the printer, did you?'

I shake my head.

Flora walks past me and stops in front of the printer, confounded.

'Maybe it's out of paper,' I suggest, the whole time feeling the weight of the manuscript like a lead brick in my bag. I can't take it out, though. What would I say? *Oh, look, how strange, it must have fallen in my bag by accident.* I'll have to feign innocence.

'I just put paper in,' Flora says, pulling out the drawer, which is almost empty. 'How weird,' she mumbles.

'I'd better go,' I say. 'Chris will be waiting.'

'OK,' says Flora, still distracted by the vanishing manuscript. 'Give him a hug and kiss from me.'

'Will do.'

I hurry to the lift but then decide to take the stairs instead. I always take the stairs when the office is mostly empty. There's something about the sound of a heel clicking on marble and the curving sweep of the banister that makes me feel like a Hollywood ingénue making her entrance at an Oscars after-party.

'Evening, Miss Crowley,' says Frank, the security guy who looks like Father Christmas, as I make my way down the stairs.

'Evening, Frank,' I say. Usually I stop for a quick chat but not tonight; I'm running late for my train.

I walk past the enormous statue that resembles a giant squid cast in bronze (or a giant's sperm, as Flora likes to joke) and past the silver PKW lettering stamped boldly on the wall, which I always think makes us sound like a management consultancy. In fact it stands for Pryor Kinnison Weng – now officially the largest entertainment talent company in the world. We're only the London office – the satellite office – but we like to think we do the work of substance while the Hollywood office does vacuous 'style'.

After the merger, the powers that be decided to ditch the London office on Euston Road with its austere post-war vibe (which I always quite liked despite the Stasi feel) and move to a building more in keeping with their aspirations. Their goal was to attract and represent only the cream of the crop: the A-listers, the Oscar and Pulitzer and Bafta winners, the ones making the lists of 'Bright young things under 30', and it's fair to say that they've achieved it.

I stick my hat and scarf on as I head towards the revolving door, thinking as I always do of how the paramedics got stuck in here that time. They had too much equipment on them and something got jammed. All those extra seconds on the clock. Did they make a difference? Who knows?

A blast of cold air hits me as I'm tipped out onto the street and I pull my coat tighter and wrap my scarf around my neck in a chic French way I learned from a YouTube tutorial. I check my phone. I've got eighteen minutes to make my train. In these heels it will be almost impossible. I weigh up whether to get an Uber home but I can't really afford it – especially with Christmas around the corner and presents still to buy – so instead I hurry as fast as I can, weaving among the tourists and late-night shoppers on Carnaby Street.

The crowd around the top of the stairs at Oxford Circus resembles a lava flow trying to force its way back inside a volcano and the heat of all those bodies after the brisk night air makes me break into an instant and itchy sweat. I love London – I love the humming, brilliant buzz of it, especially in winter when the pavements sparkle and every shop and bar you pass seems to beckon you inside with a tantalising glow – but I hate commuting, that unsettling feeling of being part of the herd; one that's galloping mindlessly towards a cliff edge.

There's a tube waiting on the platform, thankfully, the doors beeping. I throw myself inside, finding myself wedged into someone's armpit and someone else's briefcase jabbing my hip.

Two stops. Four minutes. I'll have to barge my way off the tube and run up the escalator if I've any hope of making my train. Not for the first time I regret wearing heels to work, but if they gave gold medals for weaving through rush-hour crowds, I would win one. A year ago I could never have made it – wouldn't even have bothered. I'd have dawdled my way up the escalator staring at poster after poster advertising *The Lion King* and then stopped at McDonald's for a Big Mac and fries while I waited for the next train.

Now I'm like an Olympic sprinter. I make it with seconds to spare and annoyingly all the seats are taken. I'm left standing, feet killing me from having run in heels and, to make it worse, I'm squashed between several men in suits who are managing to man-spread even while standing.

I content myself for the eleven-minute train ride by checking what's happening in the land of Facebook and Twitter and Instagram, and then, because I can't help myself, when I'm sure that the people around me are all transported to their own social media lands and wouldn't notice if someone came running through the carriage naked, I open Tinder.

Eight matches! Things are definitely on the up since I changed my profile pictures and redid my bio. I message a few of them, the ones who sound like they might actually be interested in dating and not just casual sex or threesomes – and then I start flicking through profile pictures because dating is a game and you have to be in it to win it, or at least that's what the article said in last week's *Grazia*.

I swipe left on a 'bacon enthusiast and heavy metal fan' and then on a guy who claims he's 'six foot five and those are two measurements' and keep swiping past several oiled torsos, sighing at the slim pickings. I can feel my dopamine buzz start to die off with the knowledge that finding a partner on Tinder is about as likely as finding life on the surface of the sun. But then I land on someone who makes me instantly pause, my finger hovering above his face.

It's James.

It really is him. James Wickenden. #bestboyfriendever.

Oh my god. My heart has started beating very loudly and very fast, as though I've taken speed, and I have to tug at my scarf to loosen it before it strangles me.

Why is he on Tinder? Is he single? I don't know why, but all this time I imagined him and Becca still together, possibly even married by now. It comes as a shock to learn otherwise. It's possible, I tell myself, that he is still with her. Maybe he's like several of the men I've already met on Tinder who are married and looking for some side action. I desperately hope not.

There are more photos – all linked to his Facebook account. There's one of him in boardshorts on a beach somewhere tropical, definitely not Bournemouth, that's for sure. He's tanned and gorgeous with a six-pack he must have spent a lot of time cultivating. In another one he's wearing a morning suit with a buttonhole, standing in front of the entrance to a church. His arm is around someone but he's cut them out of the shot. I wonder if it was an ex, or even Becca. He isn't wearing a wedding ring in any of the pictures.

I wonder why he and Becca broke up. There was the accident, of course. That was three years ago now.

There were all sorts of rumours but we never heard for sure what happened to Becca after she left the hospital. She took the pay-out from work and disappeared. All her social media accounts went dark. I know this because occasionally I look her up on Facebook but there's never anything new except for a couple of birthday messages from friends that she never likes or comments on.

I read James's Tinder profile again: 'Entertainment Lawyer. Good at both. And I'm nice to my mum as well.'

He's going for short but sweet with a dash of humour. Throwing in the mum line tells me he's good at turning on the charm. Not that he needs to turn on the charm with profile pictures like that and the word *lawyer*. You could be a zero in the looks department and it wouldn't matter so long as you wrote lawyer in your profile. If you're a man, that is. The same rule does not apply for women. I wonder how many girls he likes the look of and swipes right on. And how many swipe right on him. Every single one, I imagine.

I go back and look at his photos again, zooming in on them. His eyes are so blue they remind me of the colour of Brockwell Lido, and there's that dimple in his left cheek. He really is a ten. I remember the trips he used to take Becca on, to Paris and Ibiza. How she used to go on and on about how romantic he was, how he was hashtag the perfect man.

What on earth am I waiting for? I swipe right. My stomach knots in instant anticipation. Will he swipe right on me too? Is it too much to hope for? Will he recognise me? I doubt it. We only met briefly three years ago, and I've changed quite a bit since then.

Shit. I look up and see we're at my stop. The train doors are already closing. By the time I've gathered up my things it's too late. The train is moving. Damn. Now I have to get off at Peckham Rye and walk back to Denmark Hill or stand around on a cold, dark platform waiting for a train heading in the opposite direction.

I call an Uber instead. To hell with the money. There's a buzz in my belly, a tight jangling of nerves like someone repeatedly strumming the same wrong chords on a guitar. I tell myself not to get too excited. He might not respond and then I'll only be disappointed.

The lights are on at the house but I know no one is home except for Chris. I leave the lights on a timer for security purposes, and to make the place look more inviting. That lovely warm yellow glow. I look up at the three-storey brick facade and count my lucky stars for Tess and her parents. I'd never be able to afford a house otherwise, not to rent and definitely not to own. I looked it up online and it's worth close to two million pounds. It's a five-bedroom end-of-terrace Victorian; red brick with a high hedge at the front offering some privacy, and a lovely red door with stained-glass panels and a brass knocker. Sometimes when I walk through the gate and up the front path, I feel like an orphan in a Dickens novel about to knock on the door of the person who'll become my benevolent saviour.

The only downside is that it's in Denmark Hill, which is in Camberwell, not the most salubrious of boroughs, and there's a council estate diagonally opposite.

Chris lunges at me as soon as I'm through the door. He's angry that I've been gone so long and he butts his head against my shins to let me know. I reach down and pick him up.

'Silly cat,' I say and carry him into the kitchen, where he flies out of my arms and lands on the table, back arched, a face on him like one of those glowering boys that hangs about on the estate selling drugs, hood pulled up, hands stuffed in oversized tracksuit bottoms, wearing Nikes the size of small boats.

'OK, OK, I'm feeding you,' I tell him, reaching for a foil packet of overpriced meat in gelatinous gunk. 'What's it to be today, Chris Hemsworth? Salmon or chicken?'

He meows impatiently.

'OK, chicken it is.' I pour it into his bowl, holding my nose. He's Tess's cat, not mine. She has a thing for the actor. We roll along together OK, Chris and I, though I'm more of a dog person, to be honest. I feed him and empty his litter tray and he makes clear his ire that I'm not Tess. I won't let him sleep on my bed because he leaves behind half his fur. But looking after him was the price I paid for having the place all to myself while Tess went travelling. It's a shame, I joked to her, that he isn't the real Chris Hemsworth. I would definitely let him sleep on the bed if he were.

Tess's parents, who raised their kids here, retired a few years ago and moved to Portugal, but they kept the house and let Tess and me live here, paying very low rent. I wouldn't be able to afford a lock-up on the estate over the road for what I pay each month. And now she's away, travelling for six months, I have the whole house to myself.

I open the fridge and hang onto the door. I'm too tired to cook and besides, I grabbed lunch from Pret after I went to the gym on my lunch break And, OK, I also snuck a Hobnob this afternoon, which was naughty of me. I still count points even if I don't go to Weight Watchers meetings. It's become a habit.

There's smoked mackerel, some spinach and a pot of fat-free yogurt in the fridge. I sigh and let my gaze drift to the bottle of Sauvignon in the door and then to the box of pink champagne truffles that a client at work gave me a few months ago. I had been saving both as a reward for finishing the first ten thousand words of my book but what the hell. I'll take a bath, drink a glass of wine, and read that manuscript. It'll help distract me from checking Tinder every five seconds to see if James has responded.

My bedroom is Tess's brother's old room. It faces the garden and is a good size, I guess, though I'd much rather have Tess's room in the attic, which is about three times as big. The carpets in my room could use replacing but I've done my best to make it as nice as possible – the bed frame is antique, and I've got a thing for decorative pillows. I can't seem to stop buying them. Tess used to joke that the pillows were multiplying like bunny rabbits. This room is my sanctuary. I even created a vision board of what I wanted the room to look like before I started decorating, cutting out pictures from magazines and pasting them on a big pin board, which now hangs over the mantelpiece and is covered in pictures of turreted chateaux, luxury yachts and Georgian mansions. I'm a big believer in the law of attraction and you have to visualise what you want in order to achieve it. For now, though, I'm grateful for what I do have. The room is light and airy, with lots of pale hues; white and muted greys with splashes of colour. The curtains are a dusky pink and match the chair I had re-upholstered and the mountain of throw cushions on the bed.

My writing desk, which I salvaged from an antiques shop in East Dulwich, sits in front of the window, giving me a view of the house that backs onto ours. I spent way more money on it than I should have, because I thought it would inspire me to write my novel, but in fact all I use it for is book-keeping – a little side-business I have going to supplement my income.

The novel I started is languishing somewhere on my computer and now every time I look at the desk I feel a pang of guilt or a needling of my conscience, which then gives way to resentment. It's like when you keep getting a reminder on your phone to call your mother but after a few reminders you start getting annoyed at the phone and then at your mother, when really you should just pick it up and call. Maybe a new desk would help me feel less animosity towards the novel. Or maybe I should start a new novel. I need to decide and then just get on with it. It's not going to write itself.

Next to my room is a bathroom and on the other side of that there's a smaller bedroom which used to be a study before Tess's boyfriend Rob turned it into a recording suite. This was a few months before they broke up, before he did the unforgivable thing, and before Tess decided to go travelling.

There are still plenty of things around that give the house a family feel: photographs on top of the piano, old coats hanging on hooks by the front door, orphaned shoes and broken tennis rackets under the stairs, a shelf of grease-thumbed recipe books in the kitchen. There are a few random things scattered around too: a bullwhip, a hockey mask and a large statue of an owl – props that Tess brings home from the theatre as keepsakes after one of her plays finishes a run. It gives the place a slightly Bohemian, artsy feel that I like.

It sometimes makes me envious, to think that Tess got to grow up here – with two squabbling siblings and parents who cared and had so much money they sent all three to private school, then paid their way through university too. If my mother had had the money to pay for private school or university, she would have spent it on fags, booze and bingo.

I grew up an only child, in a two-up two-down in Hexthorpe, a grotty village close to Doncaster, famous for three things: a big railway accident the year I was born, an almost-riot over the number of asylum seekers being sent there (my mum was among those who wanted to riot. I tried to explain to her that they had nowhere else to go but she refused to listen, saying that *if London wanted them, London could keep 'em*). And third, having the highest level of sexually transmitted diseases in the country.

I'm not sure that last one is still true, but it was when I was a teenager. All I wanted to do, from the age of about seven (when I became aware from watching TV and movies that there was another world out there – one where the skies were actually blue, not what felt like a permanent grey the colour of wet ash), was escape. I bet those asylum seekers the government sent there felt the same way I did: unwelcome, hopeless, sick to death of the boarded-up windows, the garbage-strewn streets and the utter foulness of the weather. Most of them were probably wishing they'd never left home, because even a war zone would probably be better than Hexthorpe.

Every day now, when I walk to the station, on my way to work, I feel so happy I made it out. I'm thirty and I've only been back a few times since I left at eighteen. My mum still works double shifts at the local juvenile rehab facility. We don't have much to talk about, my mum and I. She tells me about the kids who've tried to commit suicide or smeared faeces over the walls that week, and I tell her which famous faces have walked through the doors at work, but unless they've been on *Corrie*, her favourite soap, she's not interested. She still hasn't forgiven me for moving to London. She tells me that I sound like a southern toff with a stick up my arse now.

I go into the bathroom that's en suite to Tess's parents' bedroom. It's nicer – they did it up only a few years back and it has a gorgeous claw-footed tub and a rain shower big enough for a Tinder threesome, if you were ever that way inclined. I start the bath running and light a few candles before going back to my room for my glass of wine and the manuscript. The wine is a lot of calories but I ran for the train so that cancels it out. And you shouldn't deny yourself. Denial only makes you unhappy and unhappiness makes you binge.

I slip beneath the hot water then reach for my wine and the manuscript. Three pages in, I've finished my glass and I'm fully distracted. One, the writing isn't that good, and two, the story is so derivative. If this had been written by a fat and unattractive fifty-year-old man, no one would be talking about it at all. But because the author is twenty-two, female and attractive, they've been able to PR it to the heavens and create a million dollars of hype.

Frustrated, I drop the pages to the floor and lie back until I'm almost fully submerged beneath the water. Here, in my watery cocoon, my thoughts drift away from the manuscript and to much happier thoughts of James.

The one and only time I met him was three years ago. It was the night of the PKW Christmas party.

The night of the accident.

*   *   *

'Oh my god,' whispers Flora, grabbing my arm. 'Check him out.'

I turn around, glass in hand, and get almost knocked over by a wave of vertigo. He's that gorgeous. Even better in the flesh than in the photographs Becca is forever posting all over her Instagram and Facebook.

Flora is eying him up like a piece of chocolate cake slathered in buttercream icing, practically salivating, and I tease her. She blushes the colour of her dress, a Pepto-Bismol pink, and sighs dramatically. 'Imagine going home with that. It's so unfair.'

I shrug. 'In my experience, men who look that good are normally arrogant arseholes.'

Flora still can't tear her eyes off him. 'I could forgive him that. I could forgive him anything. He looks like Christian Grey. And anyway, from the sounds of it, he's lovely.'

I wonder about that. He's scanning the crowd – all of us gathered in the outdoor courtyard, protected from the winter weather by a glass roof and a dozen space heaters firing like rocket blasters. His expression is aloof – slightly disdainful even. His top lip is slightly curled as though he's here against his will, suffering through his girlfriend's work do just so she'll sleep with him later. I'm right. He's arrogant. But then he suddenly smiles and instantly his face transforms and I'm forced to reassess.

'Oh my god, look at him!' Flora gushes again, collapsing against me in a swoon worthy of a Mills & Boon damsel.

It's true that, in his black dinner jacket, he is easily the most attractive man in the room. Everyone is looking at him, some openly, a lot surreptitiously. And Becca, as if sensing it, has come over and hung herself off him like one of those plastic baubles decorating the Christmas tree in the lobby.

'She looks amazing too,' says Flora, and the two of us involuntarily suck in our stomachs as we take in Becca and her skin-tight, knicker-skimming green dress. 'That dress would be a crop top on me. If I could even get it on over my head,' says Flora with a giggle. 'Actually it would probably be more like a headband.'

I laugh. 'You look great,' I tell her.

Flora beams at me and tugs her dress down to expose even more of her ample bosom. 'Thanks. You too,' she tells me.

I smile but shift uncomfortably from foot to foot and swallow as if I've got one of the sausage roll canapés I just ate stuck in my throat. I don't feel great. I feel frumpy. I bought a dress a size smaller hoping it would inspire me to lose those extra few pounds before Christmas, but people kept bringing tins of Quality Street and M&S mince pies into work and so now it's way too tight around my stomach and hips. I'm not sure the style is very me either. It's blue and the material is a bit cheap and shiny and is making me sweat. A dress from the Primark sale rack was all I could afford, though.

I doubt Becca is wearing Primark. Her dress looks like it cost a month's salary, despite the fact there's nothing of it. And her shoes look like they've just walked straight off the catwalk too. She's had her hair cut in one of those long wavy bobs and it frames her face perfectly. I watch her hand James a glass of champagne then put her arm proprietarily through his. He places his hand over hers and it's a gesture so tender and protective that it makes my chest ache and my gut feel as if someone is wringing it out like an old, grey dishcloth. Without knowing why, I find myself blinking back tears.

I turn away. 'Just going to the bathroom,' I mumble to Flora.

'OK,' she says, her gaze still fixed dreamily on Becca and James.

In the ladies on the first floor, where I've escaped in order to avoid the other party-goers, I stare angrily at my reflection in the mirror, swiping at the tears that are threatening to ruin my mascara. I'm being silly and I try to tell myself that, but I have been so looking forward to this evening. I wanted to wear this dress and feel good in it. Sexy even. I wanted, for just one evening, to feel better about myself. I'm an idiot.

I take a deep breath and dab at my eyes. My face has gone all shiny and my hair is starting to frizz and stick up like I've stuck my finger in a plug socket. There are sweat patches under my arms too, staining the polyester fabric. Damn. I stick some tissue in my armpits to soak it up and then dab some powder on to mattify the shine.

Donna, one of the vice presidents, fifty and confidently glamorous as only a woman who has regular Botox and a designer wardrobe can be, comes out of the toilet stall behind me. She sees me and gives me a wide berth. I'm not on her radar, working in finance as I do. She has to lean across me to access the soap holder – which isn't screwed properly to the wall and comes dangerously unhinged when she presses it.

'We've only just moved in and everything is falling apart,' she says with a sigh.

I nod, feeling flustered. 'It's beautiful though,' I say, gesturing stupidly at the bathroom walls. 'The um, renovations. It looks lovely. And the party's great.' I curse myself for being such a suck-up and sounding so vapid. At the same time I'm painfully aware of the paper towels stuffed in my sweaty armpits. Has she noticed them?

But of course, she won't have. I'm pretty much invisible to her. She mumbles an answer but is already heading for the door.

After she's gone I'm left once more staring at myself in the mirror, yanking out the damp paper towels and feeling another wave of anger and self-loathing rising up inside me. I wish I could be like Flora, who seems to look in the mirror and love what she sees, but I'm not. Whenever I stare in the mirror all I hear is my mum telling me with a sneer that no one will ever want me.

I just want to lock myself in a toilet cubicle and stay there. Stupid office party. Why did I think it would be fun? Maybe because it's about the only invite on my calendar so I put all my hopes onto it.

'No,' I tell myself. 'Don't let the negative thoughts bring you down. Focus on the good. You have great skin. Flawless, in fact. That's what the lady at the MAC counter told you. You've got pretty eyes and long eyelashes. You've got fantastic tits. You've got a great arse too, apparently, if the boys on the estate opposite meant it as a compliment when they started making grinding noises and talking about tapping it when you walked past them.'

The pep talk is something I've tried to get into the habit of, after reading about it on some psychology website. Something about diverting the neural pathways and setting up more positive feedback loops in the brain.

'You are funny and smart,' I tell myself. 'You are going to go out there and you are going to enjoy this party. You never know, you might even meet someone.'

But never anyone like James. The thought comes before I can stop it. He's so far out of my league. There is Tim in IT, I remind myself. He's not terrible looking. In fact, he's quite attractive, if a little geeky in his *Game of Thrones* T-shirts. He likes chatting to me and he told Flora that he liked me. And, if I'm brutally honest, what other options are on the table? I'm not going back on Tinder. Or any of those other dating apps. Not after what happened last time.

My eyes start smarting again and I shake my head, refusing to let things get to me. 'You are going to lose weight. That's a New Year's resolution,' I say to my reflection. 'This time next year you are going to fit into a green designer dress the size of a hankie and you're going to have a man on your arm as gorgeous as James.'

I fix my lipstick, take a deep breath, and walk outside. I walk past the breakout area, taking note of the brand-new leather sofas and the fancy art on the walls, and head for the elevators. Passing by one of the agents' offices I hear raised voices. I slow down and stop just shy of the door. I'm being nosy, but shoot me. I peer through the crack. It's James and Becca.

'Where are you going?' he shouts at her. 'You can't go.' She's walking away but he grabs her by the arm. He lowers his voice and hisses something I can't make out.

'People will be wondering where I am,' Becca tells him. She pulls her arm from his and turns on her heel.

I decide I need to make my escape while I have the chance and tiptoe towards the elevator.

Back at the party I find Flora over by the canapés. 'Where have you been?' she asks me.

'I needed the loo,' I tell her, hoping my eyes don't look too red-rimmed.

'You sure you're OK?' she asks, narrowing her eyes.

'Yeah, of course,' I tell her, faking a smile. 'I'm fine, why wouldn't I be?'

'You know you look great,' she says, squeezing my arm. Then she grins and nods across the room. 'Tim's over there, he keeps looking at you.'

I glance over her shoulder and see Tim standing in front of the DJ booth, his head bouncing like one of those nodding dogs you see on car dashboards. He isn't looking this way at all.

'Well, he was,' says Flora. 'Here, have a mince pie.' She hands me one and stuffs a second one in her mouth. 'They're so good,' she says through a mouth of crumbs, giggling.

I shake my head. 'No thanks,' I say, but I'm cut off by a bloodcurdling scream for help. It's so loud it cuts through Wham!'s 'Last Christmas' like a knife through butter. Everyone looks around, startled, trying to find the source.

Then someone – a woman – comes running, bursting into the courtyard, horror scored across her face. 'Quick . . . quick . . . someone call an ambulance!' she yells, before turning around and running back the way she came.

Flora and I look at each other and then rush after her, along with a dozen or so others.

By the time we reach the lobby there's a small crowd gathered and we have to elbow our way through to see what's going on. The first thing I notice is a splash of green. And then red. It looks almost festive against the white tile background. It takes a beat to reconcile that it's Becca, in her green dress, lying on the marble lobby floor, her leg twisted at a weird angle. Someone else screams. Another person starts shouting for a doctor, as though they've forgotten we work at an entertainment agency, not a hospital.

James appears a moment later, pushing through the crowd, elbowing Flora and me aside in his haste. He kneels in the puddle of blood that's pooling in a halo around Becca's head, takes her gently by the shoulders and starts calling her name.

It takes me another few seconds to realise that the red mess I'm staring at is the right side of Becca's face. It's mushy, like the inside of an overripe watermelon.

She doesn't respond.

James looks up and with a jolt, I realise he's staring straight at me.

'Call an ambulance!' he yells.

Partial transcript of police interview with Miss Elizabeth Crawley, subsequent to filing of Missing Persons Report

PC Kandiah – Sunday, 10 December

I always imagined it was like an egg. I can't crack one against the rim of a glass bowl now without wincing. You think skulls are fairly tough but Becca's skull broke like a soft-boiled egg smacked a dozen times with the back of a teaspoon. At least, that's what I heard the doctors said.

I've never been able to get that image out of my mind. There were so many fragments of bone that the paramedics were worried about moving her in case one of them punctured her brain. It took them at least half an hour to load her onto the stretcher. That was after they got stuck in the door and had to be freed. It was all seconds on the clock.

If I had to guess, I'd say there were, I don't know . . . probably two hundred people at the party. It was a big event. We'd just moved offices, you see. It was right after the merger and they'd bought this big townhouse on Great Marlborough Street and spent all this money doing it up. Millions. And they wanted to show it off to the press and to potential clients.

Most of the people at the party worked at PKW. Some had brought partners, husbands and wives, but not everyone. Becca brought James. And there were a few journalists and PR people.

Some clients too. The ones who'd turn up to the opening of an envelope.

The thing that really sticks in my head is that Christmas music was playing. I can't hear that song . . . oh, what is it? You know . . . 'Wonderful Christmastime' by Paul McCartney . . . without thinking about Becca. Lying there.

Lots of people started crying. Most of us were wondering what the hell had happened. No one seemed to know. We assumed she had fallen down the stairs because she was lying right at the bottom of them. And there was no other obvious explanation.

I remember my friend Flora pointing out Becca's shoes. They were so ridiculously high. Maroon strappy things. I didn't know how she could walk in them. And someone else pointed out that the floor wasn't properly laid in places. It was marble. And the banister at the top of the stairs was wobbly. I remember that myself. But all of this is documented. You can read the accident report. They had to do an investigation to decide who was to blame.

Basically, it was a mess. The powers that be at PKW had authorised the move to the new office even though the renovations weren't complete. I think it was because the lease was up on the old office and the contractors had run over time. Obviously the architects and the construction people weren't happy about it and warned them but they didn't listen, which opened them up to another lawsuit.

The judge decided that PKW were liable and they ended up settling out of court. They tried to appeal, of course. They argued that Becca was drunk and wearing five-inch heels and therefore she was asking for it (which, hello, victim shaming!) and they lost, which I was quite glad about.

Rumour had it that they paid out two million pounds in

compensation, but, like I said, I work in the finance department and see the accounts, so I know the real figure was actually five million.

That sounds like a lot of money, I know, but not when you factor in that Becca needed round-the-clock care and would likely never work again. And ask yourself if you would have traded places with her. You wouldn't. Not if you'd seen her lying there. If you'd seen the blood. There was so much of it. I had no idea there was that much blood inside a person.

Sorry, where was I? What happened to her after that? This is where it goes a bit fuzzy.

What we heard from HR was that the doctors wouldn't know if she had brain damage until she woke up. She was in a coma for ages. Weeks. Maybe it was even a couple of months. They thought at least some of her language and logic functions would be affected because the damage was to the right side of her brain. I remember that it was that side because Flora joked that if the right side of her brain was damaged, no one would likely tell the difference and it's true – Flora, bless her, she can't add two pound coins.

Someone asked a Sophie's Choice question one day: if you fell down the stairs, which side of the brain would you rather suffer damage to? Would you rather lose your logic abilities or your creativity and imagination? That's a no-brainer, surely. Sorry. Bad joke.

I guess you would probably choose logic – doing the job you do.

Anyway – she did wake up and then we heard she was in rehab. No one was quite clear on how bad her injuries were. She didn't have any visitors. She refused them. There were all these conflicting reports about how she was. Tim from IT swore blind she was a vegetable (his words, not mine) and someone said she'd been scarred for life, that her face was totally disfigured, and I can believe it because it did look like someone had taken a hammer to one side of her face.

Someone else, though – a girl who worked as an assistant to one of the agents – said she'd seen Becca out and about shopping on Oxford Street. This must have been a year after the accident. But no one believed her, and no one could verify it because after she left the hospital, she disappeared. Vanished off the face of the earth.

Her Facebook and all her social media weren't updated. Even after she was out of the coma she never posted anything. And no one ever heard from her again.

You know, I don't know what else I can tell you. I've told you everything I can. She was a liar. And she didn't have any friends. And she had an accident – the kind of accident you wouldn't wish on your own worst enemy – and what I heard is that it left her slightly unhinged. I don't mean just depression because anyone would be depressed if that happened to them, I imagine. I mean, more like, *crazy*. Obviously there's *something* not right about her. Brain injuries can lead to all sorts of weird behaviour. You should look into it. Speak to her doctors. People who knew her.

Look, I think you should be out there doing something. Looking for her. Before it's too late. Or maybe it's already too late.

I don't know.

Tuesday, 5 December
Evening

The bath is cold when I startle awake. I must have nodded off. The candle, sitting by my empty wine glass, is guttering angrily. I reach for my phone. God, it's almost eleven. I've been in the bath for two whole hours. No wonder the water is colder than the Lido in mid-winter. I'm shivering as I get out and wrap a bath towel around me, and I'm still shivering as I make a mad dash across the hallway and into my room.

It's only when I'm in my PJs and under the covers that I remember to check Tinder. There's a part of me that doesn't want to, because what if James has seen my profile and decided I'm not attractive enough or don't sound like his type? But if I don't check, I'll have a sleepless night wondering if he's responded. I'll just check it once, and then I'll put my phone out in the hallway so I won't be tempted again.

But, there it is, as soon as I open the app, a match! James has swiped right. And he's sent a message. A plain and simple 'Hi'.

I feel giddy, adrenaline fizzing through me like tiny nitrogen bubbles in my bloodstream, and also somewhat disbelieving. It's hard to reconcile: the girl in the mirror today still feels like the girl in the mirror from three years ago; awkward, self-conscious, frumpy. I take a long deep breath. 'You're not that girl,' I tell myself fiercely. 'You're a new, improved version of her.'

I read the message again. *Hi.* Short and sweet, like his bio.

What to do? Should I message him straight back or should I wait? I need to think about how best to handle it. I don't want to put him off by seeming too keen. Should I remind him that we've met in person? If you can call it that. We didn't really meet. And why would I bring that up? There's no way he'd either remember me or recognise me from that night. I'll hold off on telling him – cross that bridge if and when I come to it.

My finger hovers over the keys as I stare at that two-letter word, wondering how to answer it. It's like an exam. I want to strike the perfect note but it's impossible to know what that is. I'm not good at this whole dating game, hence reading *Grazia* magazine and every other magazine and blog with dating tips in it. Maybe I should do some digging online – find out some more about him – his likes, dislikes, that kind of thing, so I can tailor my response just so. Yes, I'll do that and then I'll message him in the morning so I don't look like I'm awake at eleven at night checking my Tinder like some desperate loser.

The thing is, I've never had a shot at someone like James before, never thought in a million years that I would, and I really don't want to blow it. What is it my mother used to say? *Everything comes to those who wait.*

I drag my laptop out of my bag and pull the duvet around me so I'm all snug and cosy, before I remember the wine in the fridge. It's cold and I don't much fancy going all the way downstairs but I should probably double-check all the doors and windows before I go to sleep. I weigh it up. The toasty warmth of bed versus two minutes of cold and a glass of wine and being able to sleep soundly knowing no one is going to break in and attack me. I'm not being paranoid. Two weeks ago, an old lady who lives about five minutes' walk away woke up in the middle of the night to find a man in a balaclava standing in the middle of her bedroom. He raped her and then beat her. It was all over the papers. They said it's a miracle she survived, the attack was that ferocious.

Ever since then I've been extra security conscious. The front door has three big Chubb locks as well as an alarm system, but that's old and on the blink. The code doesn't seem to be working. I emailed Tess about it last week but she's somewhere in India without regular Internet access and hasn't responded. Because the alarm's not working, I always make sure I lock my bedroom door too, as an extra precaution. And, even though I felt stupid doing it and I'd never admit it to anyone, I've hidden a knife under the mattress – a bloody big carving knife from the posh John Lewis set downstairs. It makes me sleep slightly better.

OK, I decide, I'm going downstairs. One. Two. Three. I swing my legs out of bed and make a dash for the hallway. Chris leaps out at me from the darkness and I scream. 'Damn cat!'

I run to the front door and check all three locks. If someone broke the stained-glass panels on either side of the knocker, they'd be able to stick their hand through and undo the bolts but they wouldn't be able to undo the final lock because it has a key, and I always keep the key in a pot on the hall table. I weighed up doing this because if there was a fire, it would be dangerous (I'm the fire safety rep at work so I know the rules) but the pros outweigh the cons.

The back door, which is through the pantry, has a bolt and a lock as well. I check those and then I lock the pantry door too. All the windows are those double-glazed ones that need a key and, because it's winter, they're all locked up tight.

My feet are turning to ice blocks on the flagstones in the kitchen but I stop to pour a nice, big glass of wine before dashing upstairs with it, taking a big gulp halfway, after I manage to spill some down my PJs.

Back in bed, I open up my laptop and, with something of the excitement I used to get settling down to watch a really good movie with a bucket of sweet and salty popcorn, I start my deep dive into James Wickenden. As I type his name into Google I wonder what Flora's reaction will be when I tell her. She won't believe it. I can hardly believe it. I can picture her face and it makes me smile ear to ear.

I find James's Facebook profile easily but it's set to private. He's not on Instagram; there's an account belonging to a *JamesWlawyer* on Twitter but that is private too. I find a mention of him in an article on LegalWeek – about a press gag he managed to win for a musician who was rumoured to be cheating on his husband – and his bio from his law firm's website. From this I discover that he graduated from Lady Margaret Hall, Oxford, with a degree in law. His clients include major international artists, brands and celebrities, and Legal 500 describes him as 'much sought-after', 'dynamic' and 'a master negotiator'.

I wonder where he lives. If I knew his birthday, I could search the electoral roll for him. That's a bit stalkerish, though. In fact, it would probably feature on a list of 'Top ten things NOT to do when trying to hook a man'.

Becca hooked him. I wonder how. Of course, the simple answer is she was blonde and attractive, but she was also not very nice. I hope James isn't so superficial that all he cares about is looks.

Taking another gulp of wine, I quickly type Becca's name into the search bar on Facebook. If all her old posts are still there – the multitude of gushy love posts – I can read them and see what I can glean about James's likes and dislikes.

That's odd. She's not coming up. Did she cull me? My initial reaction is indignation. What did I do to be unfriended? But then I wonder if she's deleted her account. I do a search to see if I can find her but there are no *Becca Zaceks*es on Facebook. I search variations including Rebecca and Becky but come up empty-handed. Her Instagram account has vanished. So has her Twitter. How odd.

I put her name into Google but I can't find a single thing about her other than an article on the BBC London website about the accident at the PKW party. That's a very hard thing to achieve these days – wiping all online traces of yourself. I take another big gulp of wine. I feel suddenly wide awake, as though I'm drinking coffee not alcohol, and my imagination is running wild. Perhaps I should have been a detective and not an accountant. It's far more fun.

I go to an online search site, enter her name and the last place I know she lived and find her. It says she hasn't lived at that address for three years and there's no new address listed. Surely she would be on the electoral roll somewhere. Maybe she's opted out of the public register, or she could have changed her name. She could even be married. Or . . . what if she's dead?

What if *that's* it? But we would have heard something at work if she had died. I quickly pull up the government registry website. It won't take a second to check, and the truth is that now I'm absolutely intrigued. I manage to do a fairly substantive search and don't find a death certificate for her – at least not one in her name. If she changed it, then that's another matter.

Absorbed in my detective work, I reach across for my glass, which I've set down on my bedside table, but find it's empty. Damn. I should have brought the bottle upstairs. Still, the last thing I need is a hangover tomorrow. I've got work and it's already late. I check the clock. Oh god, I had no idea it was *that* late. It's one o'clock already. I should really go to sleep. I have to be up in six hours. But I won't be able to sleep. Not unless I do this last thing.

It's a long shot, but you never know. I take the photo of her from the BBC and do a reverse image search. It returns several dozen images 'similar' to the one I searched on. They need to work on their facial recognition software if they consider most of these to be similar. In the photo I used, Becca is posing at a viewpoint, somewhere overlooking a windswept, choppy ocean. There are white cliffs in the background, seagulls overhead, and I assume it must be England because it looks blustery cold and pretty miserable. She's wearing a blue jacket and a scarf. She looks lovely, of course, in a blonde, green-eyed, girl-next-door type of way.

For some reason Google is confusing her with a number of Hollywood actresses. I wonder if it does that with everybody and make a note to self to check tomorrow. I wonder who it would match me with? I scan the photos one by one. I don't know why I'm so obsessed about finding her. This whole thing started with me trying to find information on James, but now it's become a mystery I urgently need to solve. All of a sudden I stop, my attention caught by one of the photos. I click on it to enlarge it.

It's the same photo exactly – of Becca on the clifftop – but when I open the URL it takes me to the website of an interior design company. There are lots of gorgeous pictures of modern kitchens filled with sleek appliances, blanket-strewn sofas next to roaring fires, carefully arranged knick-knacks on console tables, white orchids framing an antique mantelpiece, clean Scandinavian-style living spaces – the kind of photos I normally sigh over in *Elle Decor* and stick on my vision board.

And there's the photo of Becca – right at the top – beside a banner that reads BRIDGES INTERIORS.

Confused, I click on the *About Us* page and I find another picture of Becca. This time, one of her leaning against a table in what looks like a design studio. A quick scan of the blurb tells me that Becca is now Becca Bridges. So she did get married! She has her own interior design company and lives in a chocolate-box village in the Cotswolds which, when I Google it, shows me images of cobbled streets, trailing roses, Tudor-style tea *shoppes*, and a picturesque church spire.

If you were going to pick an idyllic English setting for a rom-com movie, this would be it. It's not exactly the place I imagined Becca moving to. She was always more Jimmy Choo than Barbour wellies; more nights out partying in Mayfair and Soho House than church fetes and knitting scarves for the Women's Institute.

These thoughts are fleeting. I'm more interested in Becca herself. She looks exactly the same as she did three years ago. Even her hair is the same: shoulder-length and ash blonde. There's no sign she ever had an accident, no scars are visible, though the picture is taken from a little distance and when I zoom in it becomes pixelated.

She's leaning against a desk, one leg crossed over the other at the ankle, arms folded over her chest, wearing dark jeans with a white shirt tucked in. She's also wearing knee-high leather boots. No heels. Her style seems to have changed, become way more Sloane-ranger. But I suppose it's no surprise that one might opt for more sensible footwear after an accident like hers. I'd never wear heels again if I were her.

I read the blurb beside the photograph:

Becca Bridges is a designer and stylist, focusing on interiors. Inspired at a young age by her mother's love for decorating and home renovating, Becca studied for a degree in communications and embarked on a highly successful career in the entertainment business before deciding to quit her job, leave London and pursue a career in her first love: interior design.

I re-read the first paragraph. *Quit* her job? She didn't exactly quit. And, a *highly successful* career? Still, we all exaggerate when it comes to CVs.

I keep reading:

Becca brings her passion and inspiration to work with private clients, helping them create their dream homes. She lives in a converted mill in the small village of Widford in the Cotswolds, with her husband Zac and their one-year old daughter Sadie.

Wow. I have to tell Flora. But first I need to look up Becca Bridges on Facebook.

Boom. There she is. She's using the same photo of her in the design studio on both her Facebook and Instagram profiles. She must have created new ones after she got married. Both accounts appear, from their timelines, to have been set up fifteen months ago. How strange. But then maybe not that strange, when you consider that she probably took a while to recover. If the baby is about a year old and she was pregnant for nine months, then she must have met Zac pretty soon after the accident, or else it was a shotgun wedding.

There are photos of the wedding, though, and it doesn't look shotgun, or arranged on the fly, it looks amazing. The photos look like they've been styled by an art director for *Perfect Wedding* magazine – showing Becca and her husband, from behind, strolling hand in hand through a meadow. She's wearing a stunning dress – a figure-hugging, lace, off-the-shoulder number with a mermaid silhouette – her hair knotted in an elaborate bun at the nape of her neck. Her husband, Zac – who is turning his head ever so slightly towards her – is, from the looks of it, older than her. Maybe forties, with salt-and-pepper hair and a trace of stubble. He's olive-skinned and broad-shouldered and quite handsome.

If I had any doubt this was Becca, it's totally dissipated by reading the posts that go with each photo.

Thanks for all the birthday wishes everyone! I feel so lucky and blessed to have you in my life and wish I could have shared today with you all. After a lovely lie-in (Sadie slept through the night – hurrah!) Zac took me for a lovely lunch at Manoir, then Sadie gave me my present – a yummy mummy spa day! I've been massaged and pampered and am now totally blissed out – just what I needed to get me in the mood before our trip to South Africa (my Christmas present to Zac!). #spalife #best-birthdayever #Ilovemyhusband #Christmasinthesun

Victoria Harvey Happy Birthday! Did you get the flowers I sent?

Becca Bridges I did! They're beautiful. Thank you so much!

Nicholas Routledge Happy Happy Birthday! See you
tomorrow. xx

Alby Ball Hope Zac spoiled you rotten. You deserve it.

Becca Bridges He did. :)

Nina Brown Where are you going in South Africa?

Becca Bridges Cape Town and then on safari to a private
game reserve for a week followed by a week in Namibia. I
can't wait!

Nina Brown So jealous! Sounds amazing.

Becca Bridges Thanks. It's not all play. I have a commission
to do the interior design for a winery in CT.

Nina Brown Wow. Congrats. Will they pay you in wine? x

Becca Bridges I'm still breastfeeding so unfortunately not!

Nina Brown OMG. How old is she now? Go you!

Becca Bridges 15 months. Yes. We both love it so much,
hard to stop.

Nina Brown I bottle fed both mine. I admire you for sticking
with it. I found it pure torture.

Becca Bridges You just have to push through the pain. It's
worth it in the end. And breast is best as they say.

Oh, it's Becca all right.

I read every single post with a voyeuristic delight but after-wards I feel a bit queasy, as though I've eaten an entire bowl of Angel Delight. It's addictive though. I can't seem to stop myself scrolling through photo after photo.

On a close-up of her and her husband's entwined hands with her enormous diamond engagement ring on prominent display she's written: 'Today I said I do to the love of my life, my soul mate, my other half, my best friend and the best thing that ever happened to me. I have never felt so happy, so loved or so safe. #LuckiestGirl #love #bestdayofmylife'.

It looks like the wedding was a big affair – in a barn or some place similar with bunting hanging from the eaves. There are close-ups of jars of peonies on long trestle tables, a five-tiered cake draped with pink flowers, people dancing to a band, and one of her and Zac's hands gripping a knife, plunging it through the thick white cake icing and into the red velvet interior. For a second I see Becca's skull, the oozing blood bubbling out of it, and have to look away. I'm happy that she managed to move on after the accident. Good for her.

I wonder who she invited to the wedding? It's a lot of people. Maybe they were all Zac's friends. She doesn't have many on Facebook. Only seventy-eight. Did she want to wipe away all traces of her life before the accident and start over, is that why she set up new profiles? Certainly no one from PKW made the cut, by the looks of things. That makes me feel slightly better.

Fascinated, I flick through the rest of her photos. They are carefully curated, all of them heavily filtered. Most are of her husband and baby (#happyfamily #blessed). Zac's always smiling and clearly a doting husband and father. There's a photo of him in black and white, bleary-eyed and with stubble, holding the newborn Sadie, who takes after him with a shock of dark hair but otherwise looks like ET, bless her. He doesn't seem to have noticed, as the expression on his face is one of utter awe and paternal pride. The post has thirteen likes and comments, which doesn't seem very many. I get more posting pictures of my lunch. Everyone is raving about how beautiful baby Sadie is and sending congratulations.

The baby photos trace Sadie from a smush-faced newborn who, contrary to Becca's declarations, is not 'the most beautiful baby in the whole world', to a slightly cuter four-month-old spooning puree all over her face, to an eighteen-month-old with dark curls and a cupid's bow mouth, focused intently on unwrapping a Christmas present. Every single photograph comes with a gushing description and so many hashtags I get a headache from trying to decipher them. 'Took Sadie for her first check-up. She scored top marks. #mumlife #sleepingbaby #breastisbest'.

There's a photo of Becca looking lean and lovely in blue yoga pants and matching crop top, only a few weeks after the birth. In this one she's posing like she used to back in the day, blonde hair swept into a sleek ponytail, full face of make-up, not a single sign that she's been up all night with a colicky newborn or that she's broken into a sweat doing downward dog. It's a humble-brag post about how she's already back to her pre-baby weight thanks to all the breastfeeding and yoga. I can imagine all my friends with babies would scream if they saw this.

There's yet another photo of Zac and baby Sadie, this time in a swimming pool – it looks like it might be in the South of France or somewhere Mediterranean. The water is as iridescent blue as the sky and there's a lovely old rambling farmhouse behind them. 'Soaking up the rays in Languedoc with my loves, watching Sadie teaching Zac to swim. #best-dadintheworld #familytime #Lovesofmylife'.

One of the photos is of them all together, Zac with his arm around Becca who is holding Sadie. On his other side is a dark-haired woman. Becca's written, 'What a wonderful time with Auntie Maddie. Thanks for the beautiful Burberry onesie. #gratitude #familytime #BurberryBaby'. Maddie has liked the post and written, 'I'm so happy for you two. Sadie is the luckiest baby in the world.'

I feel a slight pang of envy. I'm happy for Becca, of course, but there's a part of me that can't help but feel jealous too.

She's got it all: the gorgeous house, the perfect husband, the baby, the holidays to exotic locations, not to mention an amazing career. Never mind Sadie, some might say Becca's the luckiest girl in the world. I know she had the accident but it doesn't look like it's affected her life for the worse. She seems to be living the dream.

Zac has a Facebook profile but when I click on it I find that it's private. I can read what he posts on Becca's page, though. There's an anniversary one: 'Happy Anniversary to the love of my life, my beautiful wife. This last year has been the best. You are my everything. Thank you for giving us the gift of our beautiful daughter. I love you both forever #bestwifeever'.

I make an involuntary gagging sound. Oh god, I have to send this to Flora.

I go back to the interior design website and cut and paste the link to the home page then I go back to Facebook and open up a chat box. I paste the link into the box, along with the link to Becca's new Facebook page. It will give us something to gossip about tomorrow.

Something suddenly catches the corner of my eye – a flash of movement – the bedroom door nudging open. My heart flies into my throat, the laptop falling sideways off my lap and onto the bed as a dark shape comes barrelling into the room and charges towards me. It lands on the bed. It's the bloody cat.

I leap up, grabbing him, and then angrily toss him out the bedroom door before shutting it. He scratches at the carpet in the hall but I ignore him. He'll give up soon enough and go and sleep upstairs on Tess's bed.

As I get back under the covers I notice the clock on my bedside table. Holy crap. I really fell down the rabbit hole.

It's almost three in the morning. I'm going to be so tired tomorrow. And hungover – I shouldn't have had so much wine. I'm not used to drinking these days, and two glasses has made me quite tipsy. I should really go to sleep. I'll just send this email to Flora. I grab my laptop and open the message box again.

'Get this Flora . . . it's Becca! Who we used to work with! She's managed to bag herself a hot husband and guess what?! She's also got a kid (check out the pictures – it looks like baby Gollum!). For someone who fell on her face she really landed on her feet! LOL. Getting brain-damaged didn't kill off her hashtag habit. Some things never change. Oh, and James and her aren't together any more. I've got news about that too. You'll never guess what! He swiped me on Tinder! Let's have lunch tomorrow. L x.'

Chris is still scratching at the door. I hit send, then shut my laptop and switch off the light. I'll reply to James in the morning.

MUMSTHEWORD.NET

What should I do? (6 posts)

Hammurabi Wed-06-DEC-17 02:38
An acquaintance of mine – someone I used to work with – has just accidentally sent me a message meant for someone else. In it she basically slags me off and laughs about my daughter, calling her ugly and saying that she looks like Gollum, which she doesn't. I don't have anything to do with this person and haven't for years. My question is what should I do about it? I feel like she needs to know what she's done is wrong.

Cupcake89 Wed-06-DEC-17 02:40
Block her. Ignore it. She's obviously a bitch.

WonderWomanWow Wed-06-DEC-17 04:48
That happened to me. I confronted the person and she was mortified. She apologised. I accepted her apology but I never spoke to her again.

Yayabanana Wed-06-DEC-17 05:11
Oh that's horrible. You should never say mean things about children. No child is ugly.

Wornoutmummy Wed-06-DEC-17 06:32
I'd confront her and tell her how you feel. And then I'd block her.

Hammurabi Wed-06-DEC-17 08:33
Thanks everyone. I've dealt with it.
Wornoutmummy Wed-06-DEC-17 09:37
What did you do?

Wednesday, 6 December
Morning

Needles are being inserted into my scalp and an electric current fired into my brain. Then comes a loud droning sound, like a motorbike is being kick-started right by my ear. It takes a few seconds for me to figure out that it's the bloody cat. He's sitting on my pillow kneading my head with his claws.

I sit bolt upright, which makes me feel immediately faint, and chuck the beast off the bed. Groaning at the way the room is spinning and making me feel nauseous, I try to focus on the clock. I've left my contacts in and they're all gummed up. I realise with horror that it's gone seven thirty and I'm going to be late for work.

I stagger out of bed, tripping on the twisted-up duvet and almost doing a comic face plant on the carpet. The bedroom door is open. That's odd. I thought I locked it. I must have got up in the night to go the loo and left it ajar.

A quick shower and fresh contact lenses have me feeling still only semi-alive. I can't believe two glasses of wine did this to me. OK, it was probably more like three because they were very large glasses, and when I open the fridge I see that the wine bottle only has a dribble left in it, so in fact they must have been very, very large glasses.

That's the last time I do that, I tell myself, and on an empty stomach too. What an idiot. I'm going to pay for it today.

I feed the cat, spend thirty-five minutes doing my make-up and hair because my usual routine is not going to cut it, opt for my lowest heels, throw on my coat and scarf and head out, aiming to make a train that will get me into the office just a little after the official nine o'clock start time.

Once on the train I pull out my phone and start to compose my message to James. My recon mission last night ended up getting sidetracked and I didn't really find much out about him but if I don't reply soon, he'll think I'm not interested.

I agonise over it for a good ten minutes and finally opt for 'Hi' and I'm just about to type 'How are you?' – highly original but I can't think of anything else and I figure I can't go wrong with that – when he immediately texts back: 'Nice to meet you. How's your day going?'

Oh god. He's right there. We're talking. Actually conversing, albeit over text. OK, I need to calm down. I can't mess this up. 'Running late for work,' I tell him.

'Late night?' he texts back.

'Yes,' I tell him. 'And I'm paying for it this morning.' Instantly I regret that. It makes me sound like some kind of drunken party girl. Maybe I should have told him I was up early and pounding out circuits at the gym. This whole online dating thing is so difficult. It's like learning another language.

'Where do you work?' he asks.

'Soho,' I type, hoping that he doesn't push for more details. 'I work in finance,' I hurriedly add, then kick myself as it's hardly the most exciting career on the planet. I wish I could say I was a forensic psychologist or even an interior designer, something that at least would lead to an interesting conversation. Tell people you're an accountant and you might as well just shoot anaesthetic into their veins.

'From your profile it sounds like you like to travel,' he writes and I breathe a sigh of relief that I haven't yet blown it.

'I have a big bucket list to get through. I'm going to Thailand in April,' I tell him. I'm going to meet up with Tess. At least that's the plan. I still need to book my flight. 'What about you?' I ask. I read somewhere that asking questions makes you more likable and makes you appear smart.

'Just got back from a trip to Mexico,' he says.

'I love Mexico!' I reply. I'm not exactly lying. I love Mexican food. 'The food is the best.'

'Have you tried that new place in Soho?'

'Oh, you mean Merida? Not yet.'

There's a minute's pause and I clutch my phone, waiting and hoping and praying that he's going to follow it up. For a moment it looks like he's typing something; those little dots dance across the screen, but then nothing. Damn. I lost him with 'I love Mexico!' It was the exclamation mark. It made me seem too excitable. Not cool enough. Damn. Damn.

But then, as I'm in the midst of freaking out that I've blown it, another text arrives. 'Maybe we should try it some time.'

OK, sound casual, I tell myself. 'Sure. Sounds good.'

'How's Thursday?'

Oh my god, he's asking me out for dinner. Normally on Tinder, when men aren't asking me to show them my tits, the chat goes on for a bit longer and then, if an invite comes, it's usually to meet for a quick drink. No one has ever asked me to dinner before. I hesitate before answering because, just like the tips say to always let the man do the chasing, they also tell you not to seem too available. But what if I put him off by saying I'm busy Thursday and he hooks up with some other Tinder date, falls for her, and subsequently cancels on me? That's happened to me before. I don't want to miss my chance.

'Thursday sounds great,' I say. 'I've got a boxing class at 6, but I could do 7.30.'

'Boxing?' he answers. 'I better be on my best behaviour then!'

'Yes, I've got a savage upper cut,' I tell him and follow it with a winking emoji and a fist.

I started going to an all-women gym when I first began my mission to lose weight and one of the classes was called 'Knockout fitness'. It turns out that taking out all your frustration on a punching bag is brilliantly cathartic, and it also burns over seven hundred calories an hour.

'Consider me warned!' he texts back. 'I'll see you Thursday.'

I grin. 'Have a good day,' I tell him.

Once he's gone I find I can't wipe the grin off my face.

Starbucks is crowded with people ordering eggnog and gingerbread lattes. I join the queue and pore over the text conversation with James, re-reading every line until I have it memorised. He invited me out for dinner! I still can't get over it. Not a drink or a coffee, but dinner! I need to think about what I'm going to wear. I'll have to book a blow-dry too because what if he sees me and doesn't think I look as good in person as I do in my photos?

Someone behind me in the queue pokes me in the back and I realise I'm staring at my phone and the barista is trying to take my order. As I look up, my gaze lands on the refrigerator case filled with egg and bacon sandwiches and chocolate muffins. My hangover screams *yes*. My hangover wants me to order and devour every carbohydrate-laden sugary treat on display, but I can't succumb. Not with this date on the horizon. I need to go on a strict calorie-controlled diet from now until Thursday to make sure I fit into my favourite dress. I order a coffee and congratulate myself on my iron willpower.

'Hi!'

I turn around. It's Flora. She's waiting at the side counter, picking up four coffees in a take-out carrier.

'Oh hi!' I say, giving her a quick hug, noticing the pink Grande Frappuccino topped with a mountain of whipped cream and glittery sprinkles that she's holding. 'What on earth's that?' I ask. 'It looks like they blended a disco ball.'

Flora giggles. 'You know what I'm like, if it's pink and sparkly I have to have it!'

'Did you get my message last night?' I ask.

She shakes her head. 'What message?'

'On Facebook.'

She shakes her head. 'No. What was it about?'

'You won't believe what I found out last night.'

Her eyes widen at the excitement in my voice. 'What?'

'Remember Becca?'

She nods. Of course she remembers Becca. Everyone remembers Becca.

'She's got this whole new life. She's married and she has a baby.'

Flora's mouth drops open in surprise. 'To that lawyer she was dating?' she asks. 'James whatshisname?'

'No. To someone else. Some guy called Zac. But the most amazing thing is, you won't believe this, James messaged me on Tinder last night!'

Flora's jaw practically hits the ground. My happiness is somewhat dented by her incredulity.

'Wow,' she mutters.

'I know!' I say, trying to ignore her tone. 'We're going out for dinner. He's taking me to that new Mexican round the corner from work.'

'Wow,' she says again, shaking her head. 'That's ... amazing.'

I can see the tremor around her mouth as she tries to force a smile. Maybe it's not disbelief, so much as jealousy. I lower my voice and put my hand on her arm. 'I can't believe he actually swiped right on me. Me! I thought he'd made a mistake. I mean ... do you remember how gorgeous he is?'

'Lizzie!' Someone yells just then.

I turn around. It's the barista. 'Tall sugar-free vanilla almond-milk latte,' he says, handing me my coffee.

I take it and turn back to Flora. She's waiting for me over by the door.

'You should check Facebook,' I tell her as we head outside into the cold. 'I sent you a link to Becca's new profile page. She's deleted her old one. You can see all the pictures of her wedding and the baby.'

'Why did she delete her old one?'

I shrug. 'God knows. You'll never guess what she's doing now – she's got her own business working as an interior designer.'

'Well, she was always very stylish,' says Flora.

'I suppose. Anyway, she's got this picture-perfect life. Though the baby's got a face that only a mother could love.'

'Oh no,' Flora protests with a smile, 'all babies are beautiful.'

'Not this one,' I laugh. 'Believe me. Wait until you see her.'

'Some babies just take a while to grow into their looks.'

'Some adults too,' I say, smiling a little to myself.

We reach the office and take the revolving door into the lobby. Damn, I'm twenty minutes late. Hopefully my boss is in a meeting and hasn't noticed I'm late.

Flora makes for the elevators and I follow her.

'Do you want to go for lunch?' I ask her as she hits the call button.

'Um, I'm actually a little busy today, what with that book going out.'

'I forgot about that. I don't get all the fuss personally.'

Flora looks at me. Her expression tells me she's annoyed. 'Have you read it?' she asks.

I freeze. Oh god, I almost gave myself away. 'No,' I say. 'I just mean, it seems like a lot of hype, that's all. Whenever there's a lot of hype it rarely manages to live up to it.'

'Well, this time I think it will.'

'I hope so,' I say with a smile as we enter the elevator. 'It would be amazing. Imagine the PR.'

We get in the lift and Flora presses the button for our floor. She stares at the doors and I sense she's still annoyed so I attempt to make it up to her. 'You've worked so hard,' I say. 'It will all pay off, you'll see. Let's celebrate tomorrow instead. My treat.'

'Oh, have you got time?' she says, and I wonder if there's not a sliver of sarcasm in her tone.

'Yes,' I tell her, frowning. It's not like I've deliberately been avoiding her.

'Maybe,' she answers. 'I've got a lot on.'

'OK.' The lift door opens and Flora lets me go out before her.

'See you later,' she says and walks off.

'Have a good day!' I call out.

I watch her go, feeling a little unsettled. Maybe she's annoyed about my date with James. But that's not fair. She should be happy for me.

As I turn the corner I see my boss, Daniel, sitting at his desk. Damn. He glances up and sees me. He has a face like thunder. Did something happen? I'm only twenty minutes late. It's not a big deal. I'm always the last to leave every night so he can't possibly be annoyed.

'Lizzie,' he says as I approach, in a tone that reminds me of my head teacher at school.

Immediately I feel my throat constrict and my palms start to sweat. I'm fourteen again and have been caught bunking off PE. 'Yes,' I say.

'We need a word.'

I swallow, feeling a sudden panic crawl up my chest and into my throat, blocking my airway. 'What about?' I ask.

Oh god, is this about the manuscript I took home last night? I have it in my bag. It feels like it's glowing radioactive.

'Take your coat off and let's go into the boardroom.'

The boardroom? Bloody hell. It must be serious. I cast about the finance department, the panic now rolling down towards my legs, making me wobbly. I'm glad I opted for the low heels.

Joanne and Alison are sitting at their computers, eyes fixed to their screens, but I can tell they're listening, straining to hear every word.

'Sure,' I say, lightly, determined not to show a glimmer of fear. I haven't done anything really wrong. I know I took the manuscript but I didn't do anything with it. I didn't even read more than twenty pages of it. It can't be that. And I have no idea what else it could be, unless . . . unless they're laying people off.

But why would they be? We're doing really well. I see the annual accounts. And I just had my performance review and it was great. We even talked about the possibility of promotion.

With shaking fingers I undo the buttons on my coat and hang it up. I peer across at Joanne once more and manage to catch her eye. She looks away fast. That can't be good. We usually have a good banter in the mornings.

I take a deep breath, trying to calm myself. Oh crap. I know what this is about. They've discovered my side-gig. As per the terms of my employment at PKW I'm not allowed to work anywhere else, not that running a bookkeeping business interferes with my work hours – I do it at weekends and in the evenings. It's only a few clients too, and no one in the entertainment industry.

I follow Daniel down the hallway past the breakout area. The whole time he doesn't say a word and I feel like a prisoner being led away for execution. Maybe I should just come clean. Admit about the business but tell him I'm winding it down anyway.

No, I decide, best to wait and see what it's all about before I open my mouth. I hold my head up and straighten my spine, reminding myself that if they're going to make me redundant, then that's not the worst thing in the world. I'd get a good pay-out after five years working here, and I've been wanting to quit so I could try my hand at other, more creative pursuits anyway. I could finally finish my book. There's a silver lining.

Daniel opens the door to the boardroom and then stands to one side to let me enter. I smile thanks and step past him, only to freeze in the doorway at the sight of Moira from HR sitting at one end of the huge conference table, along with

her assistant. Oh god, they're making me redundant. That
has to be it. I look to Daniel for confirmation but he refuses
eye contact, which only convinces me further. He walks past
me, gesturing to a seat on Moira's left while he sits on the
other side of the table, beside her assistant. Helen, I think it
is. She's got her laptop open and she's tapping away. Is she
taking notes? Why is she taking notes?

I walk the length of the mahogany table. 'What's this
about?' I ask as I sit down.

The atmosphere in the room has the seriousness of a
Nuremberg Trial. Moira looks up from a pile of paperwork
and gives me a nod. No smile.

'Lizzie,' she says.

I look between her and Daniel. 'Yes?' I say.

'We've received some information, some quite troubling
information.'

'What?' I ask, my nervousness and panic starting to build.
I took such pains to hide my name on the website. I used
Elizabeth instead of Lizzie and my mum's maiden name
Cook. How could they have found it?

'We received an email this morning regarding some erro-
neous expense claims.'

It's not about my side business. The relief is so great that
for a moment I'm confused by what she's telling me. 'I don't
claim expenses.'

'The expenses forms that you handle for other employees.
The ones that you sign off on.'

'What?' I ask, dumbfounded. What can they be talking
about? I'm meticulous with my work. Daniel even commented
about it in my last review, which HR will have on file. 'What
about them?' I ask.

'We seem to have uncovered some anomalies.'

'Anomalies?' I stare at them blankly. I'm vacillating between indignation and outright panic. What am I being accused of exactly? 'What are you talking about? That's not possible.'

'This is going back some years.'

'I don't understand,' I say again. 'Can you tell me who sent the email?'

Moira shakes her head. 'I'm afraid not.'

I shake my head back at her. 'I don't . . . why would someone say that? It's not true.'

'Well, we're here to try to get to the bottom of it.'

'There's nothing to get to the bottom of. I've not done anything wrong. I don't think.' I start wondering if I have accidentally signed off on something without realising it.

'This is why we're here,' Moira says in a calm voice, 'to try and find out what's going on.'

'It sounds like you're accusing me of something.'

'We're not accusing you,' says Moira in an even tone, trying out a placatory smile. 'We just need your co-operation in figuring out what's going on.'

'With what exactly?' I'm getting impatient with all the suspense.

Moira lays out a couple of pieces of paper in front of me. They're photocopies. I pick them up and study them. 'What are these?' I ask, even though I know what they are. They're claim forms. I sign off on them when employees need reimbursing for out-of-pocket expenses. My signature is on the bottom of them.

'These forms appear to be fraudulent,' Moira announces.

I stare at her. 'Fraudulent how?'

I look back down at the form, checking the date. It's an old one – the ones we used before we went fully automated. Now employees take photos of their receipts and email them for sign-off.

'This is old,' I say. 'It's from three years ago.'

Moira nods.

I look back down at the name. 'This is Becca's.'

Moira nods again. 'Yes.'

My ears start to ring. It all feels way too coincidental. But no, it can't be. What on earth is going on?

'The form was signed off by you and reimbursed out of petty cash.'

I look back at the form. It was for two items, totalling fifty-eight pounds. The items are typed up as 'refreshments for department meetings'. Attached are two supermarket receipts, which add up to the same amount claimed. Did I make a mistake and miscalculate the total? The employees were meant to list the amounts per item, add them up, then attach all the receipts and bring them to me for signing.

'OK,' I say, doing the sums in my head. 'What's the matter? It seems like it all makes sense. The receipts add up.'

'Here's another,' Moira says, and she hands me another expense claim. 'We have sixty-three in total, amounting to an overpayment of just over four thousand pounds.'

I look over the one she's just handed me, then at the others she pushes cross the table. My head's pounding, my ears still ringing, sweat starting to trickle down my spine. 'These are all Becca's,' I say, taking in her name printed at the bottom of each piece of paper, and her signature: a giant, scrawled B with loopy Cs and a babyish A.

'Yes,' says Moira. 'Is that your signature?' She points at a scrawl at the bottom beside 'APPROVED BY'.

I nod. 'Yes.'

'How about these? Do you remember signing these?'

She hands me another pile of expense claims. 'Um, I don't know,' I say. These also have Becca's name on them but the receipts aren't original, they're copies. I figure out what the issue is. 'Wait,' I say, looking up. 'These are the same receipts!'

'Yes,' Moira says.

I start laying the expenses claims out along the table so I can study them further. 'But the claims have different dates,' I say. 'Roughly one month apart.'

'Yes,' says Moira.

'So . . .' I look to Daniel. 'Becca was making fraudulent claims?'

Daniel shakes his head. He's clearly decided not to open his mouth during this interrogation and leave all the bad-cop stuff to Moira.

'No. We don't believe she was. Compare her signature here and here,' Moira says, pointing with the tip of her Biro to Becca's signature on two separate pages. 'They're different.'

'If you say so.'

'We believe these are fraudulent claims and that you know something about it.'

'How would I know something about it? Obviously Becca submitted the same receipts twice.'

'That's not what we believe. Once the receipts were submitted along with the original expense claim she wouldn't have been able to resubmit them. Only someone in finance would have. And these don't have receipts attached – only photocopies.'

'Wait, you think that *I* submitted these?' I look at her and then at Daniel, hoping he is finally going to open his mouth and back me up, but he doesn't. He stares at me stonily.

'I . . . that's absurd,' I splutter angrily. 'Of course I didn't. Becca worked in the finance department for a time. Maybe she did it then.'

Neither of them say a word. Helen stops typing, though her fingers stay poised over the keyboard. Moira looks at Daniel.

'I'm afraid we're going to need to place you on leave while we investigate,' says Moira.

'What?' I say. 'You can't do that.'

'I'm afraid it's all part of the process. Once everything is cleared up you can return to work. I'm sure you understand.'

I don't understand. Not at all. 'But . . .' I say, 'I'm innocent. I haven't done anything. You don't have any proof, just a load of false information and slanderous allegations.' I'm on my feet, propelled by anger, and too late I realise that I'm shouting. Daniel stands up too but Moira shoots him a sharp look then turns to me and gestures for me to sit back down. The wind goes out of my sails, and I do, sinking into my seat, feeling very close to tears.

'Who sent the email?'

'That doesn't matter.'

'It does to me. I want to know who's spreading lies about me.'

Neither of them says anything. My face is getting hot. The ringing in my ears is back – it's like an orchestra of school children are playing triangles in my head.

'Lizzie,' Daniel says softly. 'We'll get to the bottom of this. For now we just need to put you on leave while we investigate things. It shouldn't take long.'

'But—'

'If you co-operate then it will be easier,' Moira cuts in.

'Co-operate?' I splutter. 'What do you mean?'

She raises an eyebrow. She means confess, not co-operate. 'But I haven't done anything,' I repeat, feeling myself close to tears. How is this happening?

'Why don't we go and collect your things?' Daniel suggests.

I nod, dazed, and get up.

'How long will this take?' I ask Moira as I pass her.

'Oh, a couple of days, no more,' she says and this time her tone is more pleasant. She does seem to have softened slightly. Maybe she doesn't believe it. Maybe she was just playing bad cop to see if I'd confess.

'OK,' I say. 'But I promise you, I haven't done anything.'

As I walk through the office with Daniel I feel dozens of eyes burning into me like lasers. I walk with my chin up, refusing to show any trace of guilt. I quickly put on my coat, gather up my things and my undrunk coffee.

Alison looks at me as I pass her desk and gives me a smile. I'm so grateful that it almost makes me burst into tears. 'Can you water my plant?' I say.

She nods.

'Thanks,' I say.

And then I follow Daniel into the elevator, across the lobby, past the PKW sign and the giant bronze squid sperm, and finally out of the building.

Wednesday, 6 December
Afternoon

I find myself at home without any clear recollection of how I got here. I stood outside the office for a good few minutes in a complete daze, before the whooshing of the revolving door behind me startled me into moving. I couldn't bear the thought of seeing anyone from work.

The first thing I do when I get in is open the fridge and drink the last gulp of wine in the bottle. It's not even lunchtime but my nerves are like frayed electrical cords. I'm in shock. I need something much stiffer but there's nothing else in the house.

I sink down at the kitchen table, still wearing my coat and scarf, and sit there for a good long while, staring into space. The postman shoving the mail through the letterbox snaps me out of it. I glance around. Chris is standing over his food bowl meowing non-stop. I get to my feet. On autopilot I reach for a box of cat food from the top of the fridge and pour a sachet into his bowl, then I walk into the hallway and pick up the mail. There's a postcard from my mum who's gone to Tenerife with some friends on a winter getaway, and a couple of bills that need urgent attention. I put the mail down, unopened, on top of the stack that's building in the hallway. Maybe I should show work my credit card bills. If I were stealing money, I wouldn't be this much in debt.

The thing that's still bothering me the most is who sent the email. Who would do such a thing? I head upstairs. I need to lie down. It's warm and safe under the covers and I curl up in a ball with my coat still on, trying to wrap my head around it all. *OK, you need to think this through,* I tell myself. But my head is pounding and my brain feels too sluggish to process anything. What if they investigate and come to the conclusion that it was me? Surely that's not possible. *But what if?* I keep asking myself. I'll be out of a job. And I'll never be able to get another one, not without a reference. They might even call the police! I could get a criminal record. *No. Stop, stop panicking. It won't get that far.*

Maybe I should look up my rights or try to get some advice from a lawyer. Reluctantly I drag myself out of my duvet cave and reach across the bed for my laptop, which is lying on the bedside table where I left it last night.

When I open it I discover that it's dead. I plug it in and while I wait for it to charge I check my phone. There's a message from Flora. 'Are you OK? I heard that you had to leave work?'

It almost brings tears to my eyes. I think about replying but what am I going to say? There's a message alert on Facebook. It's also from Flora: 'You said that you sent me a message last night? I didn't get it. Where's the link to Becca's new profile?'

That's weird. I check my messages.

Oh god. Oh my god.

Panic invades me like a swarm of hornets trapped in my chest. No. No. That can't be right. How did I do that? I sent the message I meant for Flora to Becca. With a shaking hand I open it and re-read it. Oh god, what was I thinking? I called her baby Gollum. Oh, this is bad. Very, very bad. I drop my phone and cover my face with my hands for a few moments, praying that when I open them it will all have gone away. It's still there. Wait, what if she hasn't read it yet? I can delete it! No. Shit. There's a little tick beside it. That means she's seen it. It's too late.

Somehow I'm out of bed and pacing the room, wringing my hands and talking out loud to the walls. 'OK, it's not that bad. It could be worse. No. You called her brain-damaged. It could not be worse. You likened her baby to a deformed hobbit creature.'

I pick up my phone again and re-read the message but it only makes things worse. Not knowing what else to do, I stab my finger on Becca's face to load her page. Maybe she'll have posted something this morning – a status update that will give me a clue as to whether she's upset. There's a chance she found it funny. Even as I think it, I know that's highly unlikely but I don't get to find out as the page won't load.

This page does not exist.

What? I click the reload button.

This page does not exist.

She's deleted her Facebook profile.

I sit down on the bed and hammer at my laptop to wake it up. The screen lights up. And there's Becca's Facebook page and the message I thought I wrote to Flora but somehow, drunkenly, stupidly, managed to send to the wrong person. Idiot. How could I have been so careless?

Wait.

Hang on.

The orchestra of kids playing percussion in my ears gets louder. The room seems to violently tilt in one direction and then the other, as though the house is a boat on a storm-tossed sea. My gut lurches. Becca. The email about the expenses. The coincidence that I shrugged off. But that same feeling is back – that weird, shivery flutter across my shoulders, the tightening of my airways as though invisible hands are wrapping around my neck and squeezing. What if it was Becca who sent the email to work?

But why would she want to incriminate herself? That doesn't make sense. And honestly, how would she have managed to do all that in the time frame available? I sent this just before 2 a.m. By the time I got to work they'd already received the anonymous email and gone through the expense claims.

OK, think, Lizzie, think. I take several screenshots of the page (minus my message box) because if she has deleted her account, this will be the only evidence I have that it ever existed and once I refresh the page it will be gone.

Why would she delete her page, though? I switch tabs to her interior design website and click on the contact page.

404 Error.
We are sorry but the page you are
looking for does not exist.

I go back and refresh the home page.

404 Error.
We are sorry but the page you are
looking for does not exist.

OK. This is now officially beyond weird. I search for any trace of Bridges Interiors and then Becca Bridges, even scouring cached pages and online archives but nothing comes back. Nothing at all. It's as if I dreamed it.

Partial transcript of police interview with Miss Elizabeth Crawley, subsequent to filing of Missing Persons Report

PC Kandiah – Sunday, 10 December

The first time I met her? I remember exactly. It was her first day at work and I was standing by the copier photocopying receipts for my boss. She had just started and she was being shown the ropes: where the kitchen was, how to make coffee, how to use the printers, that kind of thing. This was back in our Euston Road office, which was much shabbier than the new one.

I said hello and introduced myself and offered to show her how to use the copier because it was really old and temperamental, but she just glanced at me and told me she knew how to use a photocopier. It was like she thought I'd insulted her intelligence, when I was only trying to help. But, yeah . . .

She was hired as a receptionist but then someone was away on holiday so she covered for a few weeks in the finance department, then I think she moved to the comms team but she didn't last long there, maybe six months, before she got the job as PA to the CEO and, between you and me, it was no secret why. The CEO was known for employing *a type*. He was married, of course, but he was forever having these long business lunches on a Friday and we all knew what kind of business he was doing. I was friendly with his old PA – the one who worked for him before Becca – and she told me he was carrying on an affair with an agent at another company. She was mid-twenties. He was close to sixty. I mean, gross or what?

A few people applied to be his new PA. You have to understand that it's a very good job. Well paid. A good bonus. It can fast-track you into an agent role like *that*. There were a lot of interns and assistants who wanted that job. And Becca bagged it. I'm not saying she did anything inappropriate. In fact, I'm sure she didn't because she was dating James, but everyone else started speculating.

After she started that job, she stopped hanging out with the rest of us. She started going out to lunch with the junior agents instead. Not that we minded. She'd got a bit of a reputation by then for never paying for what she'd ordered. I think I mentioned that already.

This one time, when we were all out at lunch, celebrating something, I can't remember what, the bill came and someone didn't pay their fair share. We split it like we always do. I did the sums because everyone assumes that because you work in accounting adding up is your forte, even though everyone has a calculator on their phone and there are even apps to do it for you these days. But I did it, and everyone put in their twenty or so pounds, whatever it was, but we were short. In the end Flora put in the extra, so in effect she paid twice just to save us having to sit there and wait for someone to own up. I thought it was Becca because I was sitting next to her and I didn't see her get out her wallet. And she sat there in silence the whole time with this smile on her face like she knew what she was doing and thought it was funny. But for the rest of us, twenty quid was a lot of money. I didn't say anything at the time but Flora and I made sure to keep an eye on her the next time we went out. And she did it again, if you can believe it.

When I confronted her she told me point blank that she had paid and she picked up one of the twenties on the table and said it was hers. But that was bollocks. After that we stopped inviting her for lunch.

Thursday, 7 December
Morning

I sleep the sleep of the dead but wake up feeling like a three-day-old corpse. I'm groggy. There's slurry surrounding my brain. I took a pill around nine o'clock last night, knowing I wouldn't be able to sleep a wink otherwise.

I check the time. It's almost ten in the morning. Adrenaline floods my bloodstream, sending me lurching upright, thinking that I'm late. Then I remember I don't have a job to go to and sink back into the pillows. Slowly the events of the day before begin to pierce through the sludge. Becca. The mystery of the vanishing website and the vanishing Facebook page. It doesn't make sense. She might have blocked me on social media and made her accounts private, but what about the website? Why take down your own business website? Unless, of course, it's unrelated and nothing to do with me. I could be being paranoid.

My phone buzzes. I want to ignore it but what if it's work telling me they've cleared my name and I'm free to come back? But how on earth will I ever go back? How would I be able to show my face after this? Everyone must be gossiping about me. I reach for my phone. It's a message from Flora. She sent one last night too.

'OMG, I just heard the news. What's going on? Do you want to talk?'

And the one she sent just now says: 'Hey, how are you doing? Is there anything I can do?'

I fling the phone across the bed and flop backwards onto the pillows. There's nothing she can do. I just have to hang tight and wait for them to sort it out. But what if it takes a while? At least I'm still being paid. I should treat it like a holiday. Get on with my book. Maybe go shopping. But I know there's no way I'll be able to concentrate on that.

My phone buzzes again. I can't keep ignoring Flora but I really don't want to talk to anyone. It's not her, though. It's Google Alerts, letting me know someone has posted a review about me online. My phone buzzes in my hand. Another alert. Then another. And another. My phone is vibrating in my hand like a bomb about to go off. Fourteen alerts. And it's still going. It won't stop. What on earth is happening? I stab at the screen but it won't shut up. The alerts keep popping up, one on top of the next. Not knowing what else to do, I shove the phone under the pillows and with shaking hands I open my laptop.

I go to Yelp, which is where most of my bookkeeping clients find me. **EZ Bookkeeping.** I thought it was quite a good name, the riff on *easy*, and in the two years since I've been doing it I've earned an extra five hundred or so pounds a month; nothing that's going to allow me to retire before I'm eighty or get on the property ladder but enough to help pay the interest on my credit cards and tackle my student loan.

Overnight my rating has dropped from 5 stars to 1.5. I had twenty-eight reviews yesterday, mostly 5-star, and now I have eighty-six more reviews, all posted in the last hour, every single one giving me a 1- or 2-star review. I scan the names, a rising hysteria in my belly. Who is Jennifer J? Who is John A? And David F? I don't know any of these people. I've certainly never done any work for them.

I'm feeling slow from the sleeping pill, as though my brain is operating on an obsolete operating system that desperately needs a reboot. Is Jennifer J someone from work? I don't recognise her profile picture. I click on her review so I can read it in full.

> After reading the positive reviews I thought I'd give EZ Bookkeeping a try but after taking our books and promising to complete our tax return in time for filing we never heard back.

What? That's a lie. I've no idea who she is. I never promised her any such thing. There must be some mistake.

John A apparently hired me to do his books and I messed them up so badly he ended up owing over five thousand pounds in back taxes and fines. David F accuses me of taking his money and running.

This cannot be happening. My business will never recover. I'll never get another client again.

My phone is still bleating angrily beneath the pillow. I hurl it across the room then bury my head in my hands and start to rock back and forth. *Just breathe*, I tell myself, *just breathe*.

After a few minutes, when I'm calmer, I turn my attention back to Yelp. Methodically I start to go through the reviews.

Ravi P sounds like he's Indian, or at the very least doesn't speak English as a first language, because his grammar is all over the place: 'The taxes preparation was not to my liking and in these situations there was no recompense offered.' These are fake reviews. Someone has paid people to post negative reviews of my business. I know this happens. I've seen people advertising their services – both to post positive reviews about their own business or negative reviews about a rival. I never expected it to happen to me.

Someone called Hammurabi – who sounds like another fake reviewer from India – has posted, 'Lizzie is a liar. She's as trustworthy as Sméagol.'

My heart smashes into my ribcage. I re-read it. *Sméagol.* That's another name for Gollum. That cannot be a coincidence.

When I try to breathe in, air refuses to fill my lungs. I click on Hammurabi's profile picture. It's a double infinity sign. The person has only just set up their account. They have no friends and have only posted this one review.

And I would bet every penny I have that Hammurabi is Becca.

King Hammurabi (c. 1810 BC – c. 1750 BC) ruled Babylonia during the First Babylonian Dynasty. Known for being a just king as well as a military genius, he conquered many city states and expanded his empire. He is most well known for writing the first ever recorded laws, which were inscribed on massive stone pillars. Among these laws was 'An eye for an eye and a tooth for a tooth.'

Thursday, 7 December
Afternoon

Hammurabi hasn't replied to my email, or should I say, *Becca* hasn't replied to my email. It took me a while to compose it. I went through a dozen drafts, each of them angrier than the last, before realising I was going about it the wrong way. Belligerence is not the answer. If she's behind the situation at work too, which I'm almost certain she must be, then making her angrier isn't going to help.

The funny thing is that before she did all this I was going to apologise but now it seems like the punishment she's inflicting far outweighs my crime. I wrote a crawling apology email anyway, explaining that I was drunk and was thoroughly ashamed of my actions. I asked her to forgive me. I made no reference to the slew of online reviews she had posted and I didn't ask her to take the reviews down either. I treated her as you would treat a psychopath who is holding a knife to your throat – very carefully.

As far as the reviews, I flag each one and ask Yelp to remove them. It can take up to forty-eight hours for them to verify the false accounts and take them down, so I just have to hope that in the meantime none of my existing clients and no possible new ones read them.

By four I haven't left the bedroom except to go downstairs to feed the cat and make some coffee. I haven't heard from Becca or from work either, though I did email Moira to let her know I thought I might be the victim of a slur campaign. I didn't hear back. The problem is that I need proof or I'm the one who sounds crazy.

It's dark outside already. And it's cold, almost cold enough to snow. With the curtains drawn and the lights low, the atmosphere feels charged and ominous. If this were a Hitchcock movie, the soundtrack would be screeching sombre strings and clanging bell tones. I can't help but feel like something bad is about to happen, something worse than what has already happened. I try to imagine what, as that way I might be able to pre-empt it, but my mind runs off into a place of wild imaginings. And then I wonder if I'm the one losing my mind.

To break the spell – the torture of waiting – I decide to clean the house. I start with my bedroom. The knife tumbles out from under the mattress as I'm stripping the bed and I pick it up, pressing my thumb to the edge to test its sharpness, feeling a shiver travel down my spine as the blade pricks the flesh. I'm being stupid, I tell myself. But I wipe off the smear of blood on the tip and put the knife back where I found it.

I move on to the bathrooms next, getting down on my hands and knees and scrubbing to remove every spot of dust and grime from under the toilet rim and even behind the sink. I use an old toothbrush of Rob's to scrub away at the mould around the grouting. I'm on a real mission by now, determined to make the house shine. The more I clean, the more my mind feels clean too.

My arms and my back ache by the time I finish in the bathroom, but I hoover the hallway and stairs anyway, as well as my room and even the study that Tess let Rob take over as a recording room. He used to score movies, that was his job. From the way he acted you'd think he'd written the music for multiple Oscar-winning movies, but in fact all he'd done was a couple of small indie movies and a few radio jingles and he was flat broke the whole time and basically living off Tess.

I wasn't a massive fan of Rob's. He was kind of creepy. After Tess gave him a key I'd often come home and find him here alone, hanging out in his studio, making music. I didn't mind that. But a few times I found him watching me from the doorway in the kitchen, just standing there, not saying anything, just staring. Or I'd come out of the bathroom and he'd be there, blocking the doorway, and he wouldn't move until I asked him to.

I walked past his room once. He was in his studio, ostensibly recording something, but the door was open slightly and I heard a load of groaning and moaning, and when I went to look I saw him through the crack. He was masturbating vigorously to what was obviously some porn. It was really embarrassing because he looked up, and maybe he saw me, I don't know for sure, but he got up and slammed the door. After that he always kept it closed so I couldn't hear anything. I'm pretty sure he wasn't recording any music. I think he spent all those hours holed up in there wanking off.

When Tess found out he was cheating on her and dumped him, I was glad. My theory was that Rob was jealous of Tess's success. She made the top thirty under thirty as an up-and-coming playwright and he couldn't stand it. It made him feel insecure and so he cheated on her to reassert his male power. It was so obvious that David Attenborough could have documented it in a nature programme for the BBC. I told Tess after they broke up about his porn addiction, hoping it would make her feel better, and I think it did. She booked a round-the-world ticket in order to get some distance and do some healing.

I miss her. Particularly now, in this big house, with all this going on. I feel alone. You'd think I'd be used to it, and in some ways I am and I relish my own time. But occasionally I do think it would be nice to have someone to turn to, someone who'd always be on my side, offering unfailing support.

Halfway through emptying the kitchen cupboards of mouldering food, I discover an old packet of Jammy Dodgers. They must have been here a while because I threw all the biscuits and sweets away when I started my diet in earnest. I must have missed this packet, unless Tess had them hidden up here, out of my sight. I also discover a box of hard-shell tacos with a best before date of the mid-noughties. The tacos remind me of Mexican food, which in turn reminds me of James. Shit.

I forgot all about our date tonight. I glance at my watch. I've just got enough time to shower and get ready. I wonder for a moment if I should cancel or at least postpone, but it beats sitting at home waiting and wondering what else Becca has in store for me. Perhaps I'll be able to dig a little and find out more about who Becca is and what she might be capable of, or even how to handle her. If anyone knows, it's James.

Thursday, 7 December
Evening

He's even more attractive than I remember. One of those lucky men who get better with age. Find me a woman who improves with age like a fine wine. It's so unfair. He's got a few grey hairs, not many, just a smattering, and there are some lines etched around his eyes, which are the most phenomenal blue up close, so glacial they make me almost shiver. I'm guessing he's mid-thirties.

As I sit down I'm aware of him taking me in, his eyes scrolling down my body. It makes me nervous. It feels like someone is scraping their nails down a blackboard inside my head. I'm praying that he doesn't recognise me, though the chances are he'd never associate the old me with the new me.

I hope too that he likes what he sees, that the new me passes the test, and after I smooth down my dress and look up at him, I'm fairly sure that he does. At least I think he does. He's smiling at me, so I take a deep breath and smile back.

'Great dress,' he tells me.

'Thanks,' I say, silently high-fiving myself for buying it, even though it cost me an arm and a leg. It's Vivienne

Westwood and fits like a dream, accentuating every curve, and I see his gaze quickly flit to my cleavage before returning to my face.

'What would you like to drink?' he asks. 'Red or white?'

I hesitate, not sure I should drink, but what the hell, it's been a very stressful few days. 'Red,' I say.

'Do you like Pinot Noir?' he asks, perusing the menu.

'Sure,' I say. 'You choose.'

He chooses the most expensive one, which I take as a good sign. And he orders a whole bottle.

We make small talk as we wait for the waiter to bring the wine. He seems keen to impress, telling me that his flat is just around the corner in Marylebone, and that he bought it because it came with a twenty-four-hour concierge and a gym and swimming pool in the basement. I keep quiet about where I live, just telling him that it's in East Dulwich – a bit of a fudge, but it sounds better than Camberwell.

As he talks I smile and nod and think about how much I wish my mother could see me now. And my schoolmates. Or even Becca. My mother's words echo in my head – calling me a stupid cow and telling me that no one would ever look at me twice, that I would never amount to anything. Yet here I am, I think to myself as I twirl the wine glass stem between my fingers, in a fashionable new restaurant in Soho, wearing a designer dress, sitting opposite a man who's just paid close to a million pounds for a one-bedroom flat in the centre of London.

When the waiter comes I order oysters Mexican style, because I've heard oysters are an aphrodisiac, and a halibut ceviche with sorrel, while James orders the crispy octopus with hazelnut mole and pickled potatoes. I was expecting tacos and burritos and cheesy nachos, but this is a lot more upscale. I'm not even sure what half the stuff on the menu is. I hear my mum sneering about how fancy I am now and asking what the hell's wrong with an ordinary boiled potato, why the need to pickle them? I try to ignore these thoughts and focus on James. I'm also trying to silence another voice in my head, the voice of worry, wondering if he'll foot the bill or expect us to split it, because I can't really afford this, especially now.

'So where do you work?' James asks as the waiter pours our wine.

I knew this would come up and I've thought long and hard about what to tell him. 'PKW. It's an entertainment agency,' I say.

He freezes with his glass halfway to his lips. 'Yeah, I know it. I represent some of their bigger clients.'

I take a large sip of the wine the waiter has just poured me. 'I thought I recognised you,' I tell him. 'Did you use to date Becca?'

He frowns and cocks his head at me. 'How do you—? Did we meet?'

I shake my head. 'No. Becca was just always talking about you. And I remember seeing you at the Christmas party.'

He turns as white as the tablecloth and sets his wine glass down. I wonder if there's a slight tremble in his hand, but I might be imagining it. 'You were there?' he asks.

I nod and bite my lip. Perhaps it was too soon to mention it but if it came up later, he'd only wonder why I hadn't said anything before. 'I'm sorry,' I tell him. 'When I saw you on Tinder I thought I recognised you but I wasn't sure.'

He picks up his glass of wine and takes a big sip. 'Wow. Sorry, um, this is . . .' He shakes his head. 'Weird.'

That wasn't the reaction I was hoping for. I was hoping we could skip past it, laughing at the coincidence. I was hoping that tonight would not just be a way to take my mind off the disasters in my life, but a chance to dig for information on Becca. But I can't come right out and tell him about her harassment campaign because he'll ask what caused it and I'll have to admit that I sent that email. I don't want him to think badly of me.

James exhales loudly. 'So you and Becca were friends?' he asks.

I shake my head. 'No. Just colleagues. She didn't really have many friends at work.'

'Yeah, she said everyone was a bitch. She hated it there.' He must see my reaction because he quickly adds a flustered, 'Sorry. I'm sure she didn't mean you.'

'So, what about you?' I ask him. 'Are you still in touch with her?'

'No. Not for years.' He looks up sharply. 'You?'

I shake my head. 'No. Well, only on Facebook.'

'Facebook? She's back on Facebook?'

'Yes,' I tell him. 'I mean, she's got a new profile.'

'She does?'

I nod. He looks surprised but quickly shakes it off.

'How is she?' he asks.

I hesitate before I answer. He looks a little bit too hopeful, a little bit too eager to hear, and it jabs at me like a sharp pencil poked between my ribs. 'She's married,' I tell him. 'She's got a baby and everything.'

His face falls at the news.

'She looks really happy,' I say.

He takes another large gulp of his wine. I start to think I should have stayed quiet. I could kick myself. I knew it was a risk, that bringing up Becca might backfire, but I figured it was worth it. I reckoned that for one, they were broken up and for two, if he didn't know about Becca's new life then finding out that she was married and had a kid would work in my favour, but it doesn't feel that way. He seems peeved to hear she's with someone else.

Our food arrives and I offer him an oyster. He shakes his head but I press him and he relents. I watch him squeeze a drop of lemon juice onto it and raise it to his lips.

'What's she doing now?' he asks very casually, too casually, just before he tips the oyster into his mouth and swallows it whole.

'She's an interior decorator. Somewhere in the Cotswolds.'

I copy him with the lemon squeeze and then lift my own oyster to my lips and let it slide down my throat in what I hope is a sophisticated way. It takes every ounce of willpower in my body not to bring it right back up again and spit it onto my plate like the fat briney slug that it is. Good lord. Why do people eat these? I start coughing so hard that the waiter, who is passing by, stops to ask if I'm OK and James rises out of his seat as though wondering if he needs to try out the Heimlich manoeuvre.

I guzzle some water as James retakes his seat, and when I'm recovered I laugh in what I hope is a winsome way. 'Not very aphrodisiac-like,' I say, embarrassed.

He laughs too. 'I think you need to eat several to get the full effect,' he says, grinning and revealing his dimple.

I relax a little. Maybe all hope is not lost. Perhaps he is over Becca but simply experienced a momentary shock – as we all do when hearing something unexpected. It makes sense he'd be curious about her.

'When did you and Becca break up?' I ask, because I'm curious too. I want to know what happened.

'Oh, about six months after the accident,' he mumbles.

'What happened?' I say. 'Do you mind me asking?'

He sighs. 'She changed is what happened.'

I rest my elbows on the table and lean forward, all ears. 'How?'

'She was different. After the accident. For a start she couldn't remember much of anything. Not even my name at first. She couldn't remember the accident at all. But when that stuff started to come back, it was more that her personality changed.'

'What do you mean?'

He frowns, deep in thought. 'She was always really fun before.'

I try to keep my expression neutral. He might have thought Becca was really fun but the rest of us certainly didn't.

'You must remember that about her?' James continues. 'She was always up for a laugh.'

I nod, more to signal that I'm listening than that I agree.

He smiles as he reminisces. 'It was always an adventure being with her. But after the accident she changed.'

'Changed how?' I ask, trying to keep my tone conversational when I'm hanging on every word.

He shrugs. 'Well, she was a lot more self-conscious for one.'

'What about?' I ask

'The scar,' he says.

'What scar?' I ask.

'On her face.' He draws a line down his cheek from just below his eye to his jaw. That's weird, I think to myself. There was no scar in her photo but then again it's likely she's had plastic surgery, and make-up can cover a multitude of sins – that much I do know.

'I mean, it wasn't all that bad,' he continues, 'I remember telling her that. We got in a fight about it. It probably wasn't the most sensitive thing to say. There she was, in a wheelchair—'

The waiter interrupts with our main courses and I have to wait for him to set down James's crispy octopus and pickled potatoes and my ceviche before I can follow up.

'Wheelchair?'

'Yeah,' James answers. 'She was in a wheelchair for three or four months. She had a lot of operations on her leg, metal plates put in. Her spine had to be fused in a few places – the vertebrae. It was tough for her. She was in a lot of pain. They told her she might never walk again. She had to learn from scratch. Her fine motor skills too – like how to hold a knife and fork.'

'We never knew any of this,' I tell him, in shock.

James offers me a bite of his octopus but I shake my head. 'No. She didn't want anyone to know. And she didn't want anyone seeing her that way. I think it was also because of her hair. They had to shave it off when they operated. And the whole wheelchair thing. It made her embarrassed. She couldn't even go to the bathroom on her own. I mean, I get it, it's pretty undignified.'

'Yes,' I say, sympathetically. 'That must have been awful.' I think about the photos on Facebook. 'You could never tell now. She must have had plastic surgery and her hair's grown out.'

'Yes, the doctors talked about plastic surgery.' He takes a bite of his pickled potatoes. 'So she looks well, then?'

'Yes,' I say. 'I mean, you can't see a scar but I suppose she might have been wearing a lot of make-up. But she's not in a wheelchair any more.'

'Good,' he says, 'that's good.

I want to know more about changes on the inside – to her personality. I want to know what she might be capable of.

'So,' I say, finally tucking into my ceviche. 'You were saying that after the accident she changed.'

'Yeah,' James nods, then frowns. 'Yeah. I tried. I really tried but work was full on. I was aiming to make partner at my firm, I was working crazy hours. I'd visit her at weekends. The rehab place was close to Peterborough, not the easiest to get to. And most of the time I'd wonder why I bothered. It was like visiting a stranger. She was a totally different person. The doctors told me that often happens.'

I tilt my head, not understanding.

'With brain injuries,' he goes on to explain.

'Oh?' I say, taking a sip of wine.

'It can affect behaviour,' he goes on.

'How?' I ask, my heart starting to race.

He takes a deep breath and lets it out in a big exhalation. 'It can make people impulsive, obsessive, paranoid. They can lose their inhibitions, that sort of thing.'

'Oh wow, I didn't know,' I say, swallowing hard. 'So that happened with Becca?'

He nods. 'Yes. She was really angry.' He holds his hands up. 'I mean, I totally get it. She was frustrated and she was depressed. Who wouldn't be? Stuck there, learning how to do stuff a three-year-old has mastered, struggling to remember two plus two and what the date was. But she'd lose her temper so fast. She didn't want me visiting at first and she got all moody when I came, would get obsessed with the idea that I was lying to her. But then, when I didn't visit, she got really paranoid. You couldn't reason with her at all.'

I feel a shiver crawl up my spine. 'What was she paranoid about?'

'Oh, stupid stuff. She thought because of the way she looked I'd stopped loving her. She thought I was having an affair.' He looks at me, then quickly adds: 'I wasn't. God, I had no time for anything, let alone carrying on behind her back. And I'm not that kind of person anyway,' he says, making sure he looks me in the eye. 'It was crazy – they were accusations based on nothing. She was always the jealous type. But there's only so long you can deny something before you start to feel like a stuck record. She couldn't get over it.' He breaks off suddenly and swallows hard.

'What?' I ask quietly, putting down my fork. 'Get over what?'

He stares off into space for a beat then shakes his head. 'I tried. But then she told me she didn't want to see me any more.' He scowls to himself and I wonder once again if he's actually over her or not. 'I was pretty cut up about it. I'd tried to be there for her and she pushed me away. We fell out of touch. It was easier that way. Then she changed her number and stopped answering emails and, well, that was that. When you mentioned her name it was a shock. It's been so long since we were last in touch.'

I take another bite of ceviche, pondering that.

'Where did you say she had moved again?' he asks.

'The Cotswolds. A little village called Widford.'

James nods. I offer him some of my ceviche. He leans forward and I slide it into his mouth. 'That's great,' he says, chewing on it.

'Do you want some more?' I say, spearing another piece.

'No, you finish it,' he says. 'Anyway, god, all we've done is talk about Becca. I'm sorry. What about you? Tell me about yourself. I don't know anything about you.'

Damn, I was wanting to press him further on the kinds of things Becca did or what the doctors said about how to manage her but he's smiling at me expectantly. 'Well,' I say, 'I'm from a little town near Doncaster.'

'Doncaster?' he says, his nose wrinkling as though I've told him I grew up in a slum. It riles me but I don't show it.

'Originally,' I add. 'But I've lived in London since I graduated. I live with a friend, she's a playwright, but she's away travelling so I've got the place to myself, which is good because I'm working on a novel. I'm planning on quitting my job so I can finish it.'

His eyes light up. 'Wow,' he says. 'What kind of novel?'

'It's a secret,' I say and then I look up at him through my lashes and give him a flirtatious smile. 'But one day maybe I'll let you read it.'

He looks at me with renewed interest and I remember what I read about keeping an air of mystery. Men like that.

'Maybe one day I'll see it on the bestseller shelf in Waterstones,' he says, raising his glass.

I lift mine and chink it against his.

The waiter returns to remove our plates and refill our wine glasses. 'Dessert?' he asks, handing us menus.

I consider the desserts on offer, all of them miles more appealing than oysters, raw fish dunked in lime juice and pickled potatoes, but I resist.

'Just coffee for me,' I say.

'Same,' says James, and when we hand the waiters our menus our hands brush. It seems to charge the atmosphere between us, or maybe I'm imagining it. Probably I'm imagining it. I wish I could tell.

The waiter goes away and I head to the bathroom, taking my handbag with me so I can fix my make-up. The lights are so dim I can hardly see my hand in front of my face, and the mirrors are that fake tarnish that's meant to look antique but just looks dirty, so I can't do much except carefully reapply lipstick. I spray some perfume behind my ears and knees too (which immediately brings to mind a memory of my mother, spraying Impulse Temptation up her skirt before heading out on the town with the girls). It seems weird to be on a date with Becca's ex-boyfriend while she's out there, possibly plotting further revenge. I think about what I've learned about her from James. Truthfully it's nothing helpful, only more troubling.

I head back to the table and as we sip our coffee I stretch out my legs so my foot accidentally on purpose rubs against James's shin. He doesn't move his leg and I know that's a good sign. I wonder if he'll invite me back to his, after?

'Did Becca ever do anything, then?' I ask, trying to sound casual, even though I'm aware I keep turning the conversation back to her and he might get suspicious.

He frowns, confused. 'What do you mean?'

'You said she acted strange and paranoid, but when you broke up with her she never did anything, you know, crazy?'

He shakes his head. 'No. I just never heard from her again.' He finishes his coffee and does that air scrawl signal to summon the bill.

I sit on the edge of my seat, watching the waiter bring it over. He sets it in the centre of the table in a way that tells me he's had equality training. I reach for my handbag, worrying about which card to try and run through the machine, but thankfully James picks up the bill and pulls out his wallet. 'I'll get it,' he tells me.

I'm so relieved, especially after I see the amount. 'Thanks,'

I say, wondering if that means he expects something in return and now starting to worry about that instead.

James adds a generous tip and then signs the bill with a flourish. It's a gold card, I notice. He looks up. I smile at him.

'Do you fancy going for a nightcap somewhere?' he asks me.

Friday, 8 December
Morning

Someone is pounding on the front door. It takes me a few seconds to come to and then a few more to get my bearings. My brain is fuzzy from the wine and the late night. I lie there, frozen beneath the covers, holding my breath and waiting for whoever it is to leave but they don't. They keep knocking. Reluctantly I roll out of bed.

I creep down the stairs, keeping my back flat to the wall, pulling my dressing gown on over my pyjamas and belting it tight. The hallway is subdued by heavy shadows and as the heating is off, it's also cold as the grave.

I ease my way over the creaking floorboard on the third stair from the bottom and peer at the blurred shape looming through the stained-glass window in the front door.

Who could it be? It's not the postman. He comes before eight and it's past ten, and besides, there's a pile of letters and an Amazon parcel on the floor. Whoever it is, they're not going away. They bang the knocker again with a sense of urgency. What if it's Becca? What if she's found me?

I stand stock-still. I'm not going to answer it. There's no way. I'll pretend I'm not home. But then someone lifts the letterbox flap and peers into the hallway. I catch a glimpse of an eye and almost scream.

'Lizzie?'

Oh god. It's Flora. I stride to the door, though it takes a few moments to open it as my hands are shaking and I forget about the key in the pot on the side table.

When I finally get it open I find Flora standing there in a pink rain jacket, holding a Hello Kitty umbrella and wearing bright pink polka-dot wellies.

'Aren't you going to invite me in? It's freezing out.'

I nod absently and step aside, wondering what on earth she's doing here.

Flora removes her raincoat and I hang it on a peg by the door. She eases off her wellington boots and follows me into the kitchen.

'You weren't replying to any of my texts and I was worried about you,' Flora tells me.

'Sorry,' I say as I move about the kitchen, turning on the kettle. I think about turning on the heating too, but I don't. It costs a fortune to heat a house this big and it's only me paying the bills.

I'm a little thrown by Flora's visit and the lack of warning, self-conscious that I'm not up and dressed. I run my fingers through my hair. It's a mess. And I'm not wearing any make-up.

'I didn't get you up, did I?' Flora asks, nodding at my dressing gown.

I shrug. 'It's fine,' I say.

Her eyes go wide. 'Oh, sorry, did I wake you?'

'It doesn't matter. It's late. I overslept. Shouldn't you be at work?'

Flora shakes her head. 'It's OK, I worked so many late nights this week that I got given today off.' Her face splits into a wide grin. 'Did you hear? We sold it!'

'Oh,' I say. She means the manuscript but I don't feel like I can raise any enthusiasm. Is this why she's here? To tell me about her success? Because I'm not sure I'm in the mood.

'We sold the book rights for eight hundred thousand and the film rights for a quarter million on top. It's all over the *Bookseller* and the *Hollywood Reporter*. We've got so many requests for interviews. I'm going to be flat out next week.'

I'm glad I'm holding onto the back of the kitchen chair because I feel suddenly faint. It isn't the news so much as the fact that I haven't eaten breakfast yet, combined with the sleeping pill I took last night.

Flora sees me swaying and jumps to her feet. She ushers me into a seat. 'Sorry,' she says, grimacing, 'that was stupid of me, to bring up work ...' She tails off and busies herself with making the tea and I stare at the tabletop feeling my face burning, wondering how I can get her to leave. I'm not ready for this.

'It's fine,' I say, trying to seem bright and unfazed. 'I just had a late night.'

'Oh no,' she says, moving to get out the teabags, 'are you having trouble sleeping?'

'No. I went out last night actually. With James.'

She turns to me, clutching the mugs, her face lighting up. 'I forgot! Oh my goodness, how was it? How did it go?'

'It was great,' I tell her. 'We went to Merida.'

'Wow!' Flora says. 'How was it?'

'The food or the date?'

'Well, both,' she says.

'The food not so much but the date went well, I think.' He told me he'd call me.

'Are you going to see him again?' Flora asks.

'I think so,' I say.

Her eyes get a naughty glint in them. 'Did you . . . know?' she asks, almost winking at me. She's after the salacious details but there are none.

'No!' I say. 'He wanted me to go back to his for a nightcap but I told him maybe next time.'

'Why?' Flora asks in amazement.

I stare at her. Isn't it obvious? 'You should never give in so fast, not if you want a man to respect you. They like the thrill of the chase.' I sound like an expert, I realise, which is quite ironic. 'At least,' I admit, 'that's what all the books say.'

'No, you're absolutely right,' Flora says, nodding. 'Good to keep him hanging. But how exciting!'

The kettle boils and she pours the water over the teabags. 'So, how are you feeling otherwise?' she asks, carrying the mugs to the table.

'So you've heard then,' I say. I know that's what she's doing here. She wants to find out from the horse's mouth exactly what's happening with work and the fraud charges.

She gives an awkward shrug and focuses on pouring milk into her tea.

I may as well just confront the rumours, rather than dancing around them. 'I didn't do it,' I tell her.

'Of course!' Flora says in alarm, glancing at me. 'I never . . . of course I would never . . .'

I cut her off. 'What have they told you?'

'Oh, nothing, you know what HR are like. No one is saying anything.'

'But you must have heard something,' I push.

Another shrug, her eyes downcast, not meeting mine. 'Well, someone said that there was some kind of discrepancy with the expenses claims.'

'Yes,' I say. 'But it's a mistake. I didn't do anything.'

Flora nods then shakes her head, as though trying out which one works best. 'Of course not. It's a mistake. That's what I said. I'm sure they'll sort it soon.'

I wonder what else they're saying at work. I can imagine the gossip mill is in overdrive, though maybe the news of the book deal is overshadowing it. That's one good thing, I suppose, though when I allow myself to dwell on the figures – over a million pounds! – I feel I've swallowed not just one bitter pill but an entire packet.

Flora casts around the kitchen. 'Are there any biscuits?' she asks.

I get up and open a cupboard, finding the packet of Jammy Dodgers, the ones I found at the back of the cupboard. 'I've only got these,' I say, 'but—'

She cuts me off before I can finish. 'I love a Jammy Dodger.'

They're only a little bit out of date. I open the packet. No obvious signs of distress. I put them on a plate and set them down on the table. She takes a bite of one and I watch, but she doesn't say anything and finishes it with one more bite.

'Aren't you having one?' she asks, crumbs littering her bottom lip.

I shake my head.

She dabs at her lip. 'I keep forgetting you gave up sugar.'

'Three years now.'

She smiles. 'Amazing. I couldn't last an hour!'

'It's fine once you get past the first couple of weeks. You just need some willpower.'

'Life's too short!' she laughs.

'Oh, wait,' I say, jumping up and pulling the plate of Jammy Dodgers out of her way. 'I've got something. I forgot.' I run to the fridge and get out the pink truffle chocolates. 'Here,' I say, putting them in front of her. 'Someone gave me these months ago.'

'You don't need to open those,' Flora says but it's too late, I've already opened them.

'They've been in there for months. Have one,' I say, jiggling the box in her direction.

Flora shakes her head. 'I'm OK.'

'Go on. Just one. I'll join you.'

I take one from the box and bite into it. Flora takes that as permission to take one too. She pops it in her mouth.

The sweetness of the truffle slices like a surgical blade through the roof of my mouth and into my brain. Immediately my mouth fills with saliva. I set the other half of the truffle down on the edge of my saucer and drink some tea to wash away the taste. When you're not used to eating sugar it feels so synthetic and ghastly.

'What are you going to do?' asks Flora.

'I don't know,' I say. 'Wait, I suppose.'

I think about telling her about Becca. It would be good to have someone to bounce it off, talk it over with. I couldn't tell James last night but Flora might have some ideas. A problem shared . . . I take a deep breath. 'I think I know who might be behind it.'

'Behind what?'

'Behind the allegations.'

'What do you mean?'

'Remember I told you I'd found Becca online? Her website and her Facebook page?'

Flora nods. 'Yes.'

'Well, the thing is, I sent you an email about it but I didn't send it to *you* . . . I sent it to her, to Becca, by accident.'

'OK,' says Flora, looking blank.

I sigh loudly. 'I wasn't very nice. I was only joking, of course, but I think she's taking it personally. Like, *really* personally.'

'What do you mean?'

'I think she's the one who emailed work telling them lies about me, about the expense forms. The forms they're accusing me of falsifying are all hers. How weird is that?'

Flora is frowning, trying to wrap her head around what I'm saying.

'And then, this is the really weird thing, not only has she taken down her website, but yesterday I got hundreds of really bad reviews.'

'Reviews of what?'

Oh shit. 'Nothing,' I say quickly, clamming up.

'What?'

I knew there was a reason I shouldn't have said anything. 'Nothing. It doesn't matter.'

'No, tell me.'

'OK, but you have to promise not to tell anyone, under pain of death.'

'OK,' says Flora.

'I run a little bookkeeping business on the side.'

'You do? Why didn't you tell me?'

'We're not allowed to do any other work, it's in our contracts.'

Flora wrinkles her nose. 'I'm sure they don't mean that. I know Sian in PR takes on the occasional private client. They wouldn't care. It's not like you're stealing clients from them. And it's not like they pay us enough, especially when you consider what the agents earn. I think Tim drives for Uber sometimes.'

Somehow hearing Flora say all this makes me feel better. I push the box of chocolates towards her and she takes another.

'So what happened?' she asks.

'I got all these bad reviews yesterday. All of them posted at the exact same time, all by random people I've never met, most of them fake profiles.'

Flora frowns. 'What?'

'I know, that's what I said.'

'Who would do that?' she asks.

I shake my head. It's obvious, isn't it? 'Becca. Who else could it be?'

She stares at me in amazement. 'But why? Because you said some things that weren't nice? What did you say exactly?'

I shake my head. 'Nothing! I mean, nothing too bad. Nothing no normal person would react to. I even sent her an apology. I asked James a bit about her, about the accident. I didn't tell him about all this because I don't want him to know, but I did find out that she changed after the accident. He said she went a bit crazy.'

Flora's eyes are wide as saucers. 'Crazy?'

I nod. 'Yeah, he said she got all paranoid and angry and he barely recognised her any more. That's why they broke up.'

Flora takes a gulp of her tea and reaches for another truffle. 'Oh my goodness. Did you hear back from her after you sent the email apologising? Did she respond?'

I shake my head. 'No. And I'm worried she might do something else. Something worse.'

Flora gives me a funny look, like she's weighing it all up and can't quite figure something out. 'But you don't know for sure it's her. Could the reviews just be some kind of spam thing?'

I pull a face. 'The coincidence of it, you don't think it's too much?'

Flora shrugs. 'But to do that – that's a little over the top. You said she has a whole new life now. It seems a bit extreme to go and start a fight like this.'

Now I'm starting to feel stupid. Maybe Flora is right. From her Facebook photos it seems like Becca's living a normal life. She's married and has a kid. She certainly doesn't seem crazy. Maybe I've made it all up. Maybe it is all just a string of weird coincidences. But how do you explain the Sméagol comment or the fact she's missing from the Internet?

'I tried looking her up,' Flora says, reaching for another truffle, 'and I couldn't find her.'

'She's changed her name. She's Becca Bridges now. But you won't find her. She's vanished. I can't even find her website any more.'

Flora's eyebrows jerk upwards. 'What?'

'I know. She took down her own website. Why would you do that?'

Flora shakes her head. She pops the truffle in her mouth. 'That's strange,' she says. 'Are you sure? I mean, are you sure it was actually her website? You didn't make a mistake?'

'Yes, of course I'm sure,' I say, getting irritated. It's like she's questioning my sanity. 'It was there and then it was gone in the morning, after I sent that message.'

Flora pulls a face, like she doesn't know what to think.

'What if she does something else?' I ask, hearing the note of desperation in my voice and hating myself for it. 'What if this isn't the end? What if it's just the beginning?'

Flora puts her mug down on the table. 'Don't be silly. It's all going to be fine.' She's trying to placate me, I can tell. 'Maybe she got your email and accepted your apology.'

'Or maybe she didn't accept it.' I look out the window. A raven is sitting on the garden fence, glaring at me with its beady eye and for a moment I can almost believe that Becca has sent it, like some witch's familiar, to spy on me. I jump up and start to clear the mugs and chocolates from the table. Flora stands up, slowly, and starts to help. I'm still put out that she doesn't one hundred per cent buy my story, that she seems to think I might be making it up or losing my mind.

'If you're really worried,' she says, watching me stack the dishwasher, 'why not try to speak to her?'

'I have. I emailed her,' I say.

'No, face to face. It's always best face to face don't you think?'

'But—' I stop myself. I was about to argue that that's ridiculous but actually it's not a bad idea. Confronting Becca would surely be better than sitting around on tenterhooks, waiting for her to strike again. It's harder to reject an apology when you make it in person. 'Maybe you're right.'

I put the lid on the chocolates and hand the box to Flora. 'Here, you take them,' I say.

She protests but I insist. I don't need the temptation and she likes them more than me. 'I'll be off then,' she says, putting on her coat. 'I'll see you Monday.' She breaks off, flushing, realising that it's not certain that I'll have a job to go to on Monday.

I hurry her to the door. 'Yes,' I tell her. 'I'm sure I'll see you Monday.'

I need to find Becca. How do I do that? Bridges Interiors must be listed on Companies House. If Becca is a director, her address will also be listed. I run upstairs and dive under the covers to keep warm, opening up my laptop.

As I do, my phone buzzes. Immediately my stomach clenches. It's an email notification, though, not more bad reviews.

I half hope it's from Hammurabi AKA Becca, but it's

not. It's from Yelp, telling me they are carrying out an investigation and hope to have the issue resolved within the next twenty-four hours. There's another email from one of my bookkeeping clients. Shit. The subject reads TERMINATION.

In a two-sentence email she fires me. I can't believe it. I have done her books for three years. She can't just fire me. Well, she can, but it's hardly fair. I've always done a great job for her and I was banking on her business to help tide me over in the new year. What if she gives me a bad review too? I'm probably going to have to rebrand the business and start over and that will take forever. I'll probably have to hire some fake reviewers myself just to get me back in the game. That wouldn't be very professional, or ethical, and it would also be somewhat ironic, but what else can I do? I can't afford to lose these clients.

Feeling pissed off, I turn my attention back to Becca. There's no record of Bridges Interiors on Companies House. That raises a major red flag. Was the business never set up as a legal entity? There should be some record of her somewhere online.

I search for Zac Bridges, adding in a variety of other search terms, like Becca's name but I can't find him either. This is beyond strange.

I know they live in the Cotswolds. I have the name of the village too. I'm sure the blurb on her website said that she lived in an old mill in a village called Widford. A quick search of estate agent websites and I have it narrowed down to two possible houses but only one was bought and sold in the last three years. When I look it up on Maps I get a satellite view of the street. It's a large detached house on the outskirts of the village, set at the bottom of a long lane and beside a river.

It has fields behind it. The only other house is a little cottage opposite.

I should be able to find the details of who owns the house by searching on the land registry. It costs almost fifteen pounds and I have to dig out the only credit card that still works, but within a few minutes I've got the details of the title register in front of me. The owner is a company, not a person. That's odd enough to arouse suspicion. Usually only celebrities buy a house this way, to avoid stalkers or weirdos finding out where they live and harassing them.

Either way, I think I've found her.

Friday, 8 December
Afternoon

Tess's car – an old VW Beetle – is filled with clutter: old scripts and programmes, bin bags containing costumes that I assume from the musty swamp smell she meant to bring home to wash, and a box of props. Her last play, about a terrorist attack in London, won her an award and an offer to adapt it for TV. That's ostensibly what she's meant to be doing while travelling – working on the adaptation – though from her emails it sounds like the only things she's working on are her tan and getting over Rob with copious amounts of rebound sex. If everything goes badly here, and I lose my job, I think I'll just go to India and meet up with her.

I could scrap the novel I'm writing and start afresh. I could base it on Becca. Make it about a crazy ex-colleague who tries to ruin the protagonist's life. I think about how I would do it, then get lost in trying to figure out the ending and almost miss the turn-off on the A40 to Stow-on-the-Wold.

I can't believe I'm doing this, but once I'd put the plan into motion I didn't let myself stop to think about it. I just threw on some clothes, grabbed Tess's car keys and left. Now, as I hurtle past rolling, wooded hillsides and fields of sheep, I start to wonder if this is the most sensible thing to do. If

Becca is so unhinged she'd try to sabotage my life online, what might she be capable of in real life? Still, when I was a kid my mum used to tell me that most bullies crumble the minute you confront them. I never had the guts to do it back then but now I'm older, I feel as if I'm being given a second shot. I'm not going to back down this time, roll over and play nice. I'm going to stand up to her. I really should think about what I'm going to say to her, though. If Tess was here, she could help me script the conversation. Maybe I should have brought someone with me for backup. Maybe I should have asked Flora.

My phone rings and I glance at it. It's work. I let it go to voicemail since I'm driving, but also because I don't want to speak to them. Moira called as I was leaving and left a message asking me to come in to the office this afternoon. I couldn't tell from her tone whether it was good news or bad, and I didn't want to know if it was bad. I'm putting it off until I've spoken to Becca.

I take the turn-off to Widford and follow the directions to her house, down a long A-road with fields and woods on either side, and a couple of farms, until I turn up Magpie Lane. There's a pub on the corner. The King's Arms. A slightly shabby place with peeling paint and a sign advertising Fish and Chip Fridays and rooms which I bet are a horror of chintz. I drive past, noticing how low in the sky the clouds are hanging, like two-week-old helium balloons sagging to a grubby brown carpet.

Becca's place is just up on the left, over a little stone bridge that crosses the river. I start to slow down. I can see the house up ahead. I recognise it from Google maps. I'll drive by and see if there are any lights on first or if there's a car in the drive.

The house is bigger than I was expecting but otherwise the photos on the estate agent site did a pretty good job. It's lovely Cotswold stone – cream coloured, with a black slate roof. A low brick wall in front is covered in rambling rose bushes, and the facade with a wisteria, though because it's winter the bare branches look like gnarly witch's hands trying to strangle the house. I imagine come spring the whole grass verge will be carpeted in snowdrops and daffodils and the house will look like it belongs on the cover of *Country Living* but now it feels isolated and rather bleak. There's no car in the driveway but there's a separate garage to one side of the house. There's one light on downstairs, in the hallway, but that's it. I wonder if she's home?

On the other side of the lane, diagonally opposite, there's a stone cottage. It's smaller and quainter with a conservatory tacked on the end and a high hedge squaring off the garden. There's a huge Christmas tree in the downstairs window, its lights twinkling brightly, and a fancy wreath on the door that must have cost a fortune. A BMW is parked out front.

I carry on up the lane until I reach a lay-by in front of a field and turn around. Then I stop the car and think about what I'm doing. Now I'm here I'm losing my nerve. But I can't drive all this way and not do what I set out to. If I go home, I'll feel like I did as a kid when someone would tease me at school and I'd run home in tears only to have my mum yell at me for being a big coward and not standing up for myself.

Hearing my mum's voice in my head, urging me on, I drive back the way I came and pull over in front of Becca's house. I stare at the front door. What if her husband answers? I had a story worked out, something I came up with while driving, that I was an old friend of Becca's just passing through. But looking around at the endless fields and hedgerows and ditches filled with mud, I realise that sounds a bit suspect.

I switch off the engine, pull on my coat then get out of the car. The rushing of the river a few feet away is so loud, like static on an old TV. I'm used to the cacophony of London: sirens and beeping and people driving past with thumping music blaring out of their car speakers, loud enough to make your body vibrate. I'm not used to the sound of running water, or bare tree branches creaking in the wind, or crows cawing. For a moment I think about getting back in my car and driving back to London, wondering if I'm walking blindly into danger; but there's that voice again in my head, my mum yelling at me to stand up for myself. I set off up the driveway.

The house sits back from the road by about fifty metres. There's no sign of anyone as I approach the front door.

I ring the bell and then stand there, on the doorstep, shoving my hands deep into my pockets and hunching against the cold. I strain my ears to see if I can hear someone inside but it's all quiet.

I press the bell again. Nothing. Glancing over my shoulder, I see that the neighbours over the road would be able to see me if they looked out their front window and it makes me feel awkward, but I'm not doing anything wrong. All I'm doing is ringing a doorbell. I step to one side and peek in through the little side window. The blind is partly drawn but I can see a sliver of hallway. Coats and a scarf on a stand, including, of course, the requisite Barbour jacket and Hunter wellington boots. I can make out the bottom of the stairs. There are several doors off the hall. All of them are closed. There's no mail on the mat when I lift the letterbox to peer inside, which means that either she got no post today, or she was home earlier and has already picked it up.

I walk further along the front of the house and stop at the window to the living room. There's a cream sofa facing a large stone fireplace, a coffee table stacked with books and magazines, and two ugly sixties-style armchairs which are at odds with the rest of the design. On the other side of the living room, French windows look out onto the back garden and a big pond.

I wonder if I could walk all the way around, but when I go and explore I see that I can't. There's a twelve-foot hedge at the side of the house blocking off access and at the other side, past the garage, there's a fence. The gate through to the back is locked.

I guess no one is home but something is bothering me. I can't quite pin it down until I turn around and head back down the driveway. The top of what looks like a child's climbing frame is poking over the hedge in the neighbour's garden. That's what stops me in my tracks. There's no sign of a child at Becca's house. No little welly-boots by the front door or children's coats on the stand. No buggy or car seat in the hallway, none of the usual detritus I imagine you'd need if you had a baby. And what parent of a small child owns a cream-coloured sofa? Or leaves a garden pond uncovered?

'Hi!'

I look up. A woman is coming out of the house opposite carrying two bags. She's around forty, quite pretty, with brown hair in a ponytail. She smiles. I smile and wave, thinking how much nicer country people are than city people. If a stranger says hello to you on the street in London, you cross to the other side pronto because they're either on day release or they're a Jehovah's Witness.

'Hi,' I say, walking towards her.

She frowns. 'Can I help?'

'Actually, yes,' I say, thinking to myself that she looks familiar but not sure why. 'I wonder, do you know Becca?'

'Yes,' she nods, beeping open her car and putting the bags in it.

'Do you know where she is?' I ask.

The woman shakes her head. 'I don't know. I saw her this morning, putting the bins out.'

'Does she normally park her car in the drive?' I ask.

'No, it's always in the garage.'

We look over at the house.

'I tried the doorbell but she didn't answer.'

The neighbour shrugs. 'She might be out walking the dog.'

She has a dog?

Just then I hear the sound of a baby screaming. A man is walking out of the house, carrying a baby wearing a big pink snowsuit that makes it looks like a cartoon starfish.

'Can you take Sadie,' the man says to the woman and offers her the baby. 'I need to lock up.'

My gaze flits from the child, with her brown curls, cupid-bow mouth and slightly wizened face, to the man. I know him.

'You're Zac,' I blurt in astonishment.

The man looks at me curiously. 'Yes,' he says, with some uncertainty. 'Have we met?'

The woman casts a very sharp look between us.

'No,' I say to him. 'Is this your house?'

Now it's his turn to frown, his eyes narrowing at the intrusive questions. 'Yes,' he says.

'Why are you asking?' the woman cuts in. 'Do you two know each other?'

Zac shakes his head. 'No. We've never met.'

I look at the woman and realise with a start that she's the woman from the photo on Becca's Facebook. I hadn't seen it until now. Her hair is darker. She's the aunt. What was her name? Maddie or something? 'Who are you?' I ask.

'What?' the woman asks, confused.

I look at Zac. 'Is she your sister?'

'No! I'm his wife!' Maddie answers.

'I'm sorry,' I say, realising how bizarre my behaviour must seem to them. 'It's just . . .' *How do I explain this?* I stare at the baby she's holding, whose face is all moist with snot and tears. 'Whose baby is that?'

'Mine!' the woman says, clutching the baby tighter.

'Yours?'

'Listen,' Zac starts to say, getting quite aggressive with me now. 'How do you know my name?'

'She was looking for Becca,' the woman says, jiggling baby Sadie up and down and staring at me like I'm about to steal her baby from her arms.

'I know this sounds really crazy,' I say quickly, 'but is Becca . . . is she married?'

'What?' the woman snaps.

'Why do you want to know?' Zac asks, scowling at me.

'I can explain everything,' I say. I look to Becca's house, then back at them. 'But first of all you need to tell me, is Becca married? Does she have a baby?'

'No!' Maddie replies shrilly. 'What on earth—?'

'Oh dear,' I manage to whisper.

Maddie hands me a cup of tea and then takes a couple of steps backwards and leans against the edge of the sofa. She's positioned herself part way between me and the door, and part way between me and her husband. She still doesn't seem to understand what I've just told her, or maybe she just wants to shoot the messenger.

She pulls out her phone and I worry that she might be about to call the police. But that's fine. I'll happily explain to them. Maybe it's them I should have gone to in the first place.

Zac is sitting on the sofa opposite me. 'Let me get this straight,' he says, elbows on his knees. 'Becca has a Facebook page on which she's posted pictures of her and me and Sadie? And she's pretending that we're ... married? That Sadie's *her* baby. *Our* baby?'

I nod. 'She calls herself Becca Bridges.'

'My surname isn't Bridges.' He looks at his wife. 'It's Young.'

I frown at that but then realise it makes sense. She must have worried that if she used Zac's real name, then he or someone he knows might have stumbled across it online.

Maddie, arms crossed neatly over her chest, snorts. 'This is absurd. It's ridiculous.'

I look at her. She's old for a first-time mum, in her forties at least. 'It's the truth,' I tell her. 'How else would I know your names?'

Maddie walks over to me and holds her phone in my face. 'Then why can't I find her Facebook page?'

'She's deleted it. Or made it private.'

'Why would anyone do that?' she says, turning to Zac. 'It's insane.'

'I have screenshots,' I tell them, suddenly remembering my laptop, which is in the car. 'I can show you.'

Maddie nods. I get up and hurry outside to where I've parked – glancing over at Becca's house as I go. Is she there?

Is she watching me? Is she planning her revenge right at this very moment? I'm the one getting paranoid now. I quickly grab my laptop from the passenger seat and practically run back to Maddie and Zac's house.

I show them the photos I screengrabbed of Becca's website and Facebook page and they both lean over my shoulders to look. Maddie gasps, then covers her mouth with her hand and starts to pace the room. 'Oh my god,' she says. 'Oh my god.' Over and over. 'What kind of a nutcase is she? Who does that?'

Zac scours the screenshots without saying a word.

'Oh my god!' whispers Maddie, who's come to stand beside him. She's staring at the picture on screen of Zac and Becca on their 'wedding day', shaking her head in disbelief. She turns and looks across the room.

I look. There's a framed photo on the mantelpiece. I recognise it straight away because it's the same photo. Only, of course, it's not Becca in it. It's Maddie. Becca used their actual wedding photos – photoshopping her own face in place of Maddie's. My own jaw drops open at that.

'She stole my wedding photo!' Maddie shouts.

'And this one! Do you remember?' Zac says, pointing to the photo of the three of them; the one of Becca holding Sadie outside what looks like a church. He turns to Maddie. 'It was the church fete thing in the summer, remember?'

Maddie nods at him. Zac turns to me. 'We bumped into her and she asked someone to take a photo of us all. We thought it was weird at the time but went along with it because we didn't want to be rude.'

'She even commented as you, on her posts,' I tell Maddie.

Maddie looks at me in astonishment. 'What? I never commented on her posts. I'm not even friends with her!'

I think about the seventy-eight friends on Becca's Facebook page. Were any of them real? I bet not. 'She must have set up fake profiles,' I say.

Maddie looks at the photo of Becca holding Sadie. 'That's my baby,' she sobs. 'That's our baby! Why is she saying it's *her* baby?'

Zac takes her in his arms. 'It's going to be OK,' he murmurs. 'We'll sort it out.'

She pulls out of his arms. 'How?' she demands sharply. 'How are we going to sort it out?'

Sadie, sitting in a bouncy chair in the corner, starts to grizzle and cry and Maddie rushes over and picks her up. She starts to smother her in kisses, walking back and forth with her in her arms. 'We need to call the police. We need to report this.'

'No,' says Zac. 'She's obviously unwell. And there's nothing the police can do anyway. None of this is illegal, I don't think.'

'How is that not illegal?' demands Maddie, stabbing her finger at my laptop screen.

'She's taken it down now and I don't think she's broken any law.'

'Pretending to be someone else is fraud.'

'But she's not doing it for fraudulent reasons,' he argues.

'No, just for fucking crazy ones!'

Sadie's screams climb an octave and she waves her fists in the air as though she too feels her mother's rage.

I look between them, feeling like I'm responsible for unleashing chaos on their world. 'I'm sorry,' I say. 'Maybe I shouldn't have said anything.'

Zac shakes his head. 'No. We're absolutely glad you did.' He rubs a hand over his chin, thinking.

'Remember those clothes she gave us after Sadie was born?' he says to his wife. 'We hardly knew her to say hello and she turned up with a stack of designer Babygros.'

Maddie turns to me. 'It's true. We hardly know her. We barely ever speak to her.'

'She kept asking to babysit,' Zac adds. 'We kept putting her off.'

'We didn't know her,' says Maddie. 'We weren't about to trust our daughter with a total stranger. And thank god we never did. She probably would have abducted her.' She looks at Zac in horror, eyes widening, clutching Sadie even tighter to her chest. 'You don't think that's her plan, do you?'

'No,' says Zac, trying to calm her and Sadie. 'Of course not.'

Maddie isn't convinced. 'Why not? Why are you so sure? She was always flirting with you. I could tell. She was into you. She's probably had her eye on you this whole time. God, it's so creepy.'

'Come on, you're over-reacting.'

Maddie's face turns red. 'I'm not over-reacting!' she yells, making Sadie burst into tears all over again. She lowers her voice, bouncing Sadie on her hip to quiet her sobs. 'Every time she saw you she'd come running over with some kind of excuse. "Oh Zac, can I borrow your garden shears? Oh Zac, can you help me start my car, the battery's flat . . ."'

Zac sighs loudly. 'It *was* flat.'

'She was flirting with you,' Maddie says. 'She's obsessed with you. Oh my god. That's what it is. She's obsessed with you. And Sadie. We need to move. We can't stay here. God knows what she's capable of.'

Zac puts his arm around her. 'Calm down,' he says quietly. He ushers her to the sofa and she drops down, cradling Sadie.

She starts to rock back and forth. 'We need to move,' she repeats.

'We don't need to move,' says Zac.

'I'm not staying here, not if she is,' Maddie snaps back.

Both of them seem to have forgotten I'm here and I'm not sure what to say so I keep quiet.

Zac kneels beside Maddie. 'Listen, we're not moving. Don't be ridiculous. We just need to sort this out. I'll go over there. I'll talk to her. Make it clear we're not happy and that it needs to stop. We'll get a restraining order if we have to.'

Maddie looks at him, tears welling up. Her anger seems to have moved swiftly to upset. I totally understand where she's coming from and strangely enough, it feels quite comforting to know I'm not the only person having to deal with Becca. I'm not all alone in having to confront her. Maybe Zac and I could talk to her together. She might back off both of us if he threatens her with a restraining order. Maybe I should do the same.

On the other hand, realising that she's done this, made up a whole life and gone to so much trouble to make it seem real, makes me wonder just how unbalanced Becca is. Because that's not normal. Like Maddie says, it's really fucking crazy.

Just then another thought hits me – one so obvious I can't believe I didn't realise it until now. Has she made up *every-thing*? I clear my throat. 'I take it she doesn't have an interior design company either,' I say.

Maddie looks up from where she's sitting on the sofa, Zac with his arm around her. 'What?' she asks, her nose wrinkling in disdain. 'No. She doesn't work. At least, I've never seen her work, and she's never mentioned it. We thought she just had money.'

'You thought maybe she was someone's sugar baby,' Zac says.

Maddie flusters and glares at him. 'I never said that.'

'Yes, you did,' argues Zac. 'You used to speculate about how she could afford the house without working.'

'She had a pay-out from work,' I interrupt. 'There was an accident.'

'Oh,' says Maddie. 'What kind of accident?'

'She fell down a flight of stairs and hit her head. She was in a coma for a long time. She almost died.'

Zac frowns. 'Maybe that explains her behaviour.'

Maddie glares at him. 'Don't make excuses for her.'

'Did anyone ever visit her?' I ask, wondering how isolated Becca is or whether there's someone she's close to that we could talk to who might be able to communicate with her or act as a go-between.

Maddie shakes her head. 'We never saw anyone,' she says, turning away from her husband and towards me. 'We hardly ever saw her. She's a hermit. No friends. No family. No life.'

Except what she puts online. I bet all her followers and Facebook friends are as made up as the reviews she posted on Yelp. My god. The work involved in that. The dedication. It's . . .

'Fucking insane,' Maddie declares, as though she's read my mind. 'She's a psychopath, or I don't know . . . whatever she is, she's fucking crazy. She better stay away from my family or I'll . . .'

Zac shushes her. I gaze at the three of them and then out the window where somewhere in the darkness, just nearby, Becca is lurking.

Oh my god. What have I just done? I've gone and prodded her, exposed her whole deception. If she wasn't angry enough before, she's going to be furious now.

Part Two

Becca

Friday, 8 December
Afternoon

One doctor told me to find a hobby. He told me that would help me feel better, as though depression were something that could be fixed by stamp collecting or making crocheted owls to sell on Etsy (something he said his wife did).

Lots of doctors have told me lots of things. None of it anything I wanted to hear.

My lawyer told me that I at least had money, offering it to me like the winning prize rather than the loser's consolation that it actually was.

He handed me the cheque as I sat in a wheelchair with seventeen broken bones, some of which were still knitting back together, some of which had been surgically fused, some of which had been replaced entirely with metal plates, which James joked made me half human, half cyborg.

That was the state of my body, but don't forget the face. My face. I was used to getting second glances, and now I was getting second, third and fourth glances, but not ones of appreciation. My face looked like a Halloween pumpkin that had been carved by an angry person wearing a blindfold. It was unfortunate, I was told. I'd smashed face first into the bronze statue in the lobby before the back of my skull shattered against the marble floor.

People try to make you feel better by telling you that it could be worse. I have been told I could be a Syrian refugee, or a vegetable, or dead. At least you got compensation, they say, as though you can put a figure on a life.

Though apparently you can. Two million is what a life is worth, according to a judge. And I would give it all back in a heartbeat to have that life back. I'm not talking about my own life. I'm talking about Lucette's.

Damn. Now I've started thinking about her I won't be able to stop. Lucette. I roll her name on my tongue, say it over and over like a prayer. Or a mantra. Lucette. My little Light. Named after my sister. Lucette. The only truly good thing that ever happened to me. That ever *will* happen to me. I think maybe I'm cursed; everything I love is taken from me.

I never did take up crocheting owls. Instead, in that same doctor's surgery, waiting for a prescription for stronger painkillers, I picked up a magazine and read an article about these kids in China and Japan who spend hundreds of thousands of hours online playing games, often fantasy role-playing ones. They're so addicted that when their parents take away their computers they commit suicide. It's an epidemic, they said. I read about one boy who, after playing video games for twenty hours straight in a cyber-cafe, tried to stand up to go to the toilet and discovered he was paralysed from the waist down. As the paramedics carried him off in a stretcher, he begged his friends to keep playing his unfinished game.

A psychologist in the same article explained that spending too much time in an online fantasy world can 'jeopardise jobs, relationships, interfere in the ability to make friends and sustain a healthy social life and play sports'. I remember laughing about that. I didn't have a job or a relationship. I didn't have friends or a social life and I couldn't play sport, so what did I have to lose?

I wonder if that article was what first gave me the idea. I didn't want to battle orcs and dragons, because, well, orcs and dragons. But the idea of creating another self did appeal; someone who could walk without a prison swagger and bend at the waist and didn't have a scar that they had to spend forty-five minutes covering with concealer before they could leave the house. So, I guess I did find a hobby, and though I imagine my doctor would complain that it's not a very healthy one, it had the desired effect of improving my mental wellbeing.

When I was paralysed by grief Becca Bridges was the friend who picked up the joystick and kept playing my unfinished game.

Her first post on Instagram took only a moment to compose.

Starting over is the beautiful moment where you choose yourself.

After I hit publish on that first post I remember thinking that it felt like spring had arrived finally after a relentlessly bitter winter.

It's a big undertaking, creating a life online, almost as big an undertaking as creating a new life offline. There's Instagram and Twitter and Facebook and then, of course, Pinterest and a website, as well as all the parenting forums and chatrooms I spend time on, commenting on posts about breastfeeding and weaning and toddler tantrums. I'm starting to become something of an expert on the topic of teething because I've been through it with Sadie.

My website was easiest to let go of. I was already contemplating a career change anyway. I borrowed the content from a Dutch design company. The photo on the bio page – the one of me leaning against a desk – I took from the website of an architecture firm in Finland.

I photoshopped my head onto it using an old photo of me taken before the accident. It took a while to get it right, to line up her neck with my head, like trying to piece together two parts of an executed woman. I liked the image. It felt like Becca Bridges, mother and professional business owner, would wear what she was wearing. But I also liked the way she was leaning, bent forward at the waist. In real life, because my spine is fused, I can't bend beyond ten degrees.

I like posting photographs on Instagram the most. I find photographs on stock image libraries and use those: a child arranging colourful fridge magnets into the word 'mummy'; a chubby toddler hand dunking a carrot in hummus; a mum and her baby with faces obscured by the fairy-tale book they're reading. I get a thrill when I see the likes flooding in, the little red heart glowing.

I had been planning on announcing my next pregnancy soon. It was going to be another girl, due in the summer. I was going to call her Lucette, after my sister. I couldn't do it with my first one, name her after the real Lucette, it was still too raw, but I was ready for her to be born.

I was so excited for all the likes and comments that I'd get. I had already started collecting images of my growing bump – tasteful black-and-whites cropped just so, that first image of her little foot cradled in Zac's hand. I had started thinking about what romantic gestures and comments Zac would make as I blossomed before his eyes, carrying his child.

I'm the love of his life. He worships me.

I met Zac and Maddie when I first came to look at the house, before I bought it. They were getting into their car, going out somewhere. He had his hand on her lower back and was ushering her into the passenger seat. It reminded me of James, that gesture, and so it made me a little sad. They smiled and waved and asked me whether I was there to look at the house.

I needed a stick to walk back then, and I'd only had one operation on my face so the scar was still livid, even with make-up plastered over it. I also talked with a slight slur. I'd seen the way James looked at me – even though he tried to hide it, I knew I was hideous. I didn't want to make conversation so I just nodded yes, and then hurried as fast as I could up to the door to meet the estate agent who was waiting for me.

I turned around, halfway up the drive, and watched the two of them getting in their car. I saw the way they exchanged a look, wondering what was wrong with me. And I saw, as she bent to get in the car, pressing her coat closer to her midsection, that Maddie was pregnant.

'I'll take the house,' I told the estate agent before she'd even had a chance to pull out the keys.

I was there when they brought the baby home. Watching from the window. I went over with a gift the next day, some Babygros that I'd originally bought for Lucette and hadn't had the heart or will to throw away or donate to Oxfam. They were the one and only thing I'd bought for her, the day I found out I was pregnant. They were Ralph Lauren and covered in pale yellow polka dots.

Zac opened the door. He seemed surprised to see me standing there. We hadn't really interacted much since I'd moved in a few months before. And now I was walking without a stick and my scar had mended well, as the doctors kept telling me, and I'd found a new make-up that was better at concealing the scar and had cut my hair so it covered more of my face. He didn't recognise me at first and when he did I saw the way his eyes widened, maybe not with appreciation, but at least not with horror. It made me happy. But then Maddie appeared behind him with the baby in her arms and I made my excuses to leave. It hurt a lot more than I had thought it would.

Lucette would have been born around the same time as Sadie.

I think the alternative life I've curated for Zac as Becca's husband is better than the real deal.

But now I've lost it. Another life gone. And all because of that bitch.

My heart is beating wildly, like a bird of prey is trapped in my chest, pecking at my ribs. Lizzie's over there now. Talking to them. Telling them everything.

How did she find me? It's partly my fault. The Sméagol comment gave it away. I thought she would be too stupid to get it. That was a mistake. I was stung by what she said about Sadie and the news about her and James going on a date also hurt, made my heart feel like someone had given it a savage pinch, but I should have let it slide. I should have ignored it.

I gaze around at the refuge I've created, that I barely ever leave. The thought of stepping foot outside is hard enough, let alone having to go looking for a new place to live. It takes me days to work up the energy and determination to visit the doctor. Walking Peanut is the best I can manage, and even that isn't every day.

I hear Zac and Maddie's front door open and I peek between the curtains. I watch her leaving, scurrying out like a termite that's burrowed into the foundations, done its damage and is now running away before disaster strikes and the house collapses. I imagine a giant boot coming down out of the sky to crush her. It's what she deserves.

Zac stands behind her on the doorstep, scowling. He looks up at my house and it's almost as if I feel a physical shove backwards. I duck down out of sight and crane to hear what's happening. Zac's front door closes but I don't hear a door opening or an engine start. I wait a beat and risk another peek out the window. Lizzie is standing beside her car, looking up at the house.

Lizzie Crowley. I would never have recognised her if I hadn't seen her Facebook profile. She's tanned and blonde and thin now, almost unrecognisable from the girl that I knew. Back then she had frizzy hair, a faint moustache and always looked like she'd got dressed in the dark. Her transformation is even greater than my online one. She transformed herself in real life. It's astonishing. I don't know how she did it.

She keeps staring up at the house and I am overwhelmed with hate; a rage so great I feel like I could tear her limb from limb.

Does she realise what she's done?

She's ruined everything.

Lizzie

She's watching me. I know it. I can feel her eyes on my back like a rifle sight. I'm standing by the car, fishing the keys from my bag. I should have parked in the lay-by up the road, not out here under a street light. I catch a flicker of movement in the upstairs window. She *is* home. Oh god, that means she saw me coming out of Zac and Maddie's house. She'll have figured it out. She'll know I know that she's lying. And she'll know that they know now, too.

What will she do?

I look towards Zac and Maddie's house. They've gone back inside. They said they needed to talk about things. Zac said he'd be in touch to tell me what they'd decided about going to the police. I warned them not to confront her, that she's not stable, but I'm not sure they listened.

For a good few seconds I stand there, with the car keys in my hand, staring up at Becca's house in terror. Then I get in and lock the doors, before hurriedly starting the engine and speeding off.

Becca

It's dark when Maddie comes knocking. There's a furious pounding on the door as though she means to break it down with her fists. I stay glued to the wall by the window. I haven't moved an inch since Lizzie left.

Maddie's angry banging goes on for five minutes. I barely breathe during all that time. I'm a prisoner in my home. I've already made myself one but now I really am one.

'I know you're in there!' she yells. 'Bloody well show your face!'

I close my eyes and count to ten. What would happen if I did show my face? How could I explain it? And if I tried, would she even listen? Zac might, but not Maddie.

'Becca?'

I inhale sharply at the sound of Zac's voice. It's as if I've conjured him. For a moment I imagine he's come to rescue me, to take me in his arms and tell me it's all OK. I imagine him bringing Sadie with him and giving Maddie her marching orders, telling her it's over between them, that he's finally come to his senses. I imagine him turning to me and telling me he loves me, that he wants to start a new life with me.

'Becca, open up!' he shouts and I smile. When I hear his voice shout my name, even though he's angry, it makes me feel alive, wanted, necessary.

I can hear them on the doorstep arguing now with each other. It sounds like Zac is trying to convince her to leave it. Where's Sadie? I wonder. Did they leave her at home? They shouldn't have. That's dangerous. She's a baby. Anything could happen.

I will them to go away, but what then? They'll only be back in the morning. I can't avoid them forever. I will have to leave. Tonight even. But how? I stare around at all my things. How can I pack a car and leave in the dead of night never to return? The thought of going is almost as bad as the thought of saying goodbye to Becca Bridges.

I tell myself it's time for an upgrade. It's just like deleting an avatar in a game. I get to reinvent myself again. And this time I'll do it better. But no matter how hard I try to sell that story, it doesn't work. I don't want to have to reinvent myself again.

If I were a spy, my spymasters would be telling me to ditch everything, leave the past behind and start over with a new identity in a new place. I'm exhausted at the thought. I put so much time into Becca Bridges and into this house to just give it all up. I think of all the chatrooms I'm in, talking about Sadie and teething and the virtue of cloth nappies over disposables. I'll need to delete those accounts too. They're tainted now.

I feel exposed. A burn victim whose dressings have been ripped off, taking with them a layer of new skin and leaving behind raw nerves and bloody sinew exposed to freezing air.

I understand now why all those kids in China were so addicted to online gaming, and why they wanted to kill themselves when their online lives (which were more real to them than their actual lives) were taken from them.

They had nothing left to live for.

Lizzie

'A vodka and diet tonic,' I tell the barman at the King's Arms.

He sets it on the bar in front of me and I down half in one go. 'Another one, love?' he asks, smiling.

It's probably not a good idea because I haven't eaten anything since that chocolate truffle this morning. I could definitely use another one but I still have to drive back home. 'No, thanks,' I say, forcing a smile. 'I'm good. Maybe just some water. No ice. And um, a packet of crisps.'

'What flavour?'

'Salt and vinegar.'

The barman hands me a packet of crisps. 'Where you from?' he asks.

'London,' I say. 'Well, originally Yorkshire.'

'Couldn't tell,' he remarks. 'You don't have an accent. You here for the weekend?'

'Oh,' I say. 'No. I'm going back tonight. I just want to miss rush hour on the M25 so I thought I'd wait it out a bit. Do you have the time?'

The barman checks his watch. 'Five minutes to seven.'

I take the pint of water and go and sit at a corner table by the fire. The pub is packed with end-of-the-week revellers, most of whom seem to be local. I sit down and stare into the flames but I find my foot won't stop tapping. Maybe I should have ordered that second vodka after all. Still, a crash on the motorway is the last thing I need.

I pull out my phone and sit there for a while as I sip my drink and eat my crisps. I need to figure out my next move.

Zac gave me Becca's number. I decide I'm going to call her. I knock back the rest of my water, steel myself for a moment, then finally make the call. It rings and rings. She doesn't pick up. I'm not expecting her to, really. When her voicemail kicks in I leave a message.

'Becca, it's Lizzie. I think this game of yours has gone far enough, don't you? Please leave me alone. I'm going back to London and I don't want you harassing me any more. I know it's you behind everything, getting me fired and posting all those fake reviews. And your neighbours know all about your fake online life. I don't understand why you're doing this. Neither do they. I think you need help. We all do. Please, get some help. This has to stop or else I'm going to go the police to get a restraining order.'

I hang up. Will that do it? I wonder. Probably not.

A few minutes later my phone buzzes. For a second I think that it's Becca calling me back, but of course it's not. It's a message from Flora: 'What are u doing?' she asks.

Another text comes through, hot on its tail: 'Are U crazy?'

'What?' I text back.

'Twitter,' she responds with a row of wide-eyed emojis.

'What r u talkng abt?'

I never really use Twitter. I have an account but I don't much like tweeting. It's mostly just a swamp of alt-right women haters, trolls and self-promoters. The photo on my profile is a really old one, from before, when I had dark hair and an extra thirty pounds. That's how long it's been since I used the account.

Alerts are pinging. Retweets and comments coming so thick and fast I get whiplash trying to catch them all. I read the latest tweet.

PKW's CEO Andrew Fincher is a fuckwit who cheats on his wife and hires women based on how fuckable they are. **#ceoshit #badbehaviour #PKW**

It's been retweeted fifty-three times. I think that qualifies as going viral. There's another tweet too. Sent a minute before the other one.

The no talent talent agents at PKW regularly take the piss out of their clients and laugh behind their backs. **@CindyAlamot** is known to agents as 'moby dick' on account of how hard she was to bag and how fat she's got. **#PKW #agentgossip**

Cindy Alamot is the agency's biggest client. A multi-award winning actress in her late thirties who just had her second child and is trying to make a comeback. I'm guessing that Cindy will no longer be trusting PKW to handle that comeback.

That tweet about Cindy has over a hundred retweets and counting. And the other one too. I should delete them. Not that it matters now.

My phone rings suddenly and I jump so hard it almost flies out of my hand and into the fire. Grabbing for it I see that it's Moira again. Shit. I guess that means she's seen the tweets. And I guess that means I'm fired. I don't know whether to pick up or not. What will I say to her? How can I defend myself? If I tell her someone hacked my account, she'll never believe me. I let the call ring through to my voice-mail, then I silence my phone.

For a while afterwards I sit perfectly still, staring into the fire. My whole life is going up in flames. Everything is being destroyed but weirdly it doesn't feel like it's happening to me. I have a strange disembodied feeling as though I'm watching a movie. But in a movie the main character always finds a way to come back from the *all is lost* moment and I have no idea what to do next, or how to get control.

'It's not me sending the tweets,' I text Flora.

'OMG! Becca?' she texts right back.

'Yes.'

'What are u going to do?!' she asks.

What am I going to do? I need to get away from here. I need to get home.

I down the rest of my drink and hurry outside.

Becca

So many lives have been stolen from me. Now I think about it I wonder how I have never noticed the pattern before. The first time it happened I was a child and my parents took us off to live in a hippy commune where everything was shared, not just the dishes, and where they worshipped an Indian guru who preached spiritual wealth over material wealth but who nonetheless lived in a marble palace in India and flew first class, living off the life savings of his followers.

One day my sister and I were immersed in playschool, the park, swimming lessons and ballet, and the next we were living in a cold and draughty ex-farmhouse, being forced to meditate and chant nonsense. We were told that we no longer owned anything, even our clothes and toys. I think that's why as an adult I've never liked sharing. Or following rules. Maybe it's also why I don't trust people easily. I think most people are liars. I'd go as far as to say everyone is a liar, and most certainly everyone lies to themselves.

After my father donated his entire LED invention fortune to the guru, he got wise and we finally escaped back into the real world. We left with only the clothes on our back – clothes my mother had dyed marigold orange. You can imagine the stir we caused on the street. The four of us were like alien visitors. That third age of Becca was the happiest. We had nothing, no TV, no clothes that weren't from the charity shop, but we were happy; the euphoria of our escape buoyed us for a time and my sister and I were thrilled we were back in school and didn't have to spend our days cross-legged chanting any more. It didn't last long because then the fire came. It killed my whole family and left me untouched, and I've never understood why.

The fourth new start came when I was sent to Scotland to live with my great aunt – a woman who smelled of cigarettes and cherry-flavoured cough syrup and whose entire house was covered in cat hair so all my clothes looked like they were made of mohair. She had no use for a child. I stuck it out as long as I could, before I quit school, stole some money out of her purse (OK, all her money out of her purse) and hopped on a bus to London.

I lied about my age and got a job working the door of a club in Kensington – the kind of place where royalty hobnob with boy bands. That was the start of my fifth existence. I blagged the job using charm and bald-faced lies. Lies came easy to me. I'd had to learn very early on how to deflect questions about my past, how to fake signatures on the bottom of absence notes, how to convince newsagents I really was of legal age, how to find people online who could make me a fake ID. The list was endless.

And then I met James. I was twenty by then, though I told him I was twenty-five. He was an entertainment lawyer. He'd chatted me up to try to get entry to the club.

James had a certain way of being in the world, like it owed him something, like everyone would and should just kneel before him. In some senses, I suppose, he was a bit like the guru and maybe I drank the Kool-Aid. I learned my lesson there in the end.

I wanted to impress him and more than that, I wanted to keep him. I didn't believe that a man like James, whose father was an actual real life lord, would ever think of me in serious relationship terms unless I was something more than a door girl at a club, so when another regular visitor to the club told me he knew of a job at PKW, I jumped at the chance.

The clients were the same wealthy, privileged alpha types I was used to dealing with, but the pay was better and the hours more reasonable. And, for the first time in my life, I was doing a job that required using my brain, not just look-ing pretty and waving people past a velvet rope. I was surprised just how much I loved it. I was so used to being judged on what I looked like that I never realised how good it would feel to be judged on my abilities instead. I was good at the job too because I've always been good with people – at reading them and knowing what they want, usually before they even know themselves what that is. I guess that's the result of having to fend for myself since I was a child.

When I got the job working for the CEO I knew there were whispers, rumours that I'd slept my way to the top, but that's all they were, rumours.

I met Lizzie my first day on the job.

If only I had known back then that she'd be my downfall now. I would have tried harder to avoid her.

It's silent outside now. Maddie and Zac have given up and gone away. I can hear Peanut whining at the kitchen door to be let out. Gathering my courage, I crawl to the top of the stairs and then tiptoe down them before darting across the hall and into the kitchen. I shut the door behind me and turn on the light. Peanut bounces up and down like he's on a spring, yip-yapping incessantly. I pour food into his bowl and as he gobbles it up I contemplate my options one more time.

I came here to hide. I thought I'd be safe. That no one would ever find me. And now I have to leave and start over again. I have no choice. What if she tells James where I am?

Anger wells up inside me. It feels like there's a tornado in my chest, spiralling around and around, gathering up all the pent-up rage that I've squashed inside for all of my life – anger towards my parents, the smiling guru, towards James, and doctors and towards life, and now towards Lizzie – and that if I open my mouth, it will erupt out of me like a stream of red hot lava, destroying everything in its path.

How dare she? She has no idea what she's done. I can't – I won't – let her get away with this.

Lizzie

Saturday, 9 December
Morning

'I don't get it,' James says. He's leaning forwards, his elbows on his knees, hands pressed together like he's praying. His coffee has gone untouched.

I push my hair behind my ears, feeling myself flush. Being under his gaze is a bit like being under a searchlight. 'I'm sorry,' I say. 'After I saw you on Tinder I sort of went looking for Becca online.' He glances up at that and I shrug. 'I thought maybe you were still together and I wanted to check.'

'What?' There's a note of hostility in his voice that gives me pause.

I really didn't want to tell him all this but I don't have any other choice. Things are getting far too out of hand. I give him a timid smile along with another shrug. 'I've met a lot of guys on Tinder who are married.'

He gives me a puzzled frown, and I quickly hurry on. 'Anyway, look, long story short, I accidentally sent Becca an email meant for someone else.'

James sits back in his winged armchair. 'What do you mean?'

I swallow, looking around. We're in a small wood-panelled bar in a private members club in Soho, where James suggested we meet after I rang him very late last night to tell him I urgently needed to see him. 'I wrote an email – and I wasn't very complimentary about her.'

'What did you say?' he asks tersely.

'It doesn't matter. It was mean of me and stupid but she wasn't meant to see it.'

James purses his lips.

'I apologised, of course,' I tell him. 'But she started coming after me . . .'

'Coming after you how?'

I start ticking off the list of crazy. 'First she sent an email to my boss and got me into trouble at work. I've been fired.'

He looks surprised. 'Fired?'

'Yes. She hacked my Twitter account and posted some things . . .'

'What kind of things?'

'Things about the company. About our clients. Not very flattering things. And I can't prove that it wasn't me. So they fired me.'

'How did she hack your Twitter account?' he asks, looking at me with a highly sceptical expression.

I shake my head, frustrated. 'I've no idea but she managed to wipe every trace of herself off the Internet so I don't know . . . maybe she knows someone who can hack computers.'

'What do you mean she's wiped herself off the Internet?'

'Well, her Facebook's disappeared . . .'

He nods to himself. 'I went looking for her, after you told me she had a new profile. I couldn't find it.'

'That's because she deleted it! I've got screenshots though. Here.'

I take out my phone and swipe through the photos, showing him. He grabs the phone out of my hand and pulls it closer, zooming in on the picture of Becca on her profile page. I watch the frown fade from his face and another expression take its place; a scowl that could be anger or could be sadness. It's hard to tell which. After almost a minute I take the phone out of his hand. He looks like he wants to snatch it back but I shove it in my bag.

'And she had this whole interior design business too. Remember, I told you about it?'

He nods, his scepticism giving way to curiosity.

'There was a website. Pictures of houses she said she'd decorated, but now I'm guessing that she stole them from someone else's website or from Pinterest. Anyway, it doesn't matter because now it's gone too. The site's vanished. There's not even a record of the business on Companies House. I checked.'

A furrow appears between his eyes. 'Are you sure?'

I nod.

'But why would she take it all down? It doesn't make sense.'

'Because it's fake!' I say. 'It never existed. It was all pretend. Lies!'

He stares at me blankly.

'I went there,' I tell him. 'Yesterday. To her house. I found her.'

He looks taken aback at that. 'What?'

I lick my lips, nervous all of a sudden. I don't like his tone. It's like he thinks I did something wrong. 'I went to visit her. My friend Flora – it was her idea. She thought that if I confronted her in person, I could get her to stop.'

'You saw her?' James asks, sitting up straighter. His hands are gripping the edge of his chair.

'No,' I say. 'She wouldn't come to the door. But I found out that it's all lies. Everything she posted online. She isn't really married.'

'What?'

'She doesn't have a kid either,' I tell him. 'She made it up. She faked it all. Everything. Not just little white lies. Her whole life. I found out that it's actually her neighbour she's pretending to have a kid with. She's posting photos of him online and calling him her husband. Pictures from his wedding day to another woman! Pretending that it's *them* getting married. That their baby is hers. I went down there, to talk to her, and I met them.'

James's mouth drops open. 'That's—' He breaks off, clearly shocked into silence. He sinks back into his chair.

I supply the word he's looking for: 'Psycho.'

He exhales softly. I can't tell if he agrees with me or if he's just processing everything I've told him.

I carry on. 'So now she's pissed off because I guess I've ruined whatever fantasy she'd constructed and she's coming after me for revenge.'

He exhales slowly and I can see he's struggling to wrap his head around this. 'Do you have any proof it's her who's done all these things? Got you fired?' he finally asks.

Annoyed, I shake my head. 'No. But of course it's her. It's too much of a coincidence. All this stuff starts going wrong immediately after I sent the message. And you told me about how she changed after the accident. How she became obsessive and paranoid and angry.'

He shakes his head then looks at his watch. Damn. He wants to leave. It's too much for anyone to take on board. He clearly doesn't want to be involved.

'I don't know about you,' he says, looking up. 'But I need a drink.'

Oh, thank god. Relief almost overwhelms me. I nod and he summons the waiter.

He orders a Scotch for himself, neat, and asks me what I'd like. 'Sparkling water,' I say. I need to keep a clear head.

'Do you know what you're going to do?' James asks after the waiter disappears.

I look at him helplessly. 'I don't know. I was hoping maybe you had an idea. You know her better than me. That's why I wanted to talk you. I'm all out of ideas. The neighbours don't know what to do either. They wanted to get a restraining order.'

'It will be difficult without actual proof that she's threatened physical harm.'

I nod. 'Yes, that's what I thought. But what about the hacking? That's illegal isn't it?'

He nods. 'Yes, but you'd need proof it was her. You could go to the police but—'

I interrupt. 'I don't want to bring the police into it. I mean, it sounds like she needs help and I don't want to get her even more angry.' I pause as James picks up his drink and downs half of it in one go. 'I was thinking I could go and talk to her again,' I say. 'I know the best thing would probably be to walk away and hope she just drops it, but I need her to admit what she's done. I need her to admit she sent the tweets and faked the expenses. That way I'll have some proof so I can get my job back. And, maybe if I can talk to her face to face, I can help her see she needs help—'

'Let me come with you,' James interrupts.

'Really?' I ask, smiling widely. I didn't want to ask him directly, but I was hoping against hope that he'd offer. 'That would be amazing,' I say, and I mean it more than he could know.

'Where is it you said she lived? The Cotswolds?' he asks. 'Widford, right?'

'Yes.'

'When were you going to go?' he asks me.

'Well, I was thinking this afternoon. It's not like I've got anything else to do.'

'Maybe I should be the one to speak to her,' James says.

'You'd do that?' I ask, my voice trembling.

He shrugs. 'I could try. She might talk to me. I mean, I'm sure she would. And you're right. It sounds like if all this is true, she needs someone to talk to, someone she knows and trusts.'

My face falls.

'What?' he asks.

'It's only that,' I look away, 'what if she thinks I put you up to it? You said she gets jealous and she already hates me. What if it makes her even angrier?'

James gestures to the waiter for the bill. 'Don't worry,' he says, turning back to me. 'I'll handle Becca.'

James's car is a BMW Z4. A sporty number in blue. Or 'deep sea blue' as he informs me when we get in. He opens the door and I smile. I bet what he said in his profile about being good to his mum is true. Grudgingly, I'm starting to see that Becca with her #bestboyfriendever posts might, for once, have been telling the truth. I'm still sure that the Prince Harry thing is total bollocks, though.

I'm tempted to check my phone as James drives towards the Westway and out of London. I'm feeling jittery with nerves, wondering if this is the right thing to do or if I'm opening a can of worms. But it's too late to turn back. And the can is already open. Besides, there's nothing more Becca can do to me. *It's not like she can get me fired from the same job twice,* as I told James when he checked in with me to ask if I was certain I wanted to do this.

I sink back in the heated seat and turn so I'm facing towards James, watching him drive. I wonder at his eagerness to come with me. Is there another reason beyond him wanting to help? Is he curious to see how his ex-girlfriend is getting on without him? He smiles at me. 'Are you normally so impulsive?' he asks.

I shrug. 'Sometimes.'

James appraises me out the corner of his eye. I can't quite believe I've convinced him to come with me. For a moment I picture us as Bonnie and Clyde – there's something almost illicit about it, as if we're on the run or are about to set off on a crime spree – but then I remember that Bonnie and Clyde ended up dead, shot by the police. I'll need to find another analogy, with a happier ending.

My attention turns back to my phone, which is sitting on my lap, nagging at me. I still haven't checked my messages from Moira. I can't imagine anything more likely to put a downer on my mood, which is beginning to pick up for the first time since this whole thing started, but it's about time I faced whatever she has to say.

Moira's voice comes down the phone like a Black & Decker sander on full power, forcing me to hold the phone away from my ear. The first message is the one she sent Friday morning asking me to come into the office. Delete. Too late to respond to that one anyway. The next is the one she left Friday afternoon when I was outside Becca's house.

'Lizzie,' she starts. 'It's Moira. I was wondering if you'd got my message and if you were going to make it in? We were expecting you.' She pauses. 'Actually we wanted to share the news that Daniel's completed the investigation with the help of an external auditor, and it looks like there was some kind of mistake. All the accounts have been verified. The petty cash reconciled perfectly.'

I press my lips together to hold back my furious '*told you fucking so*'.

'So,' Moira continues, 'we were hoping we could speak to you about your return to work. If you don't call me back today, then call me over the weekend, any time. I'd like to get this resolved. I know it's been difficult.' Difficult? I told them I was bloody innocent. 'Right,' Moira finishes, at least sounding contrite. 'OK, I'll hopefully see you Monday and speak to you before then.'

Goddamn, I think to myself. If I had taken the call on Friday, would I have decided not to bother trying to talk to Becca? Would I have turned the car around and driven back to London? Maybe if I had, then I'd have a job to go to on Monday and life would be continuing as normal. But it's too late to think about what ifs.

I hit the next message button. It's Moira again.

'Lizzie,' she says, and this time there's no mistaking her tone. The contrition has gone. It's been replaced with an icy fury. 'I think you know why I'm calling. As you will be well aware, you are in breach of your contract. We have a whole section on social media and appropriate behaviour. I was hoping not to do this over the phone, but in the light of your recent tweets we are terminating your employment with PKW with immediate effect. Please do not come in to work on Monday. Our legal team will be in touch with you shortly to arrange the return of your key pass and to pass on your belongings to you. I'm also writing a formal letter. You will have it by Monday.'

I hang up and stare out the window. Well, that's that then. I hated the job anyway.

'Everything OK?' James asks.

I nod and force a smile. 'Yeah.'

'So how long have you been on Tinder?' James asks as we hurtle down the M40.

'Oh, only about six months,' I say. 'What about you?'

'On and off for about a year.'

'You haven't met anyone?' I ask, curious as to why. He's undeniably good looking, and I'm sure that if there's a list of the most eligible bachelors in London, he's near the top of it.

'Well, I've had a few casual relationships,' he admits, 'but nothing that lasted longer than a month. It's hard to find someone you connect with. You know what it's like.'

I mumble agreement. The truth is that I'm fairly new to this whole dating thing. Until recently I never had the confidence. After being teased your whole life, called Lizziesaurus by the kids at school, and having your mother telling you since you were ten that no one could ever love you, it's hard to find the confidence to go out there and fling yourself into the dating pool. There's a worry that you'll belly flop. I tried Match.com a few years back, but the first man I met up with in the flesh, who was no supermodel himself, told me in the first thirty seconds that I didn't look anything like my pictures and then he disappeared to the toilet and never came back.

There was another guy too. We texted for a bit and then, just when I thought things were going well and I'd worked up the nerve to meet him in real life, he started sexting me, telling me he wanted to do really perverted things to me. He even sent me photographs to illustrate exactly what.

'I can imagine you've got men beating down your door,' James says, interrupting my trip down memory lane.

I laugh under my breath because I could never tell him the truth. I know exactly how he'd look at me, exactly what he'd think.

'Like you said,' I tell him, 'it's hard to find someone you connect with.'

He smiles. I smile back. He looks back at the road, pressing his foot to the gas.

It's dark when we take the turn off towards Widford. James looks out at the fields and hedgerows.

'Becca always talked about moving out here, to the country. I should have guessed this was where she'd disappear to. It makes sense.'

'Why?' I ask.

He pauses for a moment. 'It's near where she grew up. Near to where her parents are buried. And her sister.'

I draw a breath. 'Oh god, I heard about that. Didn't they die in a fire?'

'Yeah. A house fire.'

So that was true after all?

'Did she ever tell you anything about her family?' James asks.

'Only that her father invented LED lights.' I can't help the slight mocking tone.

He shakes his head. 'No, he didn't invent them, he was the first person to put them into supermarket freezers.'

I burst out laughing. 'What?'

'It's true. They use them in freezers as they don't emit heat.'

I stop laughing, feeling confused. I always assumed that was a lie too.

'He made a fortune from it but then when they joined the cult he gave it all away. Lost it.'

'A cult?' I ask, incredulous. He has to be pulling my leg. Or else Becca fed him a pile of made-up crap and he bought it hook, line and sinker.

'No, I'm serious,' he says, seeing my expression. 'When she was a kid. Her parents lived in some religious commune. She didn't really remember it. I think she was about seven when they saw the light and got out, but he'd given away all his money so they were broke.'

'Wow,' I say.

'She'd been through a lot,' he says softly. 'After the fire she was sent to live with an aunt. In Aberdeen. But they didn't get on. The aunt was old, had never had kids and didn't want any either. Becca left there at sixteen, came to London and started working, if you can believe it. She got a job on the door of a club, somewhere in Kensington. Told them she was eighteen.' He laughs, almost admiringly.

He takes Magpie Lane, driving past the King's Arms. 'Her place is just up here on the left,' I say. 'About half a mile.'

We cross the bridge and I point at the house. It's barely visible. There's no moon tonight and with so few street lights it's almost pitch black. The hallway light is the only one on in Becca's house, illuminating it like a beacon.

James slows to a crawl and I peer out the window at Zac and Maddie's house. The Christmas tree lights are on, as is the porch light, but otherwise the house is dark and the car isn't parked outside either.

'Do you think she's home?' James asks, looking up at Becca's house.

I check the time. It's almost eight. 'I don't know,' I say. I feel a little strange and uncertain about the whole plan, but we're here now and I can't back out. I point out the lay-by up the road and James pulls into it.

He starts to open the door. 'Let me go,' he says, 'you stay here.' And before I have any time to argue he jumps out the car and slams the door. I sit there for a few seconds, listening to the engine tick, wondering what to do, and whether I should follow him.

I decide not to but after five minutes I start to wonder where he is. I get out the car and walk back down the road towards Becca's house – the glow in the window acting as a lighthouse as I try to navigate the blind dark of the street. That's another thing I find frightening about the countryside, besides all the strange hooting and rustling noises – the blanket darkness, as heavy as a shroud. I have to put my hands out in front of me in case I walk into a hedgerow or a ditch. And what was I thinking wearing these boots? Knee-high boots in buttery-soft brown leather with three-inch heels might look good on a catwalk but they won't look good coated in cow shit.

Halfway there, someone lunges out of the darkness at the side of the road. My automatic reaction isn't to scream, it's to punch. I surprise myself at the speed of my response, at how conditioned it is. My fist makes contact with bone and the person goes stumbling backwards.

'Shit! Ow!'

Oh god! It's James. 'Oh my god! I'm so sorry,' I say, rushing towards him.

He's stooped over and cradling his jaw in his hands.

'Bloody hell,' he grunts. I can't see his expression but his voice is two parts wary and one part impressed.

'Sorry,' I say again, 'you surprised me.'

'Who the hell did you think it was?' he asks me as we walk back to the car.

'I don't know,' I say, helping steer him towards the driver's side. 'I didn't think.'

'My god,' he says, leaning against the car door, still nursing his jaw.

'Was she home?' I ask him.

He shakes his head. 'No. At least no one was answering the door. I could hear a dog barking.'

'I wonder where she is.'

James rubs his jaw some more. 'I don't think I've ever met a woman who can throw a punch like that,' he says with an almost admiring tone. I turn back to him and by the thin sliver of moonlight I can see the glimmer in his eyes as he appraises me.

I open the door and get in the car. James follows suit.

'So what shall we do?' I ask him as he starts the engine.

He shrugs and looks in the rear-view mirror, back towards the house. He's frowning.

'What a total waste of time,' I say, feeling bad. 'You could have stayed in London and instead I've made you ferry me about all over the place.'

'Not at all,' he says smoothly. 'Maybe we could stop at that pub down the road and have a drink, then come back later and see if she's home?'

I pull a face. 'It's not a very nice pub,' I tell him, thinking of the rustic bar and shabby decor and how it compares to James's club in Soho.

James thinks about it for a moment. 'Well, we're only about twenty minutes from the farmhouse.'

'The what?' I ask.

'My club – they have a country place not far from here. It's a hotel with a bar and a restaurant. Members only. I've only been once or twice but it's nice. We could grab a bite there too, if you like.'

'OK,' I say, because why not? I know the place he's talking about. It's in the papers a lot. A celebrity hang-out. The membership cost is prohibitive and it's also invite only. You have to be in the creative industries to be accepted and it's mostly famous people: actors, artists, musicians. If the choice is there or the King's Arms, there's no contest.

It turns out that on a Saturday night the place is heaving, and walking in on James's arm gives me a strangely intense rush – a feeling like I've arrived – and I want to grasp at it, snatch it and impress it into my memory so I can replay it later. I've always imagined what it would be like to be one of those people I read about in magazines, and here I am getting to experience it first hand!

Walking through the bar, I catch sight of three famous faces, all of whom are trying hard to act incognito while simultaneously wearing outfits that scream *look at me*. I try not to seem impressed, and taking my cue from everyone else, model an expression of disinterested boredom. My mum would probably take one sneering glance around the place and say that everyone looked like *a right mardy bum*. Though maybe, like me, they're all smiling on the inside.

James says a passing hi to a couple of people he tells me are acquaintances and stops to talk to someone – a musician I recognise from a 90s indie band – who James tells me that his firm represents. He introduces me as *his friend Lizzie* and puts his hand on my lower back when he does. It feels like a warm iron pressed to a silk shirt.

I can't believe it when the man from the band kisses me on the cheek and says it's nice to meet me. He checks me out too. He definitely checks me out, making no pretence about it, and then nudges James as if to give his approval of me. At once I'm both offended and secretly thrilled to death. It's as if I'm wearing a disguise, the disguise of someone who belongs, and I've managed to trick everyone that I'm the real deal.

We get a sofa tucked into a corner of the bar area and when James tells me to order something, I choose a Malbec.

'A bottle or a glass?' the waitress asks.

I look at James who signals that it's up to me. 'A bottle please,' I say. 'Two glasses.'

James waits until the waitress goes away and then leans in to me and says, 'I'm not sure I'll be able to drive after a bottle.'

I give him what I hope is a seductive smile and look up at him through half-lowered lashes. 'I thought you said this place had rooms?'

His eyes light up and I know that I've read all the signals right. He leans further across the sofa and puts his hand around my neck to pull me closer. For a few torturous seconds he waits but then he kisses me. He's a good kisser, firm but not too firm. He's in charge but also respectful. His hands don't wander.

I let him kiss me for a few seconds before I pull away.

He frowns at me curiously, wondering what's up, and I just smile and study the menu. If you want to keep a man's interest, you have to play hard to get. If you're too eager or put out too soon, they think you're only good for a one-night stand. That's what the book said.

When the wine arrives James lifts his glass appreciatively, his eyes glinting, and we say cheers.

'To . . . new beginnings,' James says, not taking his eyes off me even for a second.

'To new beginnings,' I echo, clinking my glass against his. I smile but at the same time dark thoughts are swirling in my mind and I'm thinking not about beginnings but endings.

What is Becca up to right now? Is she finished? Is it over? Will she continue to torment me or can I start to breathe more easily?

Becca

He pulled me into a dark office, as yet undecorated and unclaimed.

'Whose desk is this?' he asked, leaning against it.

'I don't know,' I told him. The offices hadn't yet been allocated.

'Well, let's have sex on it,' he said, pulling me between his thighs.

I wriggled out of his arms. 'James, no,' I told him.

'Why not?' he asked, pouting. 'This party is so boring. Come on.' He grabbed my arm, hard enough that I knew it would blossom with fresh bruises by the morning, and pulled me closer. I resisted him, even though he dug his fingers so deep it was like he was trying to imprint himself on my bones, and I had to suppress a yelp.

'We can't go yet,' I told him, kissing him on the jaw. He softened his grip on my arm but didn't let me go. The sick part was that I didn't want him to. I liked this middle ground. Feeling needed and wanted, like I belonged to him and he was putting his mark on me. His other way of punishing me was to withhold his attention, his touch – and sometimes that hurt even more.

'I have to show my face,' I told him.

He glowered at me and then pulled me towards him. He kissed me hard on the lips. His tongue probed my mouth and his fingers started to tug at my dress, sliding up my thighs and hips and into my underwear.

'I want you,' he whispered urgently.

I had frozen when he started kissing me but when his fingers forced aside my underwear I took his hand and pulled it away.

He stared at me uncomprehending. 'What?' he asked.

'I need to talk to you,' I blurted before I could stop myself. Immediately I wished I'd kept quiet. I had planned to tell him in public. Just in case. And up there, in the quiet of the unclaimed offices, the noise of the Christmas party muted, it was too private. It was the wrong moment.

He frowned. 'What is it?'

I weighed up my choices. I could brush it aside, kiss him, let him have sex with me on the desk, but I couldn't keep putting it off, even if it was the wrong moment. He'd already made one or two comments about the extra pounds I was carrying and soon I would start showing for real and then what? He'd be angry at me for keeping it from him. I needed to bite the bullet.

He pulled me towards him again, impatient, and starting nuzzling my neck, breathing in deep. 'I want you so much,' he murmured.

I smiled and allowed my body to respond to his touch the way it always did. What was I scared of? The baby would be what we needed, it would cement us. He'd be happy. Of course he would. He loved me. He was always telling me that. I needed to trust that this wouldn't change that.

'You're not breaking up with me, are you?' he asked with a little laugh, a laugh I knew hid his insecurity. He was terrified I'd leave him. He'd told me that once, when he felt bad about the bruises. He never hit me. And he never got truly physical.

It wasn't like that. He liked to squeeze me, that's all, my wrists, my arms. He didn't want to hurt me, he just didn't know his own strength. I'd promised myself that if he ever hit me I'd leave him, but he'd never crossed that line and I doubted he would. He wasn't that kind of man.

'I'm pregnant,' I said. The words falling out of me as though squeezed by invisible hands.

James stared at me blankly, the blood draining from his face. His hand dropped from my waist as though I'd just told him I was a leper. 'Holy . . . shit.'

My heart started beating hollowly in my chest. I felt a swell of nausea, bitter bile rising up my throat, and swallowed it down. Why had I chosen now of all times to tell him? Why hadn't I done it downstairs, in a room full of people where he couldn't cause a scene?

'Are you sure?' he asked, quietly, and my heart skipped a beat. I was wrong, perhaps. He wasn't unhappy. I studied his face, scrutinised him for signs. He wasn't scowling or frowning. In fact, it looked like he was about to laugh. Was he, could he, actually be happy?

I nodded, a smile daring to break at the edge of my mouth.

'How many weeks?' he asked.

I swallowed. 'Twelve.'

He frowned.

'I only found out recently, though,' I added quickly.

He shook his head, inhaling and then exhaling in a long slow breath. 'I thought you were on the pill?'

'I am', I said, my heart rate spiking again, my throat raspy as sandpaper. 'It's not one hundred per cent effective.'

He nodded again, his face tightening ever so slightly. A muscle in his jaw pulsed. It was a giveaway, one I dreaded. A cold shiver skittered up my spine. He wasn't happy. He was the opposite of happy. I felt the prick of tears but knew I couldn't get emotional, that it would risk setting him off, so I froze and blinked rapidly, trying to clear them. James started pacing and I could feel the anger pulsating off him in waves, even though he was keeping it in check for the moment. 'What do you want to do?' he asked.

I stared at him, my legs starting to shake. 'What do you mean?'

He stopped in front of me, staring at me in alarm. 'You don't want to keep it, do you?'

All my dreams shattered like a mirror hit with a claw hammer. The scorn in his voice knocked me backwards. From the moment I saw those two pink lines I'd allowed myself to imagine James's smile, even an engagement ring and a wedding, a house in the Cotswolds, a baby called Lucette, a family of my own to replace the one I lost. Poof, and just like that, the dream was smashed to smithereens. I wasn't angry at him as much as I was angry at myself for how deluded I had been.

'I – I don't . . .' I stammered.

'You're not keeping it,' he told me, grabbing my arms and shaking me. His gaze dropped to my stomach. 'You did this on purpose, didn't you?'

I shook my head, the tears beginning to fall despite my best efforts. 'No. I didn't. I swear.'

'You're getting an abortion, you fucking whore.'

The word *abortion* was like an axe falling through my skull. It felled me. Or perhaps that's not the best way of describing it. It was more like an axe cutting through whatever invisible bonds were holding me to James. It was so sudden, so powerful and so shocking that I could feel the reverberations travelling all the way down my body and out through my feet. I took a step backwards and this time, for the first time, I didn't feel the usual tug and pull dragging me back. I took another step away from him. I felt free. Untethered, as though I was a hot air balloon drifting free of its mooring ropes.

James seemed to sense too that something had broken between us. His hold on me had vanished in an instant. New bonds had materialised in its place. Ones that he couldn't see but was still aware of. And he was jealous. I felt that. He stared at my arms wrapped around my abdomen.

'You're not keeping it,' he told me.

In that moment I felt more powerful than I have ever been, before or since. 'Yes,' I told him, savouring the note of defiance in my voice. 'I am keeping it.'

He stared at me like he was hallucinating, as though a mask had been yanked away and he'd seen another version of me, a version he didn't like. His face contorted. 'What do you mean?' he demanded. 'You can't keep it.' His expression wasn't angry so much as devastated. He looked on the verge of tears. He tried to take my hand but I pulled back, out of his reach. 'Becca, I love you and I don't want anything to come between us. Don't you understand? I just want it to be us. You and me.' He looked at me and smiled, as though that would be enough to convince me.

'I'm keeping her,' I said again.

I knew it was a girl. I turned on my heel and strode out of the room, propelled by a fierceness of purpose I'd never had before.

He grabbed my arm and yanked me back. 'Wait, where are you going?' he asked. His fingers were a vice, crushing mine, and his eyes were flashing. The desperation had morphed to rage. 'You can't go,' he growled. 'We have to talk about this. It isn't just your decision.'

'Yes, it is,' I said. I winced at the pain and he squeezed tighter, injecting a shot of fear into my veins that sedated my courage and conviction.

'James,' I said quietly, my heart beating faster. 'People will be wondering where I am.'

I saw the flicker of annoyance that crossed his face at the reminder we weren't closeted in his flat, behind a locked door. 'Let me go,' I said, seeing my moment, and yanking my arm free.

Once I was out the room I had to stop myself from running towards the elevator. I needed to get away from him, that's all I knew, put as much distance between us as possible. I needed to figure out how I was going to manage this alone.

I walked past the top of the stairs that led down to the lobby and saw the Christmas tree twinkling below and it seemed to be offering me hope; a promise of happiness. I thought about how this time next year it would just be us. Me and Lucette. The two of us celebrating Christmas together.

I didn't hear the footsteps. I just felt a sudden shove between the shoulder blades that sent me stumbling forwards. The heel of my shoe caught on something, a crack perhaps, and my eyes widened with horror as I saw the tree and all its coloured lights rising up to meet me. I grabbed for the banister, only to miss it and clutch a handful of air. And then I was suspended, floating for an instant as though I was defying gravity.

And then I was falling.

Lizzie

Saturday, 9 December
Evening

'I wasn't sure, so I got two rooms.'

I nod and let out an internal sigh of relief. I've been nervous all evening wondering what the sleeping arrangements would be and trying to figure out what I would say if he got one room. James is more chivalrous than I gave him credit for.

'I think that's a good idea,' I tell him and I trace my fingers up his shirt buttons towards his neck. One of them is loose, dangling by a thread. 'I want to take things slowly.'

He nods but I can tell he's disappointed. He has the emotional expressiveness of a toddler; out comes a pout, which I quickly kiss away. We never ended up going back to Becca's and now it's too late. He's too drunk to drive. Perhaps it's for the best. We'll go in the morning when it's light.

I let him kiss me again when we get up to the rooms. He pushes me back against the door and rubs against me, making a soft groaning noise as he buries his head in my neck, breathing deep. 'God you smell good,' he tells me.

'Thanks,' I say.

He takes another deep breath, and I feel his lips burning against my skin. 'What is it?'

'Chanel No. 5,' I tell him. It's the eau de parfum too, not the eau de toilette. Now I'm glad I decided to splurge and buy it.

His lips graze my skin and his hands grip my waist, his fingers digging into me. I pull away but he grips me tighter – refusing to let go. I can feel how hard he is. 'Oh god,' he mumbles and then says something that I don't quite catch.

I wrench myself free and stare at him.

He looks at me, blinking rapidly as though I'm out of focus, and I wonder just how drunk he is. 'Sorry,' he says. 'I'm sorry.'

I nod, mute. I can't quite be sure but I think he called me Becca.

He strokes a strand of hair behind my ear and looks deep into my eyes. 'You're just so beautiful,' he murmurs.

For an ecstatic moment time freezes. I forget what I might have heard or misheard. Hearing him say I'm beautiful gives me a buzz, the likes of which he could never imagine. No one has ever called me beautiful before. Not a single person. I've been called hot on Tinder. And fit. But never, ever beautiful. A butterfly takes flight in the pit of my stomach and I think I almost want to cry, but then I put my hands on James's chest and push him gently away. 'I don't want to rush things,' I tell him.

He nods, though I can tell he's frustrated. 'Sure, sure,' he says. 'I get it.' He bites his lip, giving me what I imagine is his most charming grin. 'We could just, I don't know, watch a movie?' He can't hide the hunger in his eyes and it makes me feel powerful, almost regal.

'I'm actually feeling a little tired,' I say.

'OK,' he says, his shoulders drooping and his pout re-appearing.

I kiss him on the jaw, on the spot where I punched him earlier. 'Thanks for everything,' I tell him. 'I really appreciate it.'

He smiles at that. I read that men love to be appreciated and treated like they're heroes and protectors. I don't know if it's true for all men but it certainly works like a charm on James. If all else fails, maybe I can take everything I've learned from reading about relationships and compile a dating manual.

I escape into the bedroom and lock the door, keeping my ear to it until I'm sure James has sloped off down the corridor to his own room. I haven't had sex. I'm still a virgin. And I'm not in any hurry either. I've done my due diligence and watched hours of material on Pornhub, even though most of it made me feel quite revolted. All the women seemed so subjugated; playthings to men, there to serve and be serviced. If that's how it has to be, it will take some time for me to work up to it.

In the bathroom (which comes complete with luxury toiletries that I make a note to nab before I leave) I undress slowly and study myself in the mirror, admiring my new nose, my pert breasts, and toned arms. I have stretch marks around my thighs but in low light you can't notice them, especially when I use fake tan, which I have done.

I drop my arms away from my stomach and stand there, looking at myself for a moment. I shed the old me like a butterfly emerging from its cocoon, but sometimes when I look in the mirror I see her looking out from behind my eyes.

I lean forwards so my nose is almost touching the glass. 'You're beautiful,' I whisper. 'You've got this. You deserve this.'

Lizzie

Sunday, 10 December
Morning

Footsteps startle me awake. I lie in the unfamiliar bed listening as they come to a stop outside my door. There's a shadow beneath it. Someone is standing in the corridor. For one terrifying moment I think it's Becca but then I remember where I am. She can't be here. We're at a hotel. There's security. I check the time. It's almost four in the morning. The person is still out there. I can feel them hovering, lurking.

Is it James? I slip from the bed, pulling on the fluffy white robe that's still damp from my bath earlier. I creep towards the door and put my eye to the peephole. Yes, it's James. He's standing in front of the door, bleary-eyed and swaying slightly. I yank the door open. He blinks in surprise and almost topples backwards.

'Hi,' he says.

'It's four in the morning,' I whisper.

'Is it?' he answers, slurring. 'I couldn't sleep. I've been down in the bar.'

I raise my eyebrows.

'I'm sorry to disturb you,' he says and makes to turn away. 'Go back to sleep.'

'You've disturbed me now,' I say. 'Do you want to come in?'

He looks delighted. 'Can I? I promise I'll be on my best behaviour.'

'OK,' I say and let the door fall open.

He walks past me and his fingers brush mine deliberately. He takes off his jacket and I notice a button missing from his shirt. He sits on the edge of the bed and when I walk towards him he suddenly grabs for me and pulls me towards him. He buries his head against my waist. I put my hands on his head and stroke his hair. What's going on? I notice his shoes are muddy. He must have been outside, but why?

'Sorry,' he mumbles.

'It's OK.' I run my hand through his hair again and he looks up at me. My robe has fallen slightly open and his gaze falls to my chest. I resist the urge to close the robe. Instead I let him look, even though it makes me feel deeply uncomfortable.

Finally he moves his hand and slides it inside my robe and up my thigh. I'm naked beneath the robe. Completely naked. He draws in a breath as his fingers slide higher. I bite my bottom lip and then take a step backwards.

'Oh god, sorry,' he says, standing up. 'I promised I'd behave myself. It's just . . . I . . . you . . .' He flops down on the bed again and buries his head in his hands for a few moments before looking up at me, eyes swimming with tears. 'She was pregnant.'

He hurls it straight out of left field. 'What?' I splutter.

'I don't know why I'm telling you. She was pregnant. Becca. With my baby.' His face starts to crumple.

'Oh,' I hear myself say. My legs start to feel a little shaky so I sink down beside him on the bed.

'She lost it,' he says. 'The accident.'

It's a lot to process and my brain has started to whir. 'I'm sorry,' I say, drawing the robe tighter around myself. I can still feel his hands sliding up my thighs and I can't concentrate.

'She was only a few weeks along. She'd just told me, the night of the accident.'

I swallow hard. Becca was pregnant. She was pregnant when she fell down the stairs. That explains a lot. I start pacing the room. Why didn't he mention this sooner. It explains everything. That must be why she's gone and created this crazy fantasy life with a husband and baby – to replace the ones she lost. James sits slumped beside me, head bowed. There's a powerful whiff of whisky coming off his breath. He's practically flammable.

'I didn't want it,' he whispers. 'I told her to get an abortion.'

I stop pacing and stare at his bowed head. I don't know what I'm meant to say to that. I bite my lip and stay quiet. He starts to cry, though at first I don't realise that's what the whimpering noise is. His shoulders heave. I put my hand on top of his knee then wrap my arm around his shoulder. He leans into me.

'She was upset,' he says. 'She could never forgive me. That's partly why we broke up. She was told she'd never be able to have more children. All the spinal damage and injuries to her pelvis made it impossible. She was so heartbroken.' He looks at me and the shame in his expression almost makes me feel sorry for him.

'I felt so bad. I hadn't wanted the baby but I didn't mean for this to happen.'

I frown at the odd choice of words.

He looks at me pleadingly, as though he's hoping I'll offer him absolution. 'She was so upset and I felt so guilty, you know, for telling her to get an abortion. She couldn't get past it.'

I nod. It makes sense. I don't think many women could forgive him for that and I'm not sure I can offer him absolution.

I almost feel sorry for Becca. It makes it much more understandable now why she went to all that trouble to invent a fake life; one complete with the baby she would never have. I can actually almost sympathise. Almost.

James is chewing on the inside of his lip and it makes me wonder once again why he came with me to see Becca. Was it really because he wanted to help me confront her or does he have unfinished business with her? Does he want to apologise and perhaps work things out? Another thought crosses my mind – one I've tried to ignore but once I allow it in it plants a flag and claims territory – could his attraction for me be something else too? Am I a stand-in for Becca?

'Do you still love her?' I ask.

He looks at me, alarmed. 'What?'

'It's OK if you do,' I tell him. 'I'd understand. She was the mother of your child. You were together for a while.'

He shakes his head. 'No, I don't love her. Not any more. I mean, I haven't seen her or spoken to her in years.' He glances at me quickly then turns away. 'I wanted to see her, though. That's why I came with you.' He bows his head, leans forwards with his elbows on his knees. 'I wanted to . . . I don't know.' He shrugs. 'I guess I was intrigued to see her again after all this time.'

I nod, keeping my face blank. So he did have an ulterior motive. I guessed as much but it still feels like an invisible punch to the gut hearing him admit it.

He takes my hand. 'But I'm glad I met you.' He smiles up at me endearingly. 'I like you,' he says and my heart flutters despite my misgivings. 'And I'd like to see where this goes.'

He likes me! He wants to keep seeing me. For the first time in my life someone likes me and wants to date me. And not just anyone either, but someone successful, rich and handsome. I've been dreaming about this my whole life. Why oh why does Becca have to be a dark shadow hanging over us?

James stands up and draws me towards him. I close my eyes. The kiss doesn't come and my eyes flash open. He's frowning. 'Your eyes look different,' he announces.

I stand up. 'I'm not wearing my contacts,' I say, and then I turn away and walk to the door. 'I think maybe you should get some sleep.'

'Yes, right, I'm sorry,' he says, rubbing a hand through his hair, mussing it up. He's like a child that needs mothering, with his shirt-tails hanging out and his cuffs undone. He shuffles towards me, eyes downcast.

'Why don't you stay here?' I suggest, softening. 'Just to sleep, that's all. No funny business.'

'Can I?' he asks, the hope on his face almost making me laugh. 'Would that be OK?'

I nod and head towards the bathroom, snatching up my clothes as I do. 'I'm just going to go and get dressed.'

'Probably a good idea,' he says, his gaze once more slipping down my body.

Becca

'You're hysterical, you're acting like a madwoman,' James hissed.

I stared at him, lips pressed together tightly to stop my rage from bursting out. I wasn't hysterical. I wasn't mad.

He took my hand and, where once he would have squeezed it, he patted it, as you would do to an elderly aunt you were visiting on her deathbed. I knew that was how he saw me now. He couldn't hide the revulsion. It was there every time he looked at me: in the twitch at the corner of his eye and the flare of his nostrils as he took in my broken body – bound in casts and suspended in traction. He could barely look at my face and when he did, he couldn't mask his horror. His mouth tightened as though he was having to hold back from throwing up.

I didn't remember much back then – my memory was like a colander, full of holes and leaking. But there was a kind of muscle memory, or animal instinct that made me feel afraid whenever I looked at him. It felt like I was screaming on the inside but my lips were sewn shut and no noise could escape. I struggled to remember the details of our relationship. When I first woke, I recognised him vaguely but I didn't know his name and I couldn't recall a single date we'd been on.

The doctors said I suffered a major brain injury and that my memories would never fully return; my brain would never work the same way again. I was like a car written off in a smash and patched up with spare parts. The car would never run as smoothly as it once did. The gears would crunch, the engine whine. And then there was the bodywork – the dings and dents and scratches that couldn't be beaten out or painted over.

That was what bothered James the most. The outside paintwork, not the workings of the engine. I overheard him once, talking to a doctor when he thought I was asleep, asking her if I'd ever look the same again. When the doctor told him no, he asked about plastic surgery options. When she said that plastic surgery would undoubtedly make a difference but that I would never look exactly like I used to, his visits became less frequent. He told me he was busy with work but I didn't believe that was the reason.

I didn't mind, though. I was too depressed thinking about Lucette.

When I woke up from the coma it was the first thing I had asked about. 'The baby?'

The nurse took my hand and squeezed. She shook her head. I closed my eyes and wished with all my might to sink back into the blackness of the coma. I wished I had died.

It was the police who put the idea into my head. They came to visit me once I was sitting up. The doctors warned them that my memory was still shot and that I was easily tired out. It was a young police officer who asked the question. Her notebook was in her hand, the pencil poised above it and she was doing her best to act sympathetic. 'Do you remember anyone being near you at the time of the accident?' she asked.

I opened my mouth and shut it. Someone being near me? What were they implying?

'Becca?' she said. I looked at her and realised I must have been staring into space for a while. 'Someone reported hearing an argument. Do you remember anything about that?' She was talking to me kindly, but with a tone you'd use on a child or someone with dementia. It made me wonder why. Was it because I looked like Frankenstein's monster? Was it because the doctors had told her I was brain-damaged? I didn't feel brain-damaged. I felt tired and I couldn't remember things and my body wouldn't obey the commands my brain was issuing, but I didn't feel my mind was broken. I felt the same person inside, even though everyone was treating me as if I was different.

'Did you argue with anyone?' the police officer asked. 'Do you remember what happened just before the accident? Is it possible someone might have pushed you?'

I looked at her, frowning. Shocked, because the idea really hadn't occurred to me until that very moment. 'Pushed me?' I repeated dully.

She nodded. I remember she had thick brown hair, pulled back in a ponytail and I wanted to reach out and touch it. My own hair had been shaved off when they operated on me and I felt a pang of longing. 'Did someone push you down the stairs?' she asked again.

'No,' I said. 'I don't think so.'

She waited a few seconds, as though I might be about to say something else, but when she saw I'd drifted off somewhere she closed the notebook and peered at the other officer, who pulled a face that said: 'Let's go, we won't get anything out of her.' So they went and the nice police officer, the one with the ponytail, left her card and told me to call her if I remembered anything, anything at all. I don't know what happened to that card. I can't even remember her name now.

That night I dreamed I was holding Lucette in my arms. She was beautiful. She had dark hair and blue eyes and I couldn't stop staring at her in wonder. I looked at the ground and saw I was standing at the top of some stairs. And then I felt a sudden shove between my shoulder blades and I fell, Lucette spinning out of my arms as the ground rose up.

I woke screaming and the nurse on duty ran into my room and administered something that put me under. I dreamed the same dream again but when I tried to turn and see who it was who pushed me, I couldn't. I couldn't move. They stayed in shadow.

'Do you remember anything?' James asked me after the police had visited and I told him what they'd asked me. I said no, despite a nagging feeling that there was something trying to force its way through, like a splinter taking its time but pushing determinedly to the surface. My frustration at not being able to just yank it out, combined with my frustration at my body, which wouldn't do what I wanted it to, and the vacant space in my now barren womb, made me furious. I started yelling at nurses and at the doctors, throwing my food and yanking out IVs, refusing medication, refusing to do my physio. All I wanted was to rip the world apart and create an abyss into which I could jump.

Then one day I woke up and, just like that, it was as if the light had been turned on inside my brain, illuminating those parts of my memory that had been in darkness. There was no reason for it whatsoever, only that the splinter had partially emerged. I remembered the fight with James. Him telling me to get an abortion. The snarl on his face and the way he gripped my arms. I remembered telling him I was keeping it and walking out of the room. I remembered the Christmas tree lights. And I remembered the shove between my shoulder blades. I hadn't imagined it. Someone had pushed me. If I closed my eyes and ran over the memories, I could even see a face emerging from the shadows.

The machine beside my bed started to beep. The ceiling felt as if it was crashing down on me. I couldn't get enough oxygen. I tried to get out of bed, pulling out several tubes as I crashed to the floor on my useless legs. The nurses came running. They shouted over my head, calling for help. It was all a dull noise in the background. Even the pain felt distant.

'Someone pushed me,' I told James when he next came to visit. I studied him for his reaction.

'You fell,' he told me. 'You tripped on the tiles. You were wearing high heels.'

'No,' I told him defiantly. 'I was pushed.'

He blinked several times. 'Did you tell the police?'

I shook my head. He took a deep breath. He seemed relieved. 'I'm going to,' I told him.

'You can't!' he shouted. 'If you do, you'll lose your compensation. PKW will only pay out if they're to blame. If you say you were pushed, they'll refuse liability.'

I hadn't considered that. I didn't care, though. I wanted the truth to be known. That was more important than money.

'What do you remember?' he pressed.

'You wanted me to get an abortion.'

He paled at that, then shook his head. 'That's not true.'

'It is true!' I yelled at him, furious that he could lie so blatantly.

His eyes flashed. He leaned over me. 'Calm down,' he spat. 'I didn't even know you were pregnant.'

'Don't fucking lie to me!' I shouted, loud enough for a nurse at the station outside my room to turn towards us. James moved away from me. 'I remember,' I hissed at James.

'You wanted me to get rid of her! You told me to get an abortion. You pushed me! It was you!'

James's face contorted and I flinched. He looked over his shoulder, glancing at the nurse's station. The nurse was occupied with something. He walked back over to the bed. He leaned over me, his face inches from mine. 'You're hysterical,' he hissed through gritted teeth. 'You're acting like a mad woman.'

'Go!' I spat at him. 'Get out!'

'If you tell anyone, they won't believe you. I'll make sure of it.'

I stared at him, wondering how I'd ever loved him. He seemed like a monster then.

'Just leave me alone. I don't want to see you again,' I whispered.

He stood up. 'Fine,' he said. 'But you don't know what a mistake you're making.'

He stormed out of the room without a backwards look. Watching him go, all I felt was relief. Now it was just me and Lucette.

Lizzie

Sunday, 10 December
Morning

When he wakes it's almost check-out time. I hand him a coffee from the room service tray I ordered earlier. 'Good morning, sleepy head,' I say with a smile.

'Good morning,' he mumbles, sheepishly. 'Oh god.' He winces as the light hits his eyes, and rubs his face before taking in the room. Then he looks at me, wide-eyed with alarm. 'Oh god, what did I do? I didn't do anything bad did I? I had way too much to drink.'

'No,' I tell him, sitting down on the bed beside him. I reach out and stroke his hair. It's sticking up all over the place.

'I behaved OK?' he asks, tilting his head a little as though he's a cat wanting more strokes.

I smile and nod, then stand up. 'You were a perfect gentleman.'

He takes a sip of coffee and murmurs approval, 'Just how I like it.' He stares at me as I stop in front of the mirror to put in my earrings. 'You look nice,' he tells me.

I spent a while getting ready. I wanted to look good when he opened his eyes. 'Thanks,' I say.

'I guess we should check out,' he grumbles once he notices the time.

'I suppose so,' I say as I sit back down on the bed beside him. 'I was thinking that maybe we could try Becca's again.'

He almost spits out his coffee. 'What?' he asks, a mild tone of panic in his voice.

'I'd like to try again. Now I know more about what's going on, what she's been through with the baby. I want to tell her how sorry I am.'

A shadow passes across his face. He's just remembered telling me about the baby. He'd forgotten. He puts the coffee mug down on the bedside table. 'I shouldn't have told you. I'm sorry.'

'No, I'm glad you did.' I put my hand over his. 'And it's OK. I think it was good for you to talk about it.'

He bites his lip and nods. 'Yeah,' he says and gazes at me. 'You're the only person I've ever told.'

I get up to pour him more coffee, feeling his eyes on my back watching me as I add the dash of milk I know he likes.

I could get used to this feeling, the warmth of his gaze against my skin. It's intoxicating. This is how Becca must have felt all the time. No wonder she couldn't cope when she lost it.

We pull up outside Becca's house. The light is still on in the hallway even though it's daytime. Zac and Maddie's car is parked outside their house so I assume that means they're home.

'Shall we?' I say to James.

'I don't know,' he replies, his hand still resting on the key in the ignition. 'I'm not sure it's a good idea. Maybe we should just leave. It doesn't look like she's home anyway.' He's anxious. Maybe it's his hangover, but his foot keeps tapping and he looks as pale and washed-out as the sky.

'We're here now,' I tell him and get out of the car. I'm determined to see this through.

'I thought you didn't want her to see us together. You were worried it might set her off.'

I shrug. 'I don't care any more. I think we should go together.'

James follows me, somewhat reluctantly it seems. Yesterday he was desperate to see her but today he seems to have changed his tune. I almost had to drag him here against his will.

He stops to pull on his coat. With his hands shoved deep into his jacket pockets and his head hunched against the cold he looks fearful; but maybe it's not fear, maybe he's nervous about the prospect of seeing her again. Annoyingly I feel a stab of jealousy at that. Maybe he still has feelings for her despite what he claims. Why else would he be acting this way? Maybe that's also why he hasn't dated anyone for such a long time.

James rings the doorbell. We wait a few minutes but there's no answer. We can hear the dog, though, barking in some far corner of the house.

'It must be locked in somewhere,' James says as he peers through the side window into the hallway.

'What?' I ask.

'The dog,' he says.

I walk along the front of the house. It really is a big house. Far too big for one person. I peek through the window into the living room. It's just as it was before, nothing out of place, and I'm about to turn away when I see it. 'James!' I shout.

He comes running. 'What?' he asks.

I point. 'There, see, the lamp!' He looks through the window, cupping his hands to the sides of his face as he presses close to the glass.

'Shit,' I hear him say.

The lamp has been knocked off the side table and is lying smashed on the floor by the French doors.

'It wasn't like that before,' I tell him.

'You're sure?' he asks.

I nod. 'Yes.'

He frowns and then peers through the window again as if searching for clues. The wind picks up, cutting like a knife, and I pull my coat tighter around me to keep out the worst of it. The place feels haunted.

'Let's go around the back,' I say to him. 'Maybe we can get a better view.' I walk off, heading towards the gate through to the back garden. It's locked. James catches me up. 'Why don't you climb over?' I suggest, pointing at the fence.

'What? That's trespassing.'

'She could be in there, hurt. God knows.'

'Then we should call the police,' he argues, pulling out his phone.

'They'll take forever to get here. Why wait? And why call them if it's nothing? Come on.'

'OK,' he finally agrees. After testing his weight on the woodpile stacked along the side of the garage he climbs up onto it and then heaves himself over the fence. After a beat I hear the lock scraping as he pulls back the bolt and then it opens and I slip inside and join him.

The garden is a big expanse of neatly cropped lawn, fenced in and bordered with hedges and rose bushes. Beyond the fence are fields, dotted with electricity pylons, and in the far distance there's a wood – the trees all bare. I shiver again. It's so isolated out here. There's a wooden gate set in one corner of the garden, leading out into furrowed fields of brown, lumpen earth.

A stone terrace runs the length of the house, bordered with empty flowerbeds. We rush towards the French doors that lead into the living room. James beats me to it.

'I can't see anything,' he says, frustrated.

I look at the flowerpot by his feet.

It's lying on its side, smashed into several pieces, the earth inside scattered across the terrace. The sight of it definitely jars. When I survey the garden I realise it's because the whole place is well tended, the grass recently cut, everything pruned back for winter. The flowerbeds are clear of weeds. The magnolia tree has shed its leaves but not a single one remains to carpet the ground. The vegetable patch at the end of the garden looks freshly turned over. Even the cast-iron table and chairs sitting on the terrace are clear of debris and fallen leaves.

'That's weird,' James says.

I try the French door and it slides open at my touch. We look at each other in alarm. I keep pushing.

'What are you doing?' James asks in an urgent whisper.

I shrug. 'It's open. We should take a look around.' I step inside the living room. 'Becca?' I call.

The dog answers from somewhere, barking wildly. It sounds yippy-yappy, terrier-like, rather than something big and aggressive like an Alsatian or Rottweiler. James follows me inside nervously. 'We shouldn't be here,' he whispers. 'We should go.'

I ignore him. I feel like an intruder but there's also something quite exciting about being inside Becca's house. We tiptoe past the broken lamp and I resist the urge to pick it up.

'Hello?' James calls. He reaches the hallway and peers around. There's nothing out of the ordinary other than a drooping poinsettia plant, its leaves starting to curl brown.

There's a pile of post sitting on the mat. I pick it up and put it on the side table.

'Don't touch anything,' James hisses.

'Why not?' I ask.

'Because it could be a crime scene.'

I dart a look at the pile of letters. It's OK, I'm wearing gloves. But what does he mean, *a crime scene*? 'That's jumping to conclusions, isn't it? Maybe she decided to run away after Zac and Maddie discovered the truth about her lies, and was in such a rush she knocked the lamp over and didn't stop to pick up the pieces.'

'But why would she leave the dog?' James asks. 'Hello? Becca?' he shouts up the stairs. There's no response. We can hear the dog louder now, scratching at a door, yapping like mad. James heads towards it, opening a kitchen door.

I open another door off the hall that leads into a little bathroom. I take note of the posh toiletries and a candle that costs more than my weekly groceries and the fact that the toilet paper is folded into a little arrow shape, like they do in hotels.

I find James in the kitchen, standing in front of a door, behind which we can hear the dog barking up a frenzy. James glances at me uncertainly. He doesn't know whether to open the door and risk being savaged.

'Wait,' I say, and open the fridge. It's very neat and clean, and a quick scan tells me that Becca likes to shop at Waitrose and eats a lot of salad. I grab an unopened packet of ham and then a knife that's lying on the side and rip the packet open. 'Here,' I say to James, handing him the opened packet.

He takes it, peeling off some of the meat and holding it in one hand while he stretches from a distance and throws open the door.

A small black and white terrier – a scruffy thing – comes hurtling out of a walk-in larder. He goes straight for James's ankles, nipping and growling. James drops the ham and it stops trying to gnaw the flesh off James's legs and dives for the ham instead, swallowing it in one or two bites. James drops the rest of the packet and the dog wolfs that down too.

'The poor thing's starving,' I say, kneeling down and reaching out to stroke it. The little bugger snaps at me and I jerk my hand out of the way.

'Who the hell locked him in?' James asks with a scowl. The larder floor is covered in dog shit and a puddle of piss. 'He must have been in there a while.'

The dog – finished with the ham – runs to a little water bowl by the back door and starts lapping like he hasn't drunk in days. He drinks the entire bowl. 'We should give him some more,' I say but James is already filling a glass from the tap and emptying it into the bowl. He reaches down and strokes the dog.

'He looks like he's hurt.'

I kneel down beside him. 'Where?'

'There's dried blood on his neck.'

I frown. 'It might not be blood. It might be mud or something.' Though when I look at James I don't think he believes it and neither do I.

'Something's not right,' James murmurs. He strides out of the kitchen and I follow him.

'I think we should call the police,' I say.

James doesn't answer me. He's making for the stairs, running up them. 'Becca?' he shouts, his voice infused with panic.

I follow him, reaching the landing as James bursts into the first room he comes to. It's Becca's bedroom by the looks of things. It's empty – the bed made. James runs into the en-suite bathroom. I wait, almost afraid, but he comes out shaking his head then rushes past me and starts opening more doors – calling her name as he explores the rest of the house.

I head further into her bedroom. The carpet is cream and the pile so thick it's like walking through a snowdrift. It needs a clean – there are patches of dried mud on it. The bedroom is decorated in neutral tones but on the wall is a striking piece of art – streaks of red splattered on a canvas. It looks like an abstract painting of a crime scene. It's not my cup of tea. To each their own, I suppose.

I walk into the bathroom. There's a large freestanding white tub and a walk-in shower. The bathroom cabinet is slightly ajar and I look inside. There are several bottles of pills without labels. I shut the cabinet door and then walk back into the bedroom.

On the chair in the corner of the bedroom is a handbag. I take a peek and see Becca's wallet. No woman goes anywhere without her handbag or wallet. On the bedside table is a pile of books – mostly cheesy romances with people kissing on the covers, though one or two are spiritual Oprah-endorsed types of book, and there's also one called *Shattered: surviving the loss of a child*.

I can still hear James searching the house, calling Becca's name. Checking over my shoulder to make sure he's not watching, I slide open the drawer to the bedside table. It feels intrusive, like I'm a burglar, but I keep my most personal things in my bedside drawer so it's worth a look.

'James?' I shout.

He appears a few seconds later.

'What's that?' he asks.

'I found it in the drawer,' I tell him.

We both stare at it. It's a photograph of Becca and James in a solid silver heart-shaped frame. James draws in a deep breath and then swears under his breath. I put the photo back in the drawer and close it because what else is there to say. Becca might have lost her memory but she's still very much stuck in the past.

'She's not here,' James says to me.

I walk back out into the hallway. 'You searched every-where?' I ask.

He nods. He's chewing on his lip. He pulls out his phone.

'Are you calling the police?' I ask him.

'No, I'm calling her phone. What's her number?'

I give him the number that Maddie gave me and he dials it.

A phone starts to ring somewhere in the house. We run down the stairs, following the sound. It leads us into the living room. We scan the room, trying to locate it.

'There!' I say. It's lying half-stuffed between the cushions. James picks it up.

'Where is she?' he asks, looking around, bewildered, as if he might find her hiding behind the sofa about to leap out and yell 'Surprise!'

'I really think we should call the po—' I break off, my eyes fixed on a spot on the floor just behind James.

'Oh my god,' I whisper. 'Is that blood?'

He turns and looks. There, hidden in the shadow of the door, beside the bookcase, is a splatter of dark brown. It looks like chocolate sauce or a red wine gravy that's been left out overnight and developed a skin.

'Yes,' says James, kneeling beside it. He looks up at me, aghast.

I swallow, looking at the congealed splatter and automatically thinking back to that night at the PKW Christmas party; the image of Becca lying there on the marble lobby floor with blood pooling all around her like an ungodly halo.

'Why is there blood on the floor?' I ask James in a whisper.

He shakes his head. He stands and rubs his hands over his face as though trying to wake himself up from a bad dream. 'Shit,' he mumbles.

I pull out my phone and start to dial 999 but James stops me, his hand circling my wrist. 'I can't be here,' he says.

I look at him. 'What?'

'I can't be here,' he repeats. 'I'm a lawyer. We're trespassing. We could be arrested. I could lose my licence. This is serious.'

'But we only broke in because we were worried about her.'

James starts pacing. 'I know how the police think. How they work. We'll be suspects.'

'Suspects for what?' I ask. 'How can we be suspects? We don't even know what's happened to her. And besides, we've been with each other the whole time.' As I say it, I break off. Because, while I went to bed last night, I don't know what James did. I can't be his alibi. There was mud on his shoes. There was mud on the carpet upstairs.

'Look,' says James, glancing around the room. 'Something's happened to her.'

'What, though?' I ask. 'What do you think could have happened to her?'

He shakes his head. 'I don't know.'

Does he know something? Is he lying?

'Look,' I say, trying to remain calm. 'Let's call the police and tell them everything. I'll tell them what's been going on. Maybe I should have done that to begin with.' James is still pacing. 'I'll tell them it was my idea, that I went into the house alone, if you like. The door was open. It's not like we broke in.'

James stops pacing. 'No, my fingerprints will be everywhere.' He walks to the back door. 'Come on, let's go.'

'What about the dog?' I say. It's standing in the hallway, watching us, its pointy little teeth bared and a low growl emanating from the back of its throat. It would be menacing but for the fact a gerbil could probably best it in a fight.

James ignores the dog and ushers me outside into the back garden. He slides the French door closed behind us and then hurries me back to the gate. I open it and step through, then let out an involuntary scream.

Zac is right in front of me, holding a shovel.

'Oh my—!' I shout at the same as he yells: 'What the hell?'

Zac looks at James standing behind me. 'Who are you?' he demands.

'This is James,' I say, clutching a hand to my heart.

'What are you doing here?' Zac asks, looking between us, suspicion clouding his face.

'I . . . we . . .' I stutter, my gaze dropping to the dirty spade he's clutching in his hands.

'Have you seen her? Becca?' James asks.

Zac narrows his eyes at James, wondering who he is.

I explain: 'He's a friend. We were worried about her, so we came to see if we could talk to her. There was no answer so we went around the back to check on her.'

'The gate was locked. How did you get through?'

How does he know that the gate was locked? I look quickly at James, who also seems to have clocked the spade in Zac's hand. Zac follows our gazes. He holds the spade up.

'I was returning this. I borrowed it.' There's something

distinctly shifty about his behaviour and James and I exchange a look.

Zac rests the spade against the woodpile. It's splotched with rust. At least I think it's rust.

'You haven't seen her, then?' James asks Zac.

Zac shakes his head. 'We haven't seen her at all.'

'What about after I left on Friday?' I ask him. 'Did you go around to talk to her?'

He shakes his head. 'No.'

'We need to call the police,' I say. Now we've run into Zac, there's a witness so we may as well just admit what we've done. James seems to realise this too because he pulls out his phone. 'I'll do it.'

Zac looks at me. 'Why do you need to call the police? She might just be out.'

I shake my head. 'There's blood on the floor.'

'What?' he asks. I scour his expression but he just looks shocked.

'Blood,' I repeat.

'Oh my god,' he says, taking a step back and staring in horror at the house.

James is speaking to the emergency operator. He looks over at me. 'What's the address?'

'The Old Mill, Magpie Lane.'

He passes that on to the operator. 'I don't know,' I hear him say. 'A burglary or a kidnapping. Yes ... a missing person. Thanks.' He hangs up.

Just then I catch movement at the end of the driveway. It's Maddie, carrying Sadie in her arms. She's come to see what's going on. She approaches almost tentatively, her eyes darting between me, James and her husband. 'What's happening?' she asks when she reaches us.

'Are these the neighbours?' James asks me quietly. I nod. He looks between them, piecing together that these are the people whose lives Becca borrowed, whose baby she passed off as her own.

'I found these two,' Zac explains to Maddie. 'They were snooping.'

'We weren't snooping,' I blurt angrily. 'We were worried about Becca. She's not home.'

'Apparently there's blood,' Zac says to her. 'But no sign of her.'

'There are signs of a struggle,' I interrupt. 'We could see it through the window.'

'There are?' asks Maddie. 'What kinds of signs?'

'A lamp's been knocked over. There's blood on the floor. And the dog was locked up in the larder.'

She frowns.

'Did you see her at all, since I left?'

She nods and I catch Zac glaring at her before shooting me an embarrassed look. He lied to me.

'I went over there straight away,' Maddie says. 'As soon as you'd gone. To confront her.'

'I told her not to,' Zac mumbles, obviously still annoyed that Maddie disobeyed him and made him look like a liar.

'What did she say?' I ask. 'Did you speak to her?'

Maddie shakes her head. 'She refused to answer the door but I saw her through the window. She ran into the living room.' She exhales with a huff. 'I mean, how dare she do all that, and then run away when I try to talk to her?'

'I told you not to go over there,' Zac huffs.

Maddie shoots him a look that could curdle cheese.

'Listen,' says James, holding up his hands and trying to

quiet them both down. 'I know she's done something bad, but you have to understand she's not well.'

'That's an understatement,' Maddie hisses. 'She's fucking certifiable.'

'Maddie,' Zac warns. 'Stop it. She's missing. Something might have happened to her.'

'We don't know that,' she says. 'Maybe she's so embarrassed about what she's done that she's fucked off somewhere.'

'How do you explain the blood?' I ask her.

Maddie shrugs. 'Maybe she's tried to kill herself.'

'Then where is she?' I ask.

'I don't know. Maybe she didn't manage to do it properly or had second thoughts. Maybe she took herself to the hospital to get patched up.'

'Her car's still here,' Zac says, glancing through a side window into the garage.

Sadie starts to blubber in Maddie's arms and then one ear-splitting sound merges with the scream of a siren approaching.

'We'll tell them the truth,' James murmurs in my ear before he walks down the driveway to meet them.

A young woman gets out of the patrol car. She's short and squat with dark hair in an unflattering bob, and the uniform is so bulky, what with all the gizmos attached to the belt, that it looks like she's a little boy playing dress up.

James points at the house and explains something. I see her nod then she walks towards us. She introduces herself as PC Isha Kandiah and asks who we are and what the problem appears to be. James tells her what's going on. When he gets to the part about how we entered the house, she scowls at us.

'You went inside?'

He nods. 'We were concerned.'

'Why didn't you call us?' she asks him.

'We weren't sure if we needed to,' he answers. 'And then we saw the blood.'

At that her expression changes. 'OK, if you could show me,' she says.

James leads her through the gate into the back garden. We all make to follow but she shakes her head. 'One is enough. If it's a crime scene, I don't want any more contamination.'

'Crime scene?' whispers Maddie, jiggling Sadie up and down on her hip. 'Oh my god.' The blood drains from her face, leaving only a bright spot of colour on one cheek that might be blusher, but could be a bruise.

I look between her and her husband. Furtive would be the word I'd use to describe both of them. I follow his eyes as they dart uneasily to the mud-spattered spade.

'Have you asked him about the spade?' I ask PC Kandiah for what feels like the fifth or sixth time.

She looks at me across the table, puts down her pen, and sighs loudly.

'What?' I say, annoyed at her attitude. She doesn't seem to be taking this seriously. 'I'm telling you, it's suspicious.'

'Yes, as you keep saying.'

I cross my arms and sit back in my seat. Two empty polystyrene coffee cups sit in front of me. I've been here over an hour answering questions. I've told PC Kandiah everything I know about Becca, how we met, what she was like at work, the accident, every detail I can think of, yet PC Kandiah is treating me in the same manner that she probably treats the elderly pensioners on her beat: with cups of tea, lashings of condescension and zero sense of urgency.

I lean forward, my elbows pressed into the table. 'I've told you, they were furious when they found out what Becca had been doing – pretending to be married to Zac, using their photographs, even ones of their wedding. Maddie told me that she went around to talk to Becca straight after I left. And believe me, she was livid. She sounded like she wanted to kill her. I think she might even have said that.'

'The neighbours are being interviewed, thank you,' PC Kandiah says, cutting me off. She's not taking me at all seriously.

'What about James?' I ask, impatiently.

'My colleague's in with him taking a statement.'

'A statement?' I ask. 'But we're not witnesses to anything. We're just here to file a missing persons report.'

'And as part of our due diligence we need to speak to anyone who came into contact with the missing person or who knew her. It helps if we can build a picture of her. Her likes, her dislikes, her routine, that sort of thing.'

'I told you. I don't know her well. I don't know what she likes or doesn't like.'

She nods. 'You and Becca hadn't had contact since the accident and the first time you spoke after that was when you accidentally sent her a message meant for your friend Flora?'

I nod, feeling my face flush.

'And in this message you described Becca in not very flattering terms, alluded in what could be called a "negative" fashion to her mental health and also described her baby as resembling "a hobbit"?'

'No. I mean yes,' I stammer, wondering why I admitted all this. 'But it wasn't her baby, was it?' I protest. 'It was a fictitious baby.'

PC Kandiah narrows her eyes at me. 'You said it was the neighbours' baby.'

'It is!' I shout. For god's sake, how many times do I need to explain it? Speaking slowly, I spell it out yet again. 'Becca was passing off Zac and Maddie's baby as hers.'

'Right.'

'And I never said the baby looked like a hobbit.'

Kandiah looks down at her notepad, then up at me. 'You said that, and I quote, "the baby looked like Gollum".'

I cringe inwardly.

'Gollum was a hobbit,' she continues, dour-faced. 'A Stoor hobbit of the River Folk.'

What? I stare at her in confusion and then sigh loudly. Oh, great, I'm being interviewed by PC Kandiah, keeper of Middle Earth Knowledge and a clear Tolkien nerd. I take a deep breath and press my lips together. Whatever happens, I must remain calm. This interview feels like it's turning into an interrogation and I need to steer her back towards the actual suspects.

'Why would Zac have a spade?' I ask her for the umpteenth time. 'You don't think that's odd? Turning up like that, with a spade. He looked like he was about to walk through into the garden with it too.'

PC Kandiah shrugs. 'He says he was returning it.'

Well, of course he says that. Doesn't mean it's true. Is she entirely obtuse? 'So you've already interviewed them?' I ask.

She nods.

'And?' I ask.

'We're gathering further information.'

'Are you looking into them? Are you checking the garden? What if he's killed her and buried her somewhere? Have you checked the vegetable patch?'

PC Kandiah sits back in her seat and stares at me. Unimpressed would be the word to describe her attitude. I want to get up and shake her. I'm not much impressed with her either. Her people skills are severely lacking and I doubt she's going to be making the jump to plain clothes any time ever. 'I'm only trying to help,' I say, with a frustrated sigh.

She smirks. 'Thanks. If I need your help, I'll be sure to ask for it.'

'Are you searching the house? Maybe there's a murder weapon,' I continue, regardless of what she's just said.

'Murder? Why do you bring up murder?' she asks me, cocking her head to one side.

'The blood!' I respond. 'There was blood on the floor! The dog was locked in the larder. Obviously someone attacked her. What if they've killed her?'

'We don't know for sure it was blood. We won't know until we get the results back from the lab.'

'Oh, for goodness' sake, what else could it have been? Chocolate sauce?'

The glare returns. She really doesn't like me but goddamn it, PC Plod needs to get off her arse and start doing some actual police work.

'Where's James?' I ask.

'Your boyfriend?'

'He's not my boyfriend,' I say.

'Oh yes, that's right, sorry, your *friend*.'

Ahhh, now I see where she's going with this. She thinks there's something dodgy going on. She's seeing a love triangle where there isn't one. Shit. I suddenly catch a glimpse of the reason she's treating me like this and it knocks most of the wind out of me. I've seen enough crime shows to know how this works.

It seems like she suspects me and James of something. But that can't be right. They don't have any evidence. Apart from the fact our fingerprints and footprints are all over the house. Suddenly a wave of anger hits me. I've had enough of this. I stand up. This isn't an official interview. 'Am I free to go?' I ask.

'Of course,' she says.

I push my chair back and make for the door.

'But if you could stay, we'd be grateful.'

I stop and turn to her. 'Why?' I ask.

She shrugs. 'We're just following up on a few things. It won't take long.'

'What things?' I ask.

'Just checking some facts. Talking to her GP, other people she knew, trying to gather a better picture of her mental state.'

'I've told you her mental state. She was *mental*. You heard Maddie say the same thing. Who else invents a whole fake life?'

'Most people tell lies online. It's not that surprising.'

I stare at her. It's a weird thing to say, as though she's normalising deeply abnormal behaviour.

'I don't know why you need me to stay,' I say, bristling.

Kandiah raises her eyebrows. 'Because one of the detectives would like a word with you,' she says. 'She'll be along in a moment.'

A moment? It's more like an hour. And then finally the door opens and in walks a woman in a dark grey trouser suit. She's probably mid-thirties, with her hair pulled back in a ponytail so tight that it's giving her a Croydon facelift. She's got sharp cheekbones and a pointy chin and she isn't wearing any make-up, as though she's trying her hardest to deny whatever femininity she does possess.

She smiles as she walks in, which softens her face somewhat. 'Hi, hi,' she says to me, 'so sorry to keep you waiting. I'm Detective Inspector Dunn.'

She takes a seat opposite me. 'It's Elizabeth, yes?' she asks brightly.

'Lizzie,' I correct her.

'Right, Lizzie, yes.' She takes a sheet of paper from a manila folder, and hands it to me across the table. 'First, if you could take a look through this list and confirm everything you touched while in the house, that would be a great help, given that you potentially contaminated the scene.'

I glance down at the list that I myself compiled. The French door, the post, the banister, the books on the bedside table, the photo in the drawer, the phone.

'Oh, the bathroom cabinet,' I say, tears burning my throat and making my voice catch. 'I touched that too.'

Dunn looks up at that. 'The bathroom cabinet?'

'Yes.'

'Why were you going through Becca's bathroom cabinet?'

I give a small shrug. 'I thought she could be on medication and perhaps knowing what medication would give me a clue as to why she was acting the way she was. I wondered if she was depressed. It sounded like she was, from what James told me.'

She smiles. 'Playing detective.'

I smile back, unsure if she's laughing at me or with me. 'I guess,' I say tentatively. 'And I was right. The cabinet had lots of drugs in. I don't know what, though, they didn't look prescription.' That alone should have their alarms ringing.

Maybe whatever drug dealer she got them from is involved in some way in her disappearance. It's a theory and all theories should be explored.

Dunn nods thoughtfully. 'I've been reading your account of her accident, by the way. Sounds awful, witnessing that.'

'Oh, it was. It was awful,' I say as the image of Becca's head exploded like an egg flashes before me.

'James told us that she was pregnant at the time. She lost the baby.'

'Yes, I just found that out. I didn't know. It's terrible. I think she was devastated. I mean, of course she would be. What a horrible thing to happen. I feel so bad.'

'Why do you feel bad?' Dunn asks.

I flush. 'I didn't mean it like that. I just mean . . . It's my fault, isn't it?'

'What's your fault?'

'This. That she's missing. It's all because of one stupid message. If I hadn't sent it, then she wouldn't have started this campaign against me. I wouldn't have found out the truth about her. The neighbours wouldn't know about it. She's missing because of me.'

Dunn nods thoughtfully.

'Have you any idea what's happened to her?' I ask.

'Not yet,' she says. 'But we'll find out, don't you worry.'

I take a deep breath. 'Do you think she's dead?' I whisper.

Dunn gives me a non-committal shrug. 'It's a possibility.'

'You checked all the hospitals?' I ask.

'Yes. And the train stations and bus stations. No sign of her.'

I ponder that. Does that mean this is a murder inquiry? Or still a missing persons case?

Dunn looks at her notepad and then smiles at me. I watch her cross one leg and rest it on the other, casually, as if we're having a little chat down the pub. 'How long have you and James been dating?'

'We're not dating.'

She gazes at me curiously, and then turns to the paperwork in the file, flicking through it. 'I thought he was your boyfriend?'

I shake my head, exasperated. 'I already told you guys. I never met him before Thursday. I mean, not really. I saw him at the Christmas party when the accident happened. But we met properly on Tinder just a few days ago. He swiped right on me.'

'Really?' she asks, glancing up at me sharply. 'He says you swiped right on him first.'

'Oh,' I say, confused. Why is she asking these questions? 'Yes. But anyway, we liked each other and then I guess I got curious because there are a lot of guys on Tinder who are in relationships already and they don't bother to tell you.'

I glance at her wedding-ring finger. There's no sign of a band and she nods. 'I know the type.'

'So when I recognised him I got curious about Becca. I went digging online to see if they were still together. Just to make sure that he really was single. It was a surprise to me that they had broken up, you see.'

Her face clouds. 'OK, and you found Becca online and that's when you say you had the unfortunate incident with the message?'

'Yes, god, I feel so bad. I'm so embarrassed.'

'It's happened to all of us,' she says.

I look up at her in relief. 'Right?' I say. 'I just can't believe I hit send. I'm an idiot.'

'It seems like Becca's response was a little over the top.'

'I'm telling you!' I say, leaning over the table and lowering my voice. 'Who does that? She got me fired!'

Dunn shakes her head, her eyes wide. 'Yeah. Seems like she had a vendetta against you. You must have been really upset.'

'I was!' I soften my tone. 'I mean, I know what I did wasn't nice but it was an accident. I apologised. She didn't have to do all this stuff.'

Dunn nods along in agreement, then she frowns. 'I did look online, did some research, couldn't find those reviews you mentioned on Yelp.'

'Oh,' I say, 'they've probably taken them down by now. I emailed them and flagged them as fake.'

Dunn purses her lips and nods slowly. I realise with a mounting sense of horror that she doesn't believe me. 'It's true,' I say in a panic. 'I can show you the email I sent to Yelp. Oh, god,' I shake my head, 'no I can't.'

'Why?' she asks.

'It was one of those forms you fill in, so I don't have a copy, but I've probably got an automatic response from them I can show you.'

She shakes her head. 'It's fine for now. I've got no reason not to take your word for it.'

I study her. Does she mean that? She reads something in the file. 'And the tweets?'

'Well, I deleted those, of course.'

'Yes,' she says. 'Of course. I would have too.' She smiles at me but I have a horrible feeling that she's playing me. This is her good-cop routine. I've seen enough TV to recognise it. She doesn't actually believe me.

'It got me fired,' I tell her. 'You can speak to my HR person at work. Her name is Moira. She'll tell you.'

'I will. First thing Monday morning. I need to ask her some more questions about Becca as well. It sounds that she was quite a piece of work. I'm sure HR will be able to back that up.'

'Well, HR aren't the most savvy. You should talk to my friend Flora, she'll be able to corroborate what I'm saying.'

She nods again and scribbles down Flora's name in her folder. 'I also did a little research and couldn't find the um, interior design company website or the Facebook page – the one where you say Becca had posted photos of her neighbours.'

'That's because she took them down.' I point at the statement in her folder. 'It's in there. I told your colleague what happened. She deleted her profile. And the website too.'

'Right. The thing is, without proof it's difficult for us to . . . really understand what was going on between you.'

'Wait,' I say, alarmed. 'There was nothing *going on* between us. And I'm not lying. Why would I lie about this? She made up a fake life. It was there, online, she even photoshopped herself into photographs, how is that not insane? And there must be a way to find deleted web pages. Some online archive. You're the police, you must know how!' Just then I remember the screenshots I took. 'I have proof. I took screenshots! They're on my phone.'

She perks up at that. 'That would be great. I'll have someone bring you your phone so you can unlock it and show us.'

My panic starts to subside a little. Dunn gets up and goes to the door. She opens it and says something to someone waiting outside. When she returns I ask, 'What do you think happened to Becca?'

She shakes her head. 'What do *you* think has happened to her?' she asks, turning the question back on me.

She's the bloody detective. 'I don't know,' I say. 'That's why we called you.'

She smiles, then leans forward across the table as though she's about to impart a secret. 'We're exploring all options,' she says in a low voice. 'But between you and me it doesn't look good.'

I sink back into my seat, eyes wide. Oh my god. 'Really?'

She nods. 'And so, we have to explore every possible avenue.' She looks over her shoulder towards the door, then back at me, and in a lowered voice asks, 'How well do you know James?'

'Not very well,' I tell her. 'Like I told you, we only just met.'

'But you spent the night together, he said.'

'We had separate rooms.'

'Whose idea was that?' she asks, jotting something down in her notebook.

'Mine. He wanted to . . . you know, but I said no.'

'So,' she says, frowning at me, 'last night you weren't together.'

I shake my head.

'He says you were.'

'Oh.' I freeze. What has he told them? I opt for the truth. 'He did show up at my room in the middle of the night and then I let him sleep in the bed. But nothing happened.'

'I'm not interested in the sex,' she says dismissively.

'There was no sex.'

She nods as though she knows I'm lying but is letting it pass and it annoys me. 'What time did he turn up at your door?' she asks.

I shrug. 'I can't remember. Around four maybe?'

'How was he behaving?'

'Odd, I suppose. Kind of drunk. He was feeling sad, I think. He mentioned the baby then. Told me about Becca being pregnant and having a miscarriage.'

Dunn is writing this all down like I'm giving her the recipe for gold. I start to wonder if I should maybe not say any more, but she says, 'Did you notice anything else about his behaviour or what he was wearing? Was anything out of the ordinary?'

'Are you suggesting something?' I ask. 'You don't think James had something to do with her going missing?

Dunn shrugs. 'I don't know. Like I said, we're looking at all possible scenarios.' She hesitates, then says, 'Did you know that he came under suspicion after the accident? When she fell down the stairs?'

'No. I didn't know that,' I say, stunned. It feels as if the ground has just been whipped from beneath my feet. Do they really think James pushed her? And that he's behind her going missing? It puts me in a tailspin. 'I can't believe it,' I say, shaking my head.

She shrugs. 'He wasn't happy about the baby. He wanted her to get an abortion. She said no. Maybe he took things into his own hands. Maybe they got into a fight and he got aggressive and shoved her and she fell. Who knows?'

'But James is . . . he's too nice. He wouldn't have hurt her,' I hear myself say.

She shrugs as though to say you can never really know or trust anyone. The thought sends a shiver up my spine. The memory of James and Becca fighting at the Christmas party flashes into my mind. I remember the way he grabbed her wrist. At the time I thought it was romantic. He wanted her so much. And Becca didn't seem to be protesting too hard.

'Did you ever ask him what happened?' I press. 'What did he say?'

Detective Dunn shakes her head. 'We never got to inter-view him about it beyond the statement he gave on the night, that he didn't see what happened – he was in the bathroom, he said. He pulled the lawyer card very fast. And because there were no eyewitnesses there was nothing we could do. The victim didn't remember what had happened either – or if she did, she kept quiet – so we had to let it go.'

I take that in, staring back at her, wondering if this is all a ploy and she's trying to manipulate me, to turn me against James. She doesn't have any actual evidence of anything. All of this is conjecture.

'Whose decision was it to come here and confront Becca?' she asks.

'Mine,' I say.

'But James wanted to come with you.'

I nod. 'Yes.'

'He wanted to see her.'

I nod again.

'I wonder why that was.'

I don't say anything. I feel like she's carefully laying traps all around me, trying to get me to walk into one.

'Do you know where he was before he came to your room?'

'He said he'd been in the bar, drinking,' I tell her warily. I think about the mud on his shoes and the missing button. Should I say something?

'We're checking with the hotel's security,' Dunn says. 'The barman doesn't remember seeing him. And in the time available he could certainly have driven back to Becca's house.'

'He was drunk. He couldn't drive.'

'People drive drunk all the time,' she tells me.

I chew on that for a moment. They seem to have set their sights on James but surely they are also looking into Maddie and Zac. 'Listen,' I say, leaning forwards across the table. 'Have you checked the neighbours?' Zac would be *my* suspect numero uno, over James. Maddie too. She looks capable of being quite vicious. 'They've got a motive,' I say to Dunn.

She raises her eyebrows. 'So do you.'

'What?' My heart explodes like a firework in my chest and I reel back in my seat. 'Why would I kill Becca?'

'Who said she was dead?'

My mouth goes so dry that I have to swallow several times before I can speak and when I do open my mouth it comes out as a whisper. 'No one . . . I just . . .'

Dunn smiles. 'Look, if we're playing this game of hypothesising, then I'd say you had a perfect motive. I mean, it sounds like there was no love lost between you two, and it also sounds like you were very angry about what you claim she did to you.'

'I'm not claiming it,' I blurt. 'She did do it!'

'And you seem very angry about it.'

I take a deep breath and try to calm myself. I'm letting her rattle me and I can't. This is ridiculous. Absurd. It no longer feels like an interview. It feels much more serious. 'Am I under suspicion?' I ask her.

She smiles and shakes her head. 'No, of course not.' She leans across the table, playing all pally-pally but I see right through her. I'm not an idiot. She's smiling but her eyes are hard, scanning me, trying to laser right through into my brain.

'If you think I was angry,' I tell her, 'you should have seen Maddie. And she told me that she went over there on Friday to confront Becca. Maybe they got into a fight and she hit her, or she pushed her and she fell and hit her head, maybe it was an accident, maybe she died. Maybe she ran home to her husband in a panic. Maybe Zac came back and buried her in the garden. That's why he had the shovel. That's why he lied to me this morning and told me they hadn't gone over there. You need to check them out. I think they're guilty.'

Dunn is staring at me wide-eyed, an amused expression on her face. 'You've given that some thought, haven't you?' she says.

'No. But you hardly need to be a detective to put two and two together,' I say, biting back my fury. 'You can check at the hotel. I never left. I was there all night.'

Dunn looks down at the file again. 'But what about the night before that, Friday night? When you visited her on your own?'

Oh god. 'I left. I went straight home.' Adrenaline empties into my blood stream like a sluice gate has opened. I feel light-headed. 'You can ask at the pub. The barman, he saw me. He'll tell you.'

'What pub?'

'The one at the end of the road. The King's Arms. I was there when she sent the tweets! That proves I didn't do it. And Maddie saw her after I left.'

She writes that down, a little furrow forming a channel between her eyebrows. My heart is still pounding loudly in my ears, so loudly I'm worried she can hear it. My breathing is shallow. I force myself to take several slow breaths and to count to ten. She's just doing her job, poking around, trying to find out more information or get a reaction. Maybe I should have stayed quiet and not said anything. Or perhaps I should have asked for a lawyer, but then that would have looked more suspicious. That would be like telling the world that you're guilty.

She makes to close the folder, which I take to mean that the interview is over. Relief joins the adrenaline, making my head feel cotton-wool woozy. But what does that mean? Am I a suspect? Can I leave? Will James be done too? Will he have waited for me? What's going to happen next? I have so many questions but I'm scared to ask anything. I just want to get out of here.

She walks to the door. 'Can I leave, then?' I ask because it appears that she isn't going to volunteer the information.

Dunn nods.

'It's funny, isn't it?' she says as I start to get up.

'What?' I ask, as I pull on my coat.

She slides something out of the folder. It's a photograph. It's Becca. The same photograph that was in the paper. Becca standing on a cliff with the blustery ocean in the background, seagulls flying overhead. Dunn pushes it across the table towards me. 'You and Becca,' she says. 'You look very alike.'

I look down at the photograph. 'I don't think so.'

She spins the photograph around. 'You don't see it? I do.'

'We're both white, with blonde hair and green eyes,' I shrug, wrapping my scarf around my neck. 'That's about it. And I'm taller than her.'

She makes a grunting noise. 'Are you a natural blonde?'

'Excuse me?' I ask, dumbfounded.

'I tried dyeing my hair once,' she says. 'I'm mousey like you, but blonde really didn't suit me.'

I stare at her. What is she talking about?

'I found a photo of you from a couple of years ago.'

I freeze. Where on earth did she find that? I've done everything I can to delete old photos of me from the Internet. I've even had my passport reissued. She seems to guess my silent question.

'The DVLA – we were checking your driving licence. I didn't recognise you at first.'

I changed my driving licence last year, told them I'd lost it so I could get a new one issued. 'It's an old photo,' I tell her.

'I can see why you'd change it.'

Bitch. I keep my face straight.

'And your eyes changed colour too.'

'They're contacts. I've got hazel eyes normally.'

'Says on your licence that they're brown. Like your hair.'

'Hazel. They're hazel.'

She makes that grunting sound again. 'Well, I hardly recognised you,' she says, with what seems like amazement. 'Neither did James.'

That's the final arrow she flings my way. She's been saving it, waiting to use it. I won't let her see a reaction, though inside, the ball of shame is burning white hot, almost blinding me. What will he think of me now? Damn her. She's ruined everything. I feel like I could punch her. She has no idea what it's taken me to get here and she's just dismissed it all in the most humiliating way possible, ruining my chances with James at the same time.

I pick up my handbag and walk past her, keeping my head raised, my back ramrod straight.

'See you later,' she says as I open the door and see myself out.

I stir my coffee, even though it's black with no sugar. It turns out that almond milk lattes haven't made it to tea shoppes in the Cotswolds. When I dart a glance up I find James is staring at me with the exact expression I was hoping not to see: one of disappointment marbled with disgust. He remembers me from the Christmas party. That horrible detective probably pitched the idea that I was some Single White Female trying to make myself into Becca so I could steal her boyfriend. It's ridiculous. And it's not true. I didn't want to look like Becca. I did this for me. I was tired of being a brunette. I wasn't mousey. How dare she say that? I went for blonde because everyone knows that blondes have more fun. But it didn't go with my eye colour, so I decided to get contacts. I needed glasses anyway. I gave myself a makeover and I had every right to do that.

James definitely looks like he can't get the image of the old me out of his head. As though I'm wearing a Snapchat filter he can't unsee. I decide the only way out of this is to make a joke of it.

'If they hadn't shown me the photo of you, I would never have believed it,' James says. 'That's quite a transformation.'

'Thanks,' I say, 'I had a great personal trainer.' I can hardly bear to look at him, I'm so humiliated. My mum had a boyfriend once who used to call me names: lardarse, ugly bitch. The memories assault me now, ones worse than just name-calling, as James looks at me. My skin starts to burn with a shame I thought I'd long since conquered.

'We spoke, didn't we?' he says. 'At the Christmas party. I was so drunk. though, it's all a bit of a blur.'

'No,' I say. 'We didn't.'

He shakes his head. He doesn't remember, clearly. 'What did you tell the police?' he asks.

'Everything,' I say. 'What about you?'

He grimaces into his coffee. 'The bare minimum.'

'Why?' I ask.

'I'm a lawyer. You never give up information that could be used to incriminate you later. I should have warned you.'

'But . . . you haven't done anything,' I argue weakly, hearing Dunn's words replay in my head like a stuck record.

'I know I haven't done anything,' James answers, 'but the

police will try to pin it on whoever they think will make the best suspect. Guilt has nothing to do with it. They want to close the case as quickly as possible.'

'But what case?' I press. 'There is no case. She's only missing.'

He wraps his hands around his mug and stares at me. 'She's not missing.'

A long moment passes. 'What do you mean?' I finally stammer.

'She's dead,' he answers, without so much as a hesitation.

My heart stops beating, the blood freezing solid in my arteries. 'What?'

'She must be,' he says, taking a sip of his coffee. 'It's the only thing that makes sense. Where is she? She didn't take her phone or her handbag. Her car's in the garage. They checked her credit cards and she hasn't used any of them since Friday. You can't just vanish these days. It's impossible. Everything is on CCTV and everything is paid for by card. You wouldn't get five miles. They would find you within hours. The only thing that makes sense is that she's dead.' As he says it his lip trembles. 'I think it's the neighbours,' he says quietly.

I shiver involuntarily. 'It's my fault,' I say, staring into the dark whirlpool of my coffee. James puts his hand over mine and I realise I'm stirring the coffee so absent-mindedly and furiously that it's spilling over the edge of the cup and onto the table.

'It's not your fault,' he says firmly.

'It is,' I answer, tears welling up. 'I'm the one who started all this.'

I see him rapidly blinking away tears too. He's trying not to show how upset he is. But is he upset at the idea she might be dead, or is it something else?

I'm not sure how I feel about him touching me, especially now, but I don't know how to extricate myself. 'I'm so sorry,' I say, moving my hand to wipe my eyes. 'I dragged you into this. I never meant for this to happen. I don't know why I thought coming here was a good idea. God, do you really think it's the neighbours?'

He picks up his coffee.

'Yeah, who else could it be?'

He looks me dead in the eye when he says it, like he's challenging me to offer another suggestion. I just shrug and take a big gulp of my coffee.

James checks his watch then rubs his face. 'Fuck,' he hisses. 'I was supposed to be somewhere.'

'Where?' I ask.

He looks at me sheepishly. 'I, er, I actually had another date lined up. Totally forgot about it.'

'Oh,' I say, my gut lurching. With everything else going on it shouldn't matter. It shouldn't matter at all. But it does.

'With my mum,' he explains, seeing my expression, which I must have failed to hide. 'I was meant to be taking her to lunch.'

He stands up. 'Let me call her and tell her I can't make it. Hang on.' I watch him walk outside into the cold and pace back and forth as he talks to her. He keeps running his hand through his hair and I notice that he's receding a little at the temples. He doesn't look as smooth and confident as he did the other night. He looks stressed and on edge. And there's that missing button from his shirt, which makes him look shabby.

I consider how most of what I know about him came from Becca's posts. He was always #thebestboyfriendever. But now I think about all the lies Becca told on social media, who's to say if this wasn't a lie too?

I think back to last night, to how James turned up at my door drunk and emotional. I wonder if he did go around to Becca's like the police are implying. There was mud on his shoes. But he could have got that walking around the grounds of the hotel. I wonder if the police noticed the button missing on his shirt. Maybe I should have pointed it out to them. What James said about the police needing a suspect and not caring about guilt but about whether they can pin it on someone has got me rattled. What if they try to pin it on me? What if they made similar suggestions to James? What if they painted me as crazy? Capable of murder? But if they had a case, surely they wouldn't have let us go. I try to take comfort from that.

He comes back into the cafe and sits down opposite me again, rubbing his hands together to get warm.

'Everything OK?' I ask.

'Yeah,' he says. 'I should probably head back, though. Do you need a ride?'

'Yes please,' I say.

We walk to the door. James has parked just outside. He opens the car door for me and I'm about to get in when someone calls out his name. We both turn. It's Detective Dunn. The other one, PC Plod or whatever her name is, stands behind her, hands tucked into her utility belt.

'Yes?' answers James, somewhat tersely.

'I'm glad we caught you,' says Dunn, approaching us. 'We were hoping you could come down to the police station.'

'Why?' James asks.

Detective Dunn ignores him and looks at me. 'Both of you, actually. We'd like to clear up a few more things.'

'What things?' I ask.

'What's this about?' James says at the same time, impatiently. 'I've told you everything I know. We both have. So unless you're arresting us then the answer is no.' He turns to me and gestures to get in the car. I stare at him, frozen.

'They can't arrest us,' he explains. 'They have no reasonable grounds.' I hesitate. Doesn't refusing to go with them make us look guilty? Shouldn't we just answer whatever questions they have?

Dunn gestures to Kandiah, who steps forwards and, quick as a striking viper, grabs me by my arm. Before I can scream out, I feel the cold metal slap of a cuff circling my wrist.

'What are you doing?' I screech as she shoves me off the kerb and against the side of the car, wrenching my arms behind my back. 'What's happening?'

I struggle but she wedges her whole body against mine and it feels as if I've been slammed by a JCB digger.

With my face squashed against the car roof I turn my head a fraction and see that Dunn is doing the same thing to James. She body-slams him against the car, even though he isn't putting up any kind of struggle.

'James Wickenden,' she grunts. 'I'm arresting you on suspicion of murder. You do not have to say anything but it may harm your defence . . .'

The rest of her words are drowned out by Kandiah – her mouth pressed against my ear, her breath searing down the back of my neck. 'Elizabeth Crowley,' she spits, 'I'm arresting you on suspicion of murder.'

Sunday, 10 December
Evening

Arrested. I've seen it so many times on TV that it feels strange to hear the words spoken to me. I keep expecting to hear someone shout 'Cut!' But of course, that doesn't happen.

I don't know how much time has passed. It seems to be stretching out interminably. I feel as if I've been locked in this room for days. I have no idea what is going on. I tried hammering on the door but no one bothered to come. After they brought us here in separate cars, me in the back of the patrol car with PC Kandiah and James in an unmarked car with Detective Dunn, they separated us. They took me in front of the custody sergeant, who asked me dozens of questions about myself then made me sign a piece of paper confirming my name and that I understood the charge and that I wasn't in need of medical care. After that humiliation they shoved me in the same room as before, with yellow-stained walls and a filthy carpet.

The last thing James said to me, before they shoved me in the car in handcuffs, was not to say anything to them. He told me to wait for a lawyer.

But I don't have a lawyer. I requested one but I was told the duty solicitor was busy and would take hours to arrive.

They also gave me one phone call but I wasn't sure who to call. In the end I phoned my mum, forgetting she was still away. I hung up before her voicemail kicked in because what was I going to say? *Hi Mum, it's only me, I've been arrested for murder, see you in twenty- to twenty-five years?* And anyway, I already could see her reaction; could just imagine her sucking on a B&H like she was trying to draw the tar into her lungs through a crushed straw, and then calling the *Sun* and the *Daily Mail* to try to sell her 'story' to the highest bidder.

I still don't understand why they've arrested us exactly. What proof do they have of murder? There's no body. There's no murder weapon. The only thing they have is a possible motive. But even with that there's no way they could prove anything beyond reasonable doubt. And if they think I have a motive, then what about Maddie and Zac?

What murderer would file a missing persons report about a person they'd just murdered? I asked them that, but they wouldn't answer. That would be the definition of stupid, I told them. But they don't seem interested in listening to me.

Rubbing my wrists where the handcuffs bit through the flesh, I get up and walk the length of the room and back, stopping in front of the two-way mirror. I wonder if some-one is standing on the other side, a few inches away, staring back at me. They're trying to make me sweat. It's a tactic.

I wish I knew the time. They can only hold us for twenty-four hours before they have to charge us. The fact that they arrested us but haven't charged us means they can't have an actual case. They need one of us to confess to something or to rat the other one out or to get some other evidence – like a body. I know how it works. I'm not stupid. Even though they must think I am. I just keep panicking when I think about what might happen. What if they actually charge me? What if I go to jail?

It feels like I'm trapped in some kind of nightmare. That this isn't actually happening.

The door opens. I turn and find myself face to face with a man in an ill-fitting suit that's shiny on the shoulders and dusted with dandruff. His tie is tugged loose at the neck and there's a stain on the end as though he mistook it for a biscuit and dunked it in his coffee.

His eyes are black and beady as a magpie's and when he sits, he doesn't take them off me, not even for a second. It feels as if I'm sitting down to play a game of chess against a grand master and I warn myself to watch out. I can tell he's a higher-level detective than Dunn. He's older, his face pouchy and pocked, bloated bags swinging beneath his eyes like pendulums, but even though he is dressed like a homeless person, he's clearly sharp as an ice pick.

'I'm Detective Chief Inspector Tallack,' he says. He has a thick northern accent from somewhere near Manchester and he doesn't smile. I wonder if he's ever smiled in his life.

I don't answer him. I'm not saying a word. I'm too scared I'll dig a hole and fall in. He waits a moment then carries on. 'Detective Inspector Dunn is busy, asked me to have a word with you, if that's all right.'

He is her superior then. I wonder if she's been bumped for someone more experienced or if she's busy. Maybe she's interviewing James.

'Is it Elizabeth, or is it Lizzie?' DCI Tallack asks me.

'Either,' I reply, my voice shaking a little.

'If it's OK with you, Elizabeth, I'm just going to press record on this.' He gestures at a remote control, presses record then sits back. I glance up at the camera screwed to the ceiling in the corner. The light is green.

'This is DCI Tallack,' he says, then the time and date. 'I am interviewing Miss Elizabeth Crowley. I must caution you again that you have the right to remain silent but it may harm your defence if you do not mention when questioned something you later rely on in court. Anything you do say may be given in evidence. Do you understand?'

I nod.

'Please give an affirmative.'

'Yes,' I say.

'Would you like something to drink, Elizabeth?'

I shake my head.

'Are those the clothes you were wearing yesterday?' he asks.

'Yes.'

'What about James? Was he wearing the same clothes today as he was wearing yesterday?'

'Yes.'

'Odd', he continues, 'that you two came away for a romantic weekend without a change of clothes. When I take the missus away she packs like we're moving house. Brings ten pairs of shoes at least.'

'We weren't meant to be staying overnight,' I explain. 'It just got late. James had too much to drink and he couldn't drive.'

'I see.' He nods and writes something down and I immediately regret having opened my mouth. I feel like I've said something wrong when all I've done is tell the truth.

'He didn't have a change of clothes either?'

'No.'

'No, OK, so he was wearing the same shirt and the same shoes?'

'Yes,' I say.

'Did you notice anything odd about what he was wearing?'

I know what he's getting at. He means the button. He's noticed.

'Was anything missing?' he presses.

I swallow and look away. I don't want to get James into trouble but I need to tell the truth or I will get in trouble. 'A button,' I say. 'From his shirt. I noticed this morning, before we got to Becca's, that it was missing.'

'Was it missing earlier?' he asks. 'When you first met him, did you notice it was missing?'

'No,' I say.

His eyebrows rise. 'No, you didn't notice or no, it wasn't missing?'

'It wasn't missing,' I whisper.

'You're sure?' he asks and there's no mistaking the urgency in his voice, the eagerness to pounce.

'Yes,' I tell him.

'So the button must have fallen off sometime between Saturday morning when you two first met and this morning, when you noticed it was gone, is that right?'

He is right. I'm not sure I should admit it, but now I've gone and opened my mouth, I can't walk it back. 'Yes,' I say.

'When did you notice that it was gone?'

'This morning, when he turned up at my room.'

He nods. 'Did you notice anything else strange at all about James's appearance this morning?'

'His shoes. He had mud on his shoes.'

'You didn't think that was strange?' he asks.

'A little, but we were staying on a farm.'

He smirks at that. 'It's not really a farm. More of a posh hotel, not for the likes of us.'

That makes my back stiffen. What does that mean? The likes of 'us'. He's suggesting I'm not posh, that I don't belong in that world. He's lumping me in with the likes of him.

'You're a Yorkshire lass, aren't you? Down the road from me. I grew up in Macclesfield.'

'That's not down the road.'

He smirks again and I shift in my seat. 'So did you and James go for a midnight stroll around the farm?'

'No,' I say. 'I didn't. I don't know about James, you'll have to ask him. I assumed he'd maybe gone for a walk.'

Tallack gives me a disbelieving look. 'In the middle of the night? In the freezing cold?'

I draw in a deep breath and let it out slowly. 'Like I said, I didn't really think much of it until—' I break off.

He leans forwards, his little eyes glinting, as though he's spotted a worm or a shiny piece of jewellery he wants to get his beak into. 'Until when?' he pushes.

I press my lips together.

'Come on,' he says, conspiratorially, 'you can tell me. I'm trying to help you out here. I've already told my colleague that you're out of the picture. We're not looking at you, we're looking at him.'

Is that true? Am I not a suspect any more? Is it the button? They must have found it in the house. That's why they suspect James.

'So why am I under arrest still?' I ask.

'It's just the process,' he says with a shrug. 'Never mind about that, we'll have you out of here soon enough.'

By soon enough does he mean once they've built a case against James? It's hard to believe that they really think he might have killed Becca. But I feel a huge sense of relief that it's not me they suspect.

'I should wait for my lawyer,' I tell him.

'It'll be hours. We know you're innocent so why bother waiting? Let's just get this over with and you can be on your way.'

I study him, lips parted, trying to figure out if he's attempting to trick me or if he's being honest. He's hard to read.

'You were saying,' Detective Tallack continues, nodding at me, 'until . . .?'

The glimmer of hope I feel that I might be released sooner if I comply overcomes any reticence. 'Until I noticed the mud in Becca's bedroom,' I tell him. 'On the carpet. I mean, it stood out because the carpet's cream-coloured. Stupid colour for a carpet, if you ask me. Really shows the dirt.'

'Yeah, doesn't it just,' he answers, nodding in agreement.

'But James did run up the stairs before me. He might have just tracked mud in from outside.'

'How did he appear to you when he turned up in the middle of the night?'

'I've already been through this,' I say.

'If you could just humour me?'

'He seemed a little upset. Drunk. He said he'd been drinking in the bar downstairs.'

'Did he cry?'

I shake my head. 'No, he didn't cry but he was upset about something.'

'Did he say what?'

I hesitate before answering but then decide that none of this is anything they don't already know. 'He told me about the baby,' I admit.

'Anything else?'

'No. He fell asleep pretty fast.'

'Was that after you had sex?'

I look up sharply at that. 'What? We didn't ... I didn't sleep with him. I told the other detective.' I shake my head and frown at him.

He smiles at me. 'Sorry, my mistake. No sex. Got it. So in the morning, whose idea was it to go back to Becca's house?' he asks.

I pause. I suddenly feel like he's playing with me, like a cat with a mouse. 'I don't remember. I think it was his.' I pause. 'No,' I say, 'maybe it was mine.'

Detective Tallack grimaces at that. 'That's odd, isn't it? After he told you that he wanted to speak to her. Originally that was the plan, right? For him to come along with you and try to talk to her, convince her to stop messing with you. He seemed excited to know her whereabouts, didn't he? Curious about how she was doing?'

'Yes,' I say, warily. This conversation is like walking across a minefield.

'OK. How did James react when you entered the house?'

'He didn't want to go in.'

'Did you suggest calling the police or did he?'

'I did ... but he's the one that called. Listen, why are you asking all these questions? I've already been through this. Why have you arrested us? What about her neighbours? I told that woman, that other detective, you should be inter-viewing them.'

'We have interviewed them.'

'And?' I ask.

'And they have an alibi. They were down in Bristol for the weekend. A great aunt's ninetieth. They've been gone since Friday evening, returned a little bit before eleven this morning.'

I frown at that. 'Did you check? Do you know they're tell-ing the truth?'

'Oh no, didn't think of that,' he responds, deadpan. 'Dozens of alibis for the whole weekend.'

It takes me a second to realise he is being sarcastic. Damn. I thought Zac and Maddie made perfect suspects. I wouldn't have put it past either of them. 'What if they did something to her on Friday night? After I left and before they went to Bristol? Zac said they hadn't gone over there to confront her but they did! What if they got in a fight and killed her, accidentally or on purpose? They would have had plenty of time to bury the body.'

'You're very determined it's the neighbours,' he says.

'I just don't know why you're not looking into them more.'

'I told you they've got an alibi and it checks out. They were en route to Bristol – they've got a receipt from a petrol station for the time those tweets were sent from your account and we've checked the CCTV too. If Becca sent those, then she was still alive on Friday evening. That takes them out of the equation.'

'Oh,' I say.

He takes a sip of his coffee. 'So if you're done with playing detective, I'd like to carry on.'

I sit back in my chair and stare at him. If Zac and Maddie have alibis, then that leaves just James as a likely culprit. And me. Because despite what he's saying I still think I'm a suspect.

'You saw the lamp was broken and entered through the back door into the living room?' he asks.

I nod. 'The door was open. We weren't breaking and entering.'

He ignores this. I guess that's the least of his concerns when there might be a murder to solve.

'Who was it that spotted the blood?'

'Me,' I say.

'And how did James seem when you spotted it?'

I shrug, playing the scene back in my head. 'I don't know. Spooked, I suppose. We both were. He was worried.'

'And did he say anything that now seems strange to you – anything that made you feel suspicious? Either at the time or later?'

I pause. 'No. Well . . . no.'

'Go on,' he says gently.

I bite my lip. I shouldn't say another word but somehow it slips out. 'He did say that she was dead.'

The detective's eyes widen. He sits back in his seat. 'That's a strange thing to say.'

'He didn't mean it like that,' I add. 'He said there was no other explanation for why she was missing, not one that made sense anyway.'

Detective Tallack nods thoughtfully to himself as though he's putting pieces together in his head.

'Do you know what I think?' he says to me. 'I think that your boyfriend—'

'He's not my boyfriend,' I interrupt.

He gives a small shrug. 'I think James went over last night to talk to Becca. I think that they got in a fight. He killed her – probably lashed out – passion does that – and then he panicked and hid the body.'

I blink at him. Now he's laid it out like that, I can't help but see it. It could very well have happened like that. He could have gone over there. They could have got in a fight. It does all make sense. But the timing doesn't really add up. How could he have killed her and got rid of her body in a couple of hours? He barely had time to get there and back.

'The question is,' Detective Tallack continues, still studying me closely, 'whether or not he had any help.'

It takes me a second to realise what he's implying. 'What?' I stammer, my heart thumping so loudly I can hardly hear myself. 'That's ridiculous. I've already told you, you can check the security footage at the hotel. I never left.'

He narrows his eyes at that. I think I might throw up.

'I'm wondering when you and James met,' he says.

I can't keep the panic out of my voice. 'I told you we met on Tinder, last week.'

He smiles at me like a parent who's caught their child in a lie. 'That's not true, though, is it? You also said you'd met at the Christmas party. That same party where Becca mysteriously fell down the stairs. You know that wasn't an accident. We've reopened the investigation.'

They have?

'I'm wondering if you two met then and that's when the affair started.'

'Affair?' I laugh out loud. 'What affair? What are you talking about?'

'You and James carrying on behind Becca's back. Did she find out? Is that why James pushed her down the stairs?'

'What?' I blurt. I would laugh at the absurdity if I wasn't quite so terrified of the implications. 'We weren't having an affair.' James himself admitted he couldn't even remember talking to me.

He interrupts. 'OK, maybe the affair started recently and Becca found out about it. It sounds like you weren't much of a fan of hers. It must have felt good, quite enjoyable, to rub that in her face. You stealing her boyfriend.'

A muscle pulses in my jaw. I didn't rub anything in her face. And he wasn't her boyfriend. They'd been broken up for years. The only thing I did wrong was sending a not-very-nice email, by accident. If you could be arrested for that, then a lot of people would be in prison.

'Did Becca find out about you two?' he presses, on a roll now. 'Did she get jealous?'

I keep my face as blank as I can. I can't give him a reaction. That's what he's looking for. He's just cycling through one hypothesis after the other, each one more desperate and absurd than the last.

'Is that why she sent the email that got you suspended?' he asks.

'No!' I burst out. 'I've told you why she sent it.'

'Do you know the whereabouts of Rebecca Zaceks?' he fires back.

'No,' I stammer.

'I'm wondering if she knew something about you that you didn't want to get out. Something about you defrauding the company.'

'The fraud charges were dropped,' I say, furiously, but I'm also nearly on the verge of tears. Adrenaline makes my breath come in fits and starts. There's a buzzing in my ears, like a TV playing static.

'I can see you're angry about it,' he continues. 'And about her sending those tweets. That's a pretty low thing to do. She got you fired. You must have been fuming.' He's enjoying this, his eyes sparking. 'I would have been. How many years have you worked at PKW? And now you've got no job and no reference. It'll be hard to get another job, won't it? Who's going to hire you now?'

He's poking me, trying to find a weakness, an Achilles heel he can exploit to get me to admit to something. He's not going to find one. Nor an admission of guilt.

'Did you come here deliberately with a plan to stop her from talking?' he asks, his voice getting louder. 'To shut her up? Was that it?' He leans across the table, his expression almost lascivious, like he's turned on by bullying a young woman. 'Were you and James in on it together?' he demands.

What? What is he talking about? I want him to stop.

'Did you kill her by accident?' he asks. 'Did she refuse to stop trying to ruin your life? Did she threaten you with worse? Was it the only thing you could do?'

I stare at him open-mouthed. 'It wasn't me,' I whisper hoarsely. 'I didn't kill her.'

He falls silent and stares at me and I finally meet his gaze, with something of defiance. He's riled me. I hate bullies.

'Do you know the whereabouts of Rebecca Zaceks?' he asks again.

'No,' I say.

His eyes bore into me as though he's trying to read my mind and I see the flicker of irritation. It's then that I realise he doesn't have anything. If he did, he would have charged me already.

And just like that, the wind seems to drop out of his sails. He's exhausted his arsenal. He leans back heavily in his seat and sighs. The adrenaline cuts off and I'm left shaking.

'So Becca's faking it, is she?' he asks.

As soon as he says it, a lightbulb goes on in my head. My mouth falls open. Of course. Why didn't I think of that? It's the only hypothesis that might actually make sense. 'What if she is?' I answer, gripping the table and leaning forwards.

He pulls a face.

'What if she's out there right now, laughing?' I ask.

He stares at me, incredulous and scornful, but I carry on. 'What if she's faked everything? Faked her death just like she faked her life? What if it's all pretend?' Oh my god. It totally makes sense. I cover my mouth for a moment. 'There was no break-in and no kidnapping,' I say, stunned that I didn't think of this before. 'She's trying to set me up!'

Detective Tallack snorts through his nose and one of his eyebrows darts towards his hairline like a caterpillar diving for cover. 'Yeah, sure. She faked her own murder just to get revenge on you.'

'What?' I ask. 'Why isn't that believable? Look at everything else she's done. Have you looked at her history? Her whole family died in a fire but she miraculously survives. You don't think that's suspicious?'

He frowns. 'The inquiry put the blame on a faulty water heater. What are you saying? That a twelve-year-old girl tampered with the wiring on a heater to murder her family?'

I glower back at him. 'Who knows with Becca?'

'Do you know how hard it is to disappear without a trace?' he asks.

I think back to what James said. Damn. He's right. They're both right. How would she have done it? How could she have disappeared?

The door bursts open before I can say another word. A woman in a pencil skirt and a dove-grey silk shirt strides in. 'OK, enough,' she says and swings her Mulberry bag onto the table in front of Detective Tallack. She stands with her back to me, staring down at him, and he looks up with a smirking expression on his face that doesn't hide the fact he's pissed off.

'You know you're not allowed to ask questions after a suspect has requested a lawyer,' she says.

'We're waiting for the duty solicitor.'

'Where are they?' the woman asks.

'Busy. Got lots on.' He smirks some more before gesturing across the table at me. 'No need to get upset. We were only having a little conversation.'

'My client doesn't have anything else to say.'

'That's a shame,' he answers, 'because up to now she's been full of useful information.'

The woman scowls. She called me her client. Who is she? 'I'll be filing a complaint,' she tells Tallack and glares at the recorder. 'None of this will be admissible in court, you realise that?'

DCI Tallack gets up from his seat, slowly, like a giant sea creature rising from the depths. He glances at me, then at my lawyer, somewhat sourly, before making a big show of gathering up his file and papers and trudging out the door.

The lawyer waits until he's gone then turns around, switches off the tape recorder and glares at me. 'My name is Ophelia Waites,' she says. 'I work in the litigation department at James's firm.' She gives me a once-over, her lips tightly pursed. 'I'm here to make sure you don't say anything that could incriminate you or James. Though it seems like I might be too late for that.'

I avoid her eye.

'I need you to tell me exactly what you've told them.'

'They think we killed her,' I blurt, my heart starting to race again as I say the words out loud. 'But—'

She cuts me off again. 'I am not interested in whether you're guilty or innocent. I don't want to know and I don't need to know.'

'But—' I start to say again and once more she holds up a hand.

'What I need you to do is listen.'

I fall silent again and watch as she takes off her jacket, drapes it over the back of the chair and then sits down opposite me. I think I preferred it when Detective Tallack was occupying that chair because Ophelia makes him seem like a pussy cat, but at least she's on my side. At least I have a lawyer.

She pulls a laptop out of her bag and opens it up. All her movements are sleek, fast, efficient like she's a robot, an image compounded by the fact her facial expression never seems to shift or betray emotion. Her make-up is perfect, her clothes expensive, her jewellery subtle but flashy all the same. She has gleaming skin the colour of honey, and black hair.

'They've arrested you both on suspicion of murder,' Ophelia tells me. 'And they're trying to find enough evidence to make the charges stick.'

I look down at the table and notice that I'm gripping the edge of it and that my nails are ragged. I must have been chewing on them without even realising. Ophelia's voice is muffled as though she's underwater. I watch her lips, trying to make sense of what she's saying. Something about bail and hearings and magistrates and defence lawyers.

'I don't understand,' I mumble. 'I didn't do anything. I just want to go home. Can I go home?'

She stares at me like I'm stupid. 'No. That's what I've just been explaining. We have to wait and see if they charge you and if they do, then they'll arraign you in front of a judge, probably in the morning, and we can request bail.'

Bail? 'I don't have any money,' I whisper, glancing at the walls. What if they keep me here overnight? What if I get sent to jail? 'I can't go to jail.'

'OK,' Ophelia says, all businesslike and ignoring me entirely. 'I need some details.'

'They kept asking me about the button,' I blurt. 'Why?'

She looks up from her laptop, her lips drawn tight as purse strings. 'They found it.'

'Where?' I ask.

'At the crime scene, close to where the blood was. I only know that because I overheard a uniform talking.'

'Oh,' I say.

'What did you tell them?' she asks, narrowing her eyes.

I swallow and look away. 'I told them that the button was missing from his shirt this morning but it had been there earlier.'

She stares at me and for a moment the polished veneer shows a crack.

'How did it get there?' I ask. 'I mean, unless . . .' I swallow hard. 'Have they charged him?'

Ophelia shakes her head. 'But they're going to. They're just trying to gather as much evidence as they can so they can make the charge stick. That's why they were interviewing you. Your confirming about the button will be all they need now. I bet they'll charge him first thing in the morning.'

I bury my face in my hands. I can't stop shaking. 'Oh my god.'

After a moment I look up at Ophelia who is texting on her phone, angrily stabbing at the keys. 'What about me?' I ask, tentatively. 'Are they going to charge me with anything?'

'Depends if they think you were party to it,' she says.

'What will happen if they do?' I ask, my head filled with a roar of static so loud I barely hear her answer.

'They'll set a trial date.'

'Oh my god,' I say, clutching onto the table to steady myself.

'Unless you plead guilty,' she adds. 'In which case, you won't go to trial; the judge will just sentence you.'

I stare at her, the blood draining from my face. 'Why would I plead guilty?'

'You'd be looking at a minimum of fifteen years without parole for murder.'

She says it so matter-of-factly, as though she's reading out her shopping list. This can't be happening. She thinks I'm guilty. She thinks I plotted all this with James. She thinks we did this!

'Unless you cut a plea deal,' she adds.

What does she mean? A plea deal?

'If you admit to it, then we can plea it down, you'd maybe get seven years, given the circumstances – with her harassing you. We could even plead self-defence.' Her eyes drill into me and my mouth falls open in shock. She really thinks I did it. Or she's trying to get her real client, James, off the hook by getting me to admit it.

'I didn't do anything,' I tell her, shaking my head.

She stands up. 'You think about it,' she says, as though she hasn't heard me.

'They don't even know she's dead!' I shout as she bangs on the door to be let out. 'There isn't even a body! What if she's alive? What if she's out there, laughing? What if this is all part of her revenge? You have to believe me. You have to!'

Ophelia looks at me over her shoulder, completely unmoved. 'I'll be back in a bit.' With that, she walks out and the door shuts behind her.

'I didn't do it!' I shout, even though there's no one to hear me.

I stare at the yellow walls feeling as though I'm underwater, drowning. My lungs are about to burst. I rest my head on the table and close my eyes. But all I can see is Becca's face. She's laughing at me.

They put me in a cell. It's like a coffin. There are no windows and I lose track of time as I pace the room, trying not to lose hope and panicking over how far out of hand this is all getting.

I run over what Ophelia said. If my own lawyer doesn't believe me, what hope do I have that the police will? If they charge me, I'm going down for it. I know it. I'll spend the rest of my life in jail. No. This isn't fair. Why won't anyone listen to me?

I think about Becca. I think about her a lot. I think about how stupid this all is. And all because of a mistakenly sent email. I think about James and Maddie and Zac and about what a fool I've been. If only I hadn't sent the message. If only I hadn't come here and opened a Pandora's box of trouble.

I'm not sure what time it is when someone finally comes and opens the door.

'Where are you taking me?' I ask PC Kandiah, who leads me out of the cell. She doesn't answer and I start to panic. Are they taking me somewhere to officially charge me? Are they taking me to court or to jail? Have they found her body?

'Did you find her?' I ask, but PC Kandiah still says nothing. 'Where are we going?'

I catch a glimpse of the sky through the window and see that it's late. Night-time already. We walk through a room where Detective Tallack is sitting at one of a dozen desks. Dunn is perched on the edge of the desk talking to him. They both look up when I walk in. Oh god, this is it. They're going to formally read the charges. I'm done for. Where's Ophelia? Why has she abandoned me?

But we walk straight past them. Neither detective says a word – they just stare at me darkly. 'What's happening?' I ask Kandiah again, my voice barely above a squeak.

Still saying nothing, she leads me into the lobby where Ophelia is standing, waiting with my bag and coat. Kandiah makes me sign for my things and then abandons me. I'm so confused, I don't know what to do. Am I free?

'What's going on?' I ask Ophelia, who is already striding towards the door.

'They've let you go,' she tells me.

I exhale in amazement and scamper after her. 'What?' As we burst outside into the frigid night air I feel as if a ten-tonne weight has been lifted off my shoulders. I'm faint with relief. I'm free!

I want to let out a scream and a cry and collapse to my knees but Ophelia is striding towards a BMW and I hurry to catch her. She beeps open the door to her car. 'Do you need a ride somewhere?' she asks.

'Um, the station?'

She nods and gets in. I get in beside her, glancing back at the squat brick police station. 'What about James?' I ask.

She starts the engine and puts on her seat belt. 'They've charged him with murder.'

I freeze with my seat belt halfway across my body. 'What?'

'They have CCTV footage of him getting into his car and driving away from the Farmhouse. He returned forty minutes later to the hotel. He's refusing to say where he went. That and the button they found at the scene was enough for them to charge him.'

'Oh my god,' I whisper, my hand flying to my mouth. For some reason I never fully allowed myself to believe they'd charge him with anything. I mean, there's no body. It's guesswork. How can they have moved so fast to this conclusion? Though the evidence does seem irrefutable. 'I can't believe it,' I whisper in shock. 'I just . . .' I look at Ophelia. 'Do you really think he did it?'

She doesn't answer and the silence expands to fill the car until even she senses it and, growing uncomfortable, switches on the radio. I turn my head and stare out the window. How could anyone believe it? He's so charming. And so nice. He really doesn't seem capable, not the killing per se, because honestly most people could probably kill if they were forced to, but the covering it up and lying about it. Besides, forty minutes doesn't seem realistic when you think about it. It took twenty minutes to drive from the hotel to Becca's. How could he have driven there, killed her, buried her or dumped her body somewhere and then driven back to the hotel? I wonder if Ophelia has thought about that or if I should mention it. I don't think she's the kind of person who'd take kindly to someone telling her how to do her job, so instead I ask: 'What will happen now?'

'We'll see tomorrow. Now they've charged him, it's a case of trying to get bail. I'm not sure the judge will grant it. Not in a case like this.'

'Why not?' I ask.

'Because it will be all over the press.'

I stare at her. 'What will?'

'The media love a story like this. An attractive blonde, missing presumed murdered. A guilty-looking ex-lover. What's important is getting ahead of the story, trying to stop him being tried in the court of public opinion before he even gets in front of a judge and jury.'

'How do you do that?'

She turns to look at me while she's driving. 'Well, the first thing is that you need to say nothing. Not a word. They'll try to spin the story and paint you and James as lovers.'

'But we're not.'

She sighs. 'Doesn't matter. From now on, it's not about truth.' She looks at me again. 'It's about perception. Remember that. And don't get too relaxed. They might still charge you as an accessory. The Crown Prosecution didn't think there was enough evidence as it stood but that doesn't mean they won't find some.'

I come crashing right back to earth with a thud. I had thought this nightmare was over, but it might just be the beginning.

'You need to get yourself a lawyer,' Ophelia says as she indicates right.

I study her, the gold watch on her wrist and the diamond studs in her ears and the car's swish leather interior. What she's saying is that there's no way I could afford someone like her. And she's right.

'Yes,' I say quietly. 'I'll find someone.' God knows how.

'I would give you a ride back to London,' she tells me as she pulls into the station, 'but I'm staying over tonight so I can be here in the morning for the arraignment.'

I nod numbly.

'Thanks,' I say as I get out of the car. 'For everything. I appreciate it.'

She nods, rather curtly, and drives off the moment I shut the door, leaving me standing all alone in the dark, with just the palest sliver of moon for company.

An owl hoots somewhere off in the distance and I shiver. I'm cold and exhausted and my brain is struggling to compute. I walk over to the ticket machine and rummage around in my wallet, trying to scrounge up enough money to buy a ticket back to London.

I wonder again at the idea I had earlier – that Becca's still out there. That she's framing me and now James. Maybe I should tell Ophelia.

I take a seat on a bench and, shivering, wait for the train.

After all of this, Becca bloody well better be dead or I'll kill her myself.

Part Three

Becca

Friday, 8 December
Evening

I've decided on a plan and it infuses me with purpose. I'm not one hundred per cent sure I can pull it off but I'm going to try, because what do I have to lose? I need to be gone by morning. I just have a few things to organise first.

Peanut's whining interrupts my thinking. He is standing by the back door looking at me imploringly. I've forgotten to let him out. I unlock the door and the second it's open he flies between my legs and disappears into the void of the garden. The moon is waning, blanketed by clouds, and it's impossible to see a thing.

Shivering against the cold I wait in the doorway, hugging myself. 'Hurry up!' I shout into the darkness. It's all come together in that moment. I've figured out what to do but I have to move fast, before I change my mind or lose my courage.

'Peanut!' I shout.

He starts barking in reply. Angrily. Growling through his teeth, as though he's spotted a fieldmouse or a fox.

'Peanut!' I shout again. 'Come here!'

He barks for several more seconds before I hear a sharp-pitched yelp. Then it goes silent.

'Peanut?' I say, keeping my voice low, fear stroking its fingers softly up my spine.

I strain into the darkness, one hand on the door, torn between stepping out into that vacuum or back into the light and bolting the kitchen door. But I can't leave Peanut out there.

'Peanut?' I hiss.

Nothing.

Something isn't right. I step back into the kitchen and move to slam the door behind me. Adrenaline is flooding through my system. She's out there. Another voice in my head tells me not to be paranoid. I'm overreacting. The dog's probably disappeared down a rabbit hole or got into it with a fox. He's done it before.

As I push the door shut it bounces towards me, slamming me with the force of a brick. I stagger backwards, seeing stars, my hand flying to my head. It feels sticky and hot but I don't have time to process what's happening because Lizzie is flying at me, kicking the door shut behind her. I cower back against the island in the centre of the kitchen, my brain firing weakly, trying to make sense of it. What is she doing in my house?

She strides towards me and instinctively I stretch my hand out, scrambling blindly for the knife block or any kind of weapon. My hand drops to my side as I see the gun in her hand.

She looks calm, not crazy. She's acting like this is a normal thing to do – burst into someone's house with a gun and hold them hostage. She's still pointing it at my chest and it's all I can focus on, all I can see. I press the tea towel to my head, trying to fight the wooziness stealing up on me and the nausea roiling the pit of my stomach.

She sneaks a quick look around the living room where we're seated, me on the sofa and her opposite in one of the armchairs. She's drawn the curtains and turned on a table lamp that's throwing shadows across the room and across her face.

'What do you want?' I ask, glancing towards the window. I'm hoping that Maddie will see the light on and come over again. That's my only hope. I can't see myself launching up out of my chair and throwing myself at Lizzie, or running for the door.

'You and I need a talk,' Lizzie says in a firm but measured voice. She sounds different from how she used to. No more blunt Yorkshire accent. She's talking like she's had elocution lessons. 'I know it was you who sent the email to Daniel with the expense claims.'

I don't say anything because she's right.

'And I know it was you who arranged for all those fake reviews. They're being taken down, by the way, so that was a bit of a pointless effort.'

Still I say nothing. My gaze flits to the cast-iron poker by the fire. It's too far to reach. And what would I do even if I could reach it? I've got no strength in the right side of my body. I couldn't lift it, let alone swing it.

'You've got a very nice house,' she says now. 'I like the sofa. Though I'm not sure about the colour.'

My eyebrows shoot up. She wants to talk decor?

'I thought you'd be totally disfigured but you're not completely,' she says, tilting her head to one side and examining me, her nose wrinkling. 'Though I can see why you'd want to hide your face. It isn't pretty, is it?'

My hand automatically goes to the scar running up my cheek.

She sits up straighter and smiles. 'What do you think of my transformation?' she asks and I notice she's had her teeth fixed and bleached as white as a Colgate commercial. Up close, the change in her is remarkable. Not just the teeth and the hair and the tan. Her face is different – I think she's had a nose job. It's like one of those make-over shows where they take someone dowdy and unfashionable and transform them with the help of a stylist and a hair and make-up artist.

'You look . . . great,' I say, swallowing hard and trying to remember where I left my phone. It's upstairs, I think, or in the kitchen.

'I worked really hard,' she tells me. 'I was inspired, you could say, after hearing your boyfriend talking about me. What was it he said? Oh yes: Who's that fat, ugly cunt? She looks like her mother had an accident with a coat-hanger.'

I bite my lips together.

'You laughed when he said it, do you remember? It was at the Christmas party.' She frowns harder. 'But maybe you don't remember. It was just before your accident.'

I do remember that. It's fuzzy but I do remember it. And I didn't laugh. I remember telling James to shush.

'Can you not point that at me?' I say, nodding at the gun.

She looks down and seems shocked to see the gun in her hand. 'Oh,' she says. 'Sorry. I didn't mean to . . . you went for the knife so . . . I only want to talk, that's all.'

She sets the gun down on the table. 'What do you think?' To my blank look she responds: 'Of talking about this? Sorting it all out like adults.'

I tear my eyes off the gun and look at her. Is she serious? She holds up her hands as though she's surrendering and smiles warmly.

There's a huge gulf, I realise, in her understanding of what constitutes normal, adult behaviour. It's like she's missing a vital part of her brain. Does she not realise she has burst into my home without an invitation and is threatening me at gunpoint? I can hear Peanut barking at the French door outside. Scratching to be let in.

'This is all getting a bit out of control, don't you think?' she continues without waiting for a response. 'Is it because I called the baby Gollum? Because she's not even your baby! And you have to admit she is kind of odd-looking. Was it about that?'

She rolls her eyes and I stare at her, mute, too stunned to answer and also too scared, because how do you reason with madness?

'Or was it because of James?' she presses. Her eyes spark with something and she leans forward. 'Were you jealous?' she asks me.

I take the tea towel away from my face. The bleeding has stopped. I shake my head at her, ignoring the dull throb behind my eyes. She looks at me with suspicion, not buying my denial.

'They've suspended me, you know,' she says, sitting back in her seat. 'Work. Though they'll realise their mistake soon enough. I thought you'd forgotten all about it, after the accident.'

'You thought you'd got away with it,' I tell her. The thing is, she almost did. If she hadn't sent the message, I wouldn't have remembered but it triggered something in my subconscious – another splinter that was long buried rose to the surface: a confrontation we had over her faking expense claims. I remembered showing her the copies I'd made. It was a vague memory, still a little fragmented. I know she started crying, telling me that she had made a huge mistake and was sorry. It didn't amount to very much, she said. She promised she would repay it all and she begged me not to say a word. She needed the money. Her mother was sick and had been evicted. She was desperate. She told me she'd shred the fake expenses forms and no one would ever know.

I didn't tell on her because the next day I was lying in a hospital bed in a coma and when I woke up I'd forgotten all about it.

When she messaged me, I remembered I still had those copies somewhere on the cloud. It wasn't so hard to find them and send them to Daniel from one of my anonymous email accounts. Now I wish I had never remembered.

Lizzie's face has hardened, her eyes like flint. After a beat she relaxes slightly. 'I paid the money back anyway, just in case,' she tells me. 'So everything will reconcile when they do an audit and then they'll beg me to come back to work. It got me into a huge amount of debt, paying all that money back. I had to take cash out on my credit card. I'm still paying it off. It was worth it though. The course I did was amazing. It changed my life. It taught me that we all have extraordinary potential and showed me how to reach mine. It was worth every penny, don't you think?' She smiles at me, hands on hips, as though striking a pose. I don't know how to respond. She glances around the room and her lips pinch and her nostrils flare. 'Of course you wouldn't know what that's like, being in debt up to your eyeballs.'

'Listen,' I say, softly, my heart a solid lump in my throat and my voice little more than a croak. 'I think you're absolutely right. You did something wrong. I did something wrong. Why don't we forget all about it and move on?'

She smirks. 'Move on? Like you've done, you mean?'

I glare at her but stay silent.

'I can tell you think I'm crazy,' she says angrily, 'that there's something wrong with me, you always have; you've always thought you were better than me, better than everyone, but look at you now.' She does an impression of me, limping, one eye pulled slightly down at the corner. 'No one would look twice at you. James likes me now.'

Still I say nothing. I'm long past caring about what I look like or what James thinks.

'They do say pride comes before a fall.' She laughs.

I frown at that. I want to answer her back. I want to tell her that she's got it wrong. I've never been proud. And I've never thought I was better than anyone. After my family died and I was sent to Scotland to live with my aunt, I became introverted. I didn't make friends easily. Ironically I was as insecure as Lizzie —always feeling like an outsider.

'You've brought everything on yourself, you know that, don't you?' says Lizzie, stabbing her finger at me. 'This is all your fault.'

'I didn't do anything wrong,' I tell her. 'I didn't hurt anyone. I didn't steal from anyone.'

'Why did you do it?' she asks. 'Why did you go to so much trouble? I mean, inventing a whole fake life. What was the point?'

'I just wanted . . .' I break off and stare out the window towards Maddie and Zac's house. The Christmas tree lights are twinkling in the window and it takes me right back to the second before I fell. I lose my train of thought.

'Wanted what?' Lizzie presses.

I shrug. 'What they had.'

I turn away from the window and find her staring at me. There's no way she can ever understand. I don't know why

I'm even trying. But for a moment her mask slips and I see the old Lizzie – the one who wasn't poised and polished – and who I know understands what it's like to want to be someone else. I wonder if I can use that to get through to her. She wanted what she didn't have too and she created a whole new life for herself to get it. Really we're not so different. Immediately I shake the thought off. I'm nothing like her.

I decide that now's my chance, while she is still frowning at me, thinking about what I've just said.

I make to stand up, slowly, watching her the whole time as though she's a rabid dog, in case she reaches for the gun. She glowers at me. 'Where are you going?'

I sink back into the sofa, my panic infusing every muscle and cell with adrenaline.

'That's exactly what I was hoping for,' she says, her tone switching to friendly again. 'That's why I came here. Flora thought face to face would be the best idea. I didn't mean to discover your big secret.' She says that with a sly smile, as though she didn't mean to but she's bloody glad she has. She leans forwards again. 'It's really none of my business why you've done all this, made up a fake life, and I never meant to mess it up. I'm sorry about that.'

Sorry? There's that apology again. She sent me a sorry email too, once she realised I was Hammurabi. She grovelled and begged forgiveness. But does she think I care about sorry? Sorry is the least useful word in the English language. I know it's meant to make things better, take away the pain and the resentment and the anger like a magic pill, but it doesn't work like that.

'You have to admit it's a little bizarre,' she continues, looking at me like *I'm* the crazy one. 'And I'm not sure your neighbours are that happy about it.'

'I think you should go,' I say through gritted teeth. I'm aware I'm slurring slightly. It's the combination of the bang to my head and the stress. Sometimes my speech and motor skills get affected when I'm under pressure.

I see her pull a face as she tries to decipher my words and then she smirks. 'You think I should what?'

She's teasing and it riles me even more. 'Please leave.'

'OK,' she says and she stands up. Oh thank god. She's actually going to leave. I realise that I'm gripping the sofa cushions, my knuckles white and my breathing rapid and shallow. Please go, I think. I just want her to get out of my house. I can feel tears of shame and anger burning like acid behind my eyes.

She's standing now, putting her bag over her shoulder. As soon as she's gone I'll call the police. They'll have to arrest her. You can't bring a gun into someone's house and threaten them. But I need to get her out of here first, which means not antagonising her.

'Before I go,' she says, 'I just want to make sure nothing else is going to . . . come out.'

I fall silent and we stare at each other for a few seconds; seconds that seem to stretch to the end of time. 'Like what?' I finally manage to say because I don't know what she's talking about.

'Oh my god, you don't remember.' She bursts out laughing.

'What?' I ask, a sense of dread creeping up on me.

'I was always worried one day it would come back. That you'd remember it was me that pushed you.' She giggles. And then reaches for the gun. And just like that, in an instant a sluice gate opens and the memories flood in.

Lizzie. In a blue dress. Smiling as she watched me fall.

It was her, not James. It was her who pushed me down the stairs. Of course it was. How did I not put two and two together? I was so fixated on it being James, so convinced it was him, that I didn't even stop to consider Lizzie as a suspect. But of course. It all makes sense.

I watch her, unable to tear my eyes off the gun, which she's holding against her side. I can't breathe for fear. My brain is rapidly trying to process this new information. She tried to kill me. She killed my baby. And now she's here to finish the job. But then the fear dissipates ever so slightly with the realisation she isn't here to kill me, she's here to buy my silence by reminding me what she's capable of.

'I was pregnant,' I whisper. 'I lost my baby.'

'Sorry about that,' she answers, matter-of-factly.

'Her name was Lucette,' I shout, then wish I hadn't. I don't want her knowing the name, sullying it.

'Lucette,' she says and I cringe hearing the name on her lips. 'How many weeks pregnant were you?'

'Twelve,' I tell her, wondering if I'm managing to elicit any sympathy, wondering if she even knows what sympathy is.

She frowns. 'Twelve?'

I nod.

'That's hardly a baby. It's just a blob of cells. It's not even a miscarriage – it's just a heavy period.'

I stare at her in disbelief, her words poison darts sinking deep. I have no comeback. I look quickly at the gun but I know I'd never have a hope of wrestling it out of her hand. I'm not fast enough or strong enough.

She has no idea that I was planning on leaving tonight. If she'd just waited an hour, I would have been gone. I was going to drive to Southampton and catch the first ferry to France. I was going to disappear; walk away from my life and start over somewhere new. I was going to reinvent myself. It's not like I don't know how to do that. And, after my initial upset and rage, there was some relief in looking around the house, which has become something of a prison, and deciding to go. I'd no longer be Becca. I'd choose a whole new name this time, something entirely different.

I was going to take Peanut and a suitcase – just the one – and be gone before sunrise, before Zac and Maddie could come knocking again. As for revenge on Lizzie, I'd decided enough was enough. Despite how much I wanted to see her suffer, it was more important to get away and start over.

Lizzie would likely lose her job. There was a sweet irony in knowing she and James were together. The two of them deserved each other.

'So, if we're both on the same page,' Lizzie says.

Same page? She's warning me not to go to the police. She killed my baby. Of course I'm going to the damn police.

'I'll leave you in peace and you leave me in peace.'

I nod in understanding – though not agreement. Whatever it takes to get her out of the damn house.

'Good,' she says and slips the gun into her handbag as though it's her phone or a notebook. I breathe out a huge sigh of relief.

She starts walking towards the hallway. I get up to follow her. I want to make sure she leaves. My legs are stiff, though, and my right leg drags as though I'm walking through wet concrete. I lurch and fall against the table, knocking over the lamp. It crashes to the floor, smashing into smithereens and on my next step I trip over the electrical cord and go stumbling towards her.

Lizzie turns and her arms come up instinctively – like a boxer's. As I fall towards her she pushes me away. I spin into the bookcase just behind the door and bang the side of my head before tumbling backwards. She's looking at me like I just tried to attack her, shock giving way to rage. She steps towards me.

I feel panic clawing at my throat and a deep-seated urge to get away from her. I stumble towards the French doors, throw the lever and yank them open.

Peanut comes tearing inside and flies at Lizzie, who screams and kicks out at him. He's only a toy dog – a Scottish Terrier mix – but he's fierce, and he nips and yaps furiously at her. Lizzie draws back her leg and kicks him hard in the ribs. He goes flying across the room, landing by the sofa with a sickening thud and a yelp.

I glance out into the garden. I could try to make it around to the side gate and maybe to Maddie and Zac's but there's no way I can outrun her.

I turn back into the room, grabbing for the nearest thing I see from the side table – a shard of broken vase as big as my palm and I clutch it in front of me – waving it at her in warning to stay back.

She cocks her head as she walks towards me.

'Stay back!' I sob. 'Get away from me.'

Her fist comes out of nowhere, connecting with my jaw, and I go down in the carpet of broken glass on the floor. Groaning, the floor rocking, I look up through a blood-red haze and see Lizzie bending over me, her face blurring in and out of focus like a moon skittering behind dark clouds.

'Look what you made me do,' she hisses.

My skull is a gong being struck repeatedly with a hammer. The clanging reverberates through my whole body, down my spine and legs, all the way to my feet, a trail of fire. Beyond the awful pounding in my head I can hear Peanut barking but it's muffled, as if he's locked in another room.

For a while, I don't know how long, it's all I can do to focus on managing the pain and trying not to black out again. It's hard to breathe but every time I do, it's like adding gasoline to the flames.

Finally I'm able to open my eyes. I'm on the living-room floor, lying on my side, knees drawn up towards my chest. It's dark. The lamp is lying on the floor in pieces. I can see a pair of high heels. It's Lizzie. She's doing something.

I try to move my legs but they're bound with something, tied at the ankle. My wrists are bound too. A belt perhaps. Oh god. It hurts to breathe; my heart feels too big, beating too fast. I tell myself to calm down, to take long, slow deep breaths but it doesn't help. The panic doesn't abate. What is she doing? What is she planning? I try not to make a sound. I don't want her to know I'm awake. This might be my one opportunity to get free. If only I could get to the phone in the hallway.

Lizzie steps over me just then, crossing to the French doors. Through half-closed eyes I watch her. She's using a duster and some cleaner from the kitchen to wipe the door handles and all the surfaces. She moves to the armchair next and the side table, wiping them down. She hesitates by the lamp, staring down at all the pieces, then steps over them and heads out towards the kitchen.

There's a sudden bang on the front door. I jump. It must be Maddie! I'm saved! I open my mouth to yell but Lizzie is suddenly rushing back into the room and throwing herself on top of me, her hands covering my mouth. She pushes the gun to my head, ordering me in a hissing whisper to stop making noise. There's another sharp bang. Maddie's not

going away. I could kiss her. *Please don't give up*, I beg silently.
She's yelling at me to come to the door and talk to her.

Tears start to fall silently down my cheeks as I hear Maddie
shouting 'This isn't over!' The knocking stops. She's leaving.
No! I listen hard but I think she's gone.

After a minute Lizzie stands up. She backs out of the room
but only for a second before she returns, holding my scarf.
She wraps it around my head, gagging me. 'Now shhhhhh,'
she says, holding a finger to her lips, and then leaves.

I wait a beat, frozen in terror and also despair, but I can't
let her win. I've got another opportunity and this could be
my last. With some difficulty I push myself up so I'm in a
sitting position. I try to tug the gag off but it's too tight. I turn
my attention to the belt around my ankles. It's from the coat
hanging in the hall. Though my wrists are also bound, I have
just enough freedom to get at the knot binding my ankles. I
work at it, on the verge of hysteria, but it's tight as a padlock
and with limited reach and my screwed-up motor skills, I
can't manage to untie it. Damn. I look around the room and
spot the ceramic shards from the broken lamp. Throwing
myself across the floor, driven by urgency and sheer panic,
because god knows what she has planned, I pick up one of
the shards and wedge it between my knees and start sawing
frantically at the belt around my wrists, but it's leather and
it's impossible. Shit.

She's going to be back any second. I need to get to the
phone. I crawl to the hallway on my knees. The front door
is in sight – tantalisingly close. I can see Lizzie moving
about in the kitchen. What is she doing? It looks like she's
cleaning. And I can hear Peanut barking. She's locked him
in the pantry, I think. I hear Lizzie yell at him to shut the
fuck up.

The landline is on the table across the hallway. Can I get to it without her seeing me? I don't think so. What are my other options, though? I won't be able to open the front door because I can't stand and even if I could I wouldn't be able to run anywhere. The phone is my only option.

I glance once more at the kitchen. Lizzie is standing just a few feet away from me – her back to the door. It's now or never. I start to crawl across towards the table, holding my breath and hoping that she's so absorbed in whatever she's doing that she doesn't turn around or hear me.

I make it and now I'm pretty much out of sight. I can't see into the kitchen any more. I reach for the phone and ease it off its base, cringing at the buzzing tone. It's so loud she has to hear it, but when I steal a glimpse over my shoulder there's no sign of her.

I fumble with the keys, hit 9 twice, but then my grip slips and I hit the 8 by accident. I manage to press cancel and start to redial but before I can even hit 9, the phone is yanked out of my hands.

Lizzie is standing over me, glowering. 'What are you doing?' she asks, as though I'm a child she's caught out of bed after lights out.

My eyes dart to her other hand, looking for the gun. But she's not holding it. She's holding my iPhone.

'Were you trying to call the police?' she asks me. 'Because that wouldn't be a good idea.'

She bends down in front of me and I instinctively cower away from her, against the table, and a sob erupts out of my throat.

'What are you doing?' I ask her. 'Please just let me go. I won't say anything.'

'It's too late for that,' she says, kneeling down beside me. 'I didn't want it to come to this,' she sighs. 'This isn't what I wanted at all.' She tilts her head to the side pityingly, but her eyes are devoid of all emotion, and it hits me then that she's planning to kill me.

The knowledge comes but I don't get a rush of adrenaline that makes me want to flee. I freeze. My limbs feel leaden. I can't move at all.

'I really didn't want this,' Lizzie says again, and I could almost be convinced by the look of anguish. 'But now I've got no choice.'

'You do!' I say. 'You can just go and I'll pretend it never happened. I won't call the police. I swear.'

She snorts with laughter. 'Oh, come on, of course you would. You were just about to.'

She puts the phone back on its base and then exhales loudly, hands on her hips. 'Right, it's time.'

I stare up at her in sheer, paralysed horror, sprawled across the hallway, my skull still ringing, and for a moment I'm back, lying on a marble floor, skull broken, looking up at the person who just pushed me, as she smiles down.

It's pitch black, the cold piercing my thin sweater and sweat pants. I'm wearing a pair of slip-on shoes I normally reserve for gardening that Lizzie forced me to put on after she undid the belt around my ankles.

She shoves me out through the French doors and I stumble and fall into a flowerpot. It falls over and smashes, and Lizzie swears. She seems more nervous out here – less in control.

She has put on a pair of my gloves – black leather ones so she doesn't have to worry about leaving fingerprints.

'Move,' she hisses at me, prodding me in the back.

With a whimper I start to shuffle towards the end of the garden, tears sliding hot down my face. I know I'm losing my chance. I know I should put up a fight. But my limbs are heavy, everything is heavy, even my eyelids are dropping. She made me take three small white pills. I struggled until she held my nose and when I opened my mouth to breathe, she shoved the pills in and then forced me to swallow like I was a dog.

'What was that?' I asked her afterwards.

She wouldn't answer.

'Don't fall asleep,' Lizzie warns, pinching my arm and shoving me towards the garden gate.

I look back towards my house – it's melting into the darkness and I wonder if this is the last time I'm ever going to see it. I think of my mobile, which Lizzie shoved down between the cushions of the sofa. She used it to send some tweets, laughing to herself as she did. What is she going to do now? Kill me and bury me out here in the field? Did she give me enough of whatever it was to kill me? Maybe that's her plan – to lead me into the woods and leave me there so it looks like a suicide. I'm sure I've read a story where that happened once – it was a scientist. Some government cover-up conspiracy. Or maybe it was real. I don't know any more.

She forces me through the gate at the back of the garden and into the field. 'Where are we going?' I slur.

'Stop asking questions,' she hisses at me and I sense she's anxious. She hasn't planned this out. Maybe there's still a chance I can talk her round.

'What are you going to do?' I say and I can hear myself crying, and I hate myself for being so weak, for not being able to fight back. I keep stumbling, flat-footed and weak-kneed – further into darkness. The woods are looming up ahead – their branches clawing the sky.

My knees buckle.

Lizzie drags me back to my feet. 'Move!' she orders.

The woods are not our destination. We trudge through the field and I don't know where we're going – the horizon keeps slanting and I am stumbling so much that Lizzie has stopped hissing at me and is now half holding me up by the elbow. We reach a fence and she's making me climb over a metal cattle gate and I recognise it. We're a quarter of a mile from my house. This is Magpie Lane. There's a car parked in the layby right by the gate.

For a moment I think maybe there's someone in it, some-one who can help me, but then Lizzie beeps the door and I realise it's her car. She opens the boot and pushes me into it. I lie down, curled on my side, my eyes already shut. I feel her lay a blanket over me and I almost murmur thank you.

The blanket covers my head. Then something else gets laid on top of me. I can't push it off. It feels like a box or something.

The door shuts. The engine starts. We move. I try to kick – remembering reading something about how the best thing to do if you're ever kidnapped and thrown in the boot of a car, is to try to kick out the brake lights so if the cops see, they'll pull the driver over – but my limbs won't co-operate and for a bewildering few seconds I am convinced I'm back in the hospital, that I'm dreaming all this and I'm still in a coma.

We don't go far before I feel the car start to slow down. We're turning. We stop. Where are we? I want to sit up and look out the window but I'm sinking, being dragged into a black hole, invisible tentacles pulling me into the void.

This is it.

The black hole swallows me.

When I come to it's to the sound of the Cranberries and someone singing over the top in a fake Irish accent. It takes me a while to realise it's Lizzie. Everything is black. I'm in a coffin. No. It's not a coffin. I'm moving. I'm still in the car. I hear a groan. It's me. I try to speak, to say her name, but I'm gagged. When did she do that? I struggle and start whimpering. The gag is cutting into my cheeks. The radio switches suddenly off.

'Is that you? Are you awake?' Lizzie asks.

She's talking to me. I ignore her. My mouth is gummy as if I've been chewing on a glue stick. Whatever she gave me feels like it could have tranquillised a horse. Maybe it was ketamine. All I know is that I need to find a way to wake up.

'We're almost there,' Lizzie calls cheerfully from the driver's seat. Where? I want to ask. Where is she taking me? Does the fact I'm not dead mean she's not planning on hurting me? Maybe she just wants to scare me some more.

After a few more minutes I feel the car reversing and then the engine cuts out. My breathing becomes more ragged and a slight spurt of adrenaline pulses through my limbs. I try to flex my ankles and feet. They don't respond. It takes me back again to when I was in the hospital, waking from the coma, but still sedated because of all my injuries.

Lizzie gets out of the car. She opens the boot and yanks off whatever is covering my face. I blink. It's still night-time. Over her shoulder I can see a house. *Houses*, in fact. A row of them. Victorian terraces. There's an orange street light illuminating Lizzie. And the gun she's holding.

'OK, up you get,' she says in a whisper, darting a glance over her shoulder.

I don't move. She reaches down and hauls me upright. I struggle and she punches me in the side of the head, enough that I see stars.

'Don't be difficult,' she tells me.

She grabs hold of my arm and heaves me out of the boot. I stare at the gun – fully awake now, though my limbs are still asleep. I slip and tumble out of the car and Lizzie curses under her breath and drags me to my feet. She's much stronger than she looks. She hooks one arm through mine and digs the gun into my ribs with her other hand.

'Walk,' she says and starts dragging me towards the closest house.

I drag my heels. Where are we? I think we might be in London. Maybe she's brought me back to her place. Where was it she used to live? Somewhere south of the river. Peckham or Kennington? I turn my head left to right, praying for a person or a car to pass by. There's no one but I do see a street sign. Leonard Road, I think it says.

Lizzie pulls me towards the front door. I look up at the house we're heading towards. I don't want to go inside. I feel as though if I go inside, I'll never come out again.

Something primal, deep inside me, stirs like an animal waking from hibernation. The voice in my head orders me to fight, no matter the cost. I struggle, my limbs finally starting to respond, strength returning in a sudden blast, and I pull away from Lizzie, managing to wrest my arm free.

She grabs me by the hair and yanks me backwards, shoving the blunt nose of the gun between my ribs. I scream but it's muffled by the scarf and she hisses at me to shut up and drags me towards the door.

She grips me with one hand and with the other she starts unlocking it. It opens and she drags me inside. I hold the door jamb and fight with every ounce of strength left in me but she closes the door on my fingers, crushing them until, with a gasp, I let go.

As I sink to my knees, clutching my hand and sucking in air, she pulls me inside the house and slams the door behind me.

When the scream comes, there's no one to hear.

The room is sound-proofed. At first I wonder at how she must have planned this, but then I see the speakers and some kind of recording equipment and realise that it must have already been here. Someone built this room to record music. Now my screams bounce off the walls with nowhere to go. She doesn't need to keep me gagged because I can't be heard outside of this eight-foot by twelve-foot room. My throat is raw from trying and my ears are ringing.

I don't know how long I've been here or what time it is. I lean against the wall and squeeze my eyes shut, trying not to cry. I need to stay calm. Crying isn't going to help. I have to think. She hasn't force fed me any more drugs, which is good because I can think again, but I don't know what she's planning.

I'm not dead yet, which has to mean something. I tell myself that if she wanted me dead, I already would be. She could have made me overdose and faked it to look like a suicide. Maybe she does plan on letting me go. But I have trouble really believing that. It's gone too far. And, most importantly, it's Lizzie I'm dealing with. She's not like other people. She doesn't reason like normal people.

I always knew there was something wrong with her. It was hard to put a finger on but something was off about her. Like she was wearing a disguise all the time, maybe that's how best to describe it; she was like an alien wearing a human disguise. She always seemed to be pretending.

Back then I dismissed it as someone slightly odd, desperately trying to fit in and be liked. It was as if she'd read a book on etiquette or *How To Win Friends and Influence People* but hadn't quite mastered the skills. She reminded me of the kids at school who were always on the outskirts, never quite accepted because of the way they looked or acted; the kids who, at risk of being bullied and knowing their lowly place in the playground pecking order, offered allegiance to the most popular kids, laughing extra loud at their jokes, complimenting them on their clothes or hair, but secretly seething on the inside and plotting their downfall. She'd always ask me where I got my clothes from and make comments that on the surface seemed like compliments but weren't. 'Nice dress,' she'd say, or 'Wow, your style is so unique!' It was particularly hurtful because the clothes had belonged to my mother. I'd found them in the attic at my aunt's and they were the only things I had left to remind me of her.

I remember the time she offered me a piece of chocolate cake, smiling at me brightly, though her eyes told me she wanted me to choke on it. It looked like she'd gouged the slice out with her bare hands but I took it because I didn't want to be rude. But when she turned her back I threw it in the bin. I had this thought that maybe she'd done something to it, spat in it, or worse.

I don't know if it was just me who saw through her. No one else seemed to. She was friends with a lovely girl called Flora and I never understood that.

Now I'm remembering everything else Lizzie did. The gossip she started about me. I think it was because I got the job as assistant to the CEO and she wanted it. She applied but didn't even get an interview. Shortly after that, things started to happen: my food would disappear from the fridge or someone would take a big bite out of my sandwich. She started a rumour that I'd told everyone I once dated Prince Harry, which was absurd. I had met him at the club when I worked the door, he was a regular, but we never dated.

It was other small stuff too. If I walked into the breakout area and she was there with the other girls, they'd all stop talking. I overheard her in the toilet once, complaining to her friend Flora that I hadn't paid my share of the bill at lunch one time. They stopped inviting me for lunch after that.

Now she's undergone this total physical transformation and it's even creepier; like she's upgraded the outside and it's hiding the monster inside. Looking at her, you'd never think she was capable of doing anything bad. But exactly what kind of bad is she capable of? I keep coming back to that.

Does she want money? Perhaps that's what it is. She mentioned her credit cards and I saw the way she looked around my house. Maybe I could offer her money. That's what I'll do. I'll tell her about all my savings accounts. I'll tell her that I need to go to the bank to get them to issue a cheque. Then when we get to the bank I'll cause a big drama – scream and yell – and security will come running. But even as I think it, I know it's a fantasy.

I look around the room. It's like a prison cell in here. Is that her plan? I don't understand how she thinks she'll get away with this. She can't keep me here indefinitely. Someone will come looking for me.

At that thought I start crying. No one is going to come. No one cares. No one will even know I'm gone. I'll vanish into thin air and it will be like I've never existed. If Zac or

Maddie come knocking again, they'll just assume I'm still hiding from them, or that I've left because I'm too embarrassed to show my face. Then I remember Peanut locked in the pantry. Maybe they'll hear him barking. They might not, though. And what if he doesn't have any food or water? How long will he last? A day or two? A week at most. I don't know. I need to get out of here. I yank my arm on the handcuff locked to my wrist that she attached to the radiator.

It's one of those old Victorian-style radiators with pipes but the handcuff doesn't clank against it because it's red and fluffy, like something from a sex shop.

I rattle the handcuff against the radiator. It won't budge. I've tried squeezing my hand through the hole but she's ratcheted it so tight there's no way, not if I dislocated every bone in my hand. And the radiator is screwed so tight that even if I had the strength of two men, I wouldn't be able to pull it off the wall.

I need water too. I'm so thirsty. My headache is back with a vengeance, pounding angrily against my skull. I'm used to headaches, they're near permanent when you have a metal plate screwed in your skull, but this one is so intense it hurts to blink.

Somehow I must drift off to sleep or pass out, because I wake with a jolt at the sound of the door opening. Lizzie stands in the doorway with a smile on her face. She steps quickly into the room and shuts the door behind her before I can try to scream. She's changed her clothes. She's wearing a green dress and heels. She's done her hair and make-up and I can smell the perfume wafting off her – Chanel No. 5. Does she know that I used to wear that? Once again I'm struck by her complete transformation. I don't think I once saw her wear heels when we worked at PKW, or make-up.

'I'm off out,' she tells me. 'I've got a date with James.'

I stare at her, speechless.

'Any advice?' she asks. 'Dos and don'ts?'

'Let me go,' I say, my voice a rasp.

'I can't,' she answers with a shrug.

'I'll give you money. I'll pay you. I've got money. I've got lots of money.'

Her eyes light up. 'Yes, I know. I know all about your little payout. Big payout really. How lucky were you!'

I frown at her. It's so hard to know when she's joking or if she's actually being serious. 'You can have it all,' I tell her. 'Just let me go.'

She pulls another face and sighs. 'I can't. It's too late now. Everything is in place. I've got a plan.'

For a beat I stare at her. The excitement vibrates off her.

'What plan?' I ask with dread.

'I can't tell you that,' she says. 'Well, OK, I'll give you a clue. I'm going to meet James and I'm going to convince him to come with me to your place and then I'm going to make him call the police and report you missing.'

I don't get it. How will that help her? Why is she getting James involved? This doesn't make any sense.

'I'm going to make it look like he might have had something to do with your going missing,' she explains.

'What?' I ask.

'I know I'll be a suspect, you see. Of course I will, there are witnesses who've seen me at your house. Zac and Maddie will point the finger. You can bet she will. She's a total bitch. But if I can get James there, have him tramp around the house and leave a few fingerprints, maybe some other clues too, then there's someone else for the police to look at and frankly he'll seem a lot more suspicious than me.'

'That's insane. It will never work.'

'I don't know. I've got away with worse. And there's no body to find so they might not even think it's murder. They might assume you've just fucked off because you're so embarrassed about the fact you stalked your neighbours.'

I'm hung up on the 'worse'. 'You won't get away with it,' I stammer.

She smiles. 'I will get away with it because I'm very convincing. It's amazing really. I never realised quite how much being thin and pretty made a difference to how you're treated. It isn't fair. It isn't fair at all. James would never have swiped right on me if I still looked like I used to. But now he's going to regret calling me names.'

'Please don't hurt him,' I say.

She crouches down beside me. 'He told me how he couldn't bear to visit you in the hospital, you know, because you were so ugly.'

I wince at her words, even though I know they're true.

Lizzie stands up and walks to the door.

'What are you going to do with me?' I ask her.

'I'm not going to do anything.'

That wasn't what I expected to hear. Nothing? 'So you'll let me go?' I ask, feeling a flicker of hope ignite.

She shakes her head. 'No. You're staying here. I'm going to lock this door and then I'm going to leave you, probably for a week. I could do two to be sure but then you might start to smell.'

'What?'

'I think it only takes a few days, but some sites say it can take up to a week.'

'Oh god.' She means to leave me here without water. Or food. 'You're going to leave me here to die?'

She shrugs like it's not up to her. 'It's not really my idea. I got it in a book. I read a lot of thrillers. I watch a lot of TV too, so I know how to clean up a crime scene and dispose of a body. And whatever you may think, I'm not a killer. I mean, I don't think I could actually pull a trigger or slit a throat. Or maybe I could. But this way there's far less blood.'

'Please!' I say, hating the begging tone in my voice. 'Please. I'll pay you whatever you want. You can't leave me here like this.'

'I have to.'

'You don't have to.' I'm crying now, despite the fact I know it won't make any difference at all. She's impervious to anyone's hurt or pain. She's some kind of sociopath, maybe even a psychopath. The difference is something to do with fear, I think. Psychopaths don't feel fear. And they act in cold blood. I think she qualifies.

How am I only seeing this now? I wonder. She was always manipulative and deceitful but I never saw the full picture. How many people do we meet in life that we never really see? Who hide their dark truth from the world? It's terrifying to think about all these monsters hiding in plain sight.

'This is your fault, you know,' she says.

'How?' I ask in a whisper. Fear is a living thing, a spider crawling up the inside of my throat.

'Because you hit your head,' she tells me, pointing at the scab on my forehead. 'I was going to just threaten you. The gun's not even real. It's a prop. My housemate had a box of things in the car. She's a theatre director. That's what gave me the idea, actually. I saw the props and thought, hmmm, maybe I could stop being an actor in my life, and instead start writing and directing the story myself. I think I heard that on a podcast. I shouldn't take credit for it.' She smiles. 'I might write a book about this eventually. My version of what happened.'

'You're insane,' I hiss at her.

Her smile fades. 'That's not nice. I could have force fed you drugs and made you overdose. I did think about it. But then they would have found your body and it would have looked too suspicious with that big bloody cut on your head. You're so clumsy, aren't you? Falling down stairs and then falling into furniture.'

I stare at her. She's trying to blame me for this?

'You should have died the first time. But hey, fate has given me a second chance. And this time I'm going to do it properly.'

'You won't get away with this.'

'The police will suspect James. I'll make sure of it. You'll be missing, presumed murdered. He'll be a suspect. They'll charge him. I'll be the poor victim who lived to tell the tale.'

'And what if it goes wrong?' I ask her, clutching at straws, trying to find a way to keep the conversation going, to keep her here. I can't have her leave. Then there's no chance. I'll die in this room. 'What if,' I say, 'the police arrest you and then get a search warrant for the house? They'll find me.'

'They won't arrest me,' she says. 'I'll have alibis.'

'You're insane,' I say again.

'Stop saying that,' she frowns, her lips pursing. 'I don't like it. Besides, who's the one who looks insane? You're the one who victimised a poor, innocent colleague. You're the one who faked an entire online life. You're the one who has no one who'll even bother to look for you.' She checks her watch. 'Anyway, I'm late. I can't keep James waiting.' She moves for the door but then turns back. 'Do you think he'll like the dress?'

I can't find any words in response, but she isn't looking for any.

She smiles and opens the door. A black cat darts between her legs. She glares down at it with disgust then draws back her foot and kicks it hard. It flies across the room and into the wall. Back arched, tail flicking, it turns and hisses at her.

'Now you'll have some company,' she says, and shuts the door.

My mouth feels as if it's stuffed with wadded-up paper towels. My head is still pounding, the pain made worse by the cat's endless meows. It's over by the door, scratching pointlessly to be let out. It's been hours. My senses tell me that Lizzie hasn't come home and that I'm alone but the truth is, I couldn't hear someone talking in the hallway right outside the door because of the sound-proofing. The only noise I can hear is the ticking of the central heating, the pipes under the floorboards hissing and clanking. She's cranked it right up. The radiator is so hot that when I brushed against it, it almost peeled off a layer of skin. I'm having to sit with my arm at a weird and painful angle so it doesn't touch the metal.

I'm sweating so much that my top is soaked through and I can feel my pulse throbbing in my temples as the moisture is wicked out of me.

I'm bursting for the bathroom too. I think I wet myself in the car when I was passed out, because I can smell it and my knickers and trousers are still damp, while my thighs feel like they're burning. I'm forcing myself to hold it in. I don't want to wet myself – I can't stand the thought of it – but I'm also aware that every drop of moisture out of me will hurry along dehydration. I know you're supposed to drink your urine but the thought makes me feel ill and besides, what would I capture it in?

I can't stand fully upright but if I crouch, I can just about get a view of the desk that runs along the opposite side of the room where there's a dusty piece of recording equipment and some tangled bits of wire. I stare at the door. Even if I can find a way to get the handcuffs off, I still have to find a way out of the room.

Panic sends my breathing through the roof – black spots dance in front of my eyes and I have to tell myself to stay calm. It's difficult, though. How am I ever going to get out? I'm going to die in here with this damn cat. I remember a story I read about men who were shipwrecked and floating for days, drawing straws to see who would become the human sacrifice. Would I ever be able to kill a cat with my bare hands and drink its blood to stay alive? I don't think so.

I tell myself to focus on one thing. First the handcuffs. They're cheap but surprisingly strong. I've tried breaking them by levering them against the radiator pipe and using my weight to snap the lock but they refused to give, and now the pipe is too hot to touch without getting a serious burn. I need to find something I can use to jimmy the lock instead. Stretching as far as I can, my fingers barely touch the desk on the other side of the room, certainly not far enough to reach the equipment up there. I figure that if I could get hold of that, then I could try to smash it open and find a piece of metal or something, which I could use to jimmy the lock.

There's a power cord dangling over the edge of the desk. I can't reach it with my hand but when I stretch out on the floor my toes just touch it. I try snagging the cord and when that doesn't work I pull off my sock and try with a bare foot. After half an hour or more I'm exhausted and still haven't managed to get hold of it. I collapse face down and sob dry tears into the floor before the darkness envelopes me.

When I wake up, my head is throbbing even harder. My lips have cracked and are bleeding and the dull ache in my bladder is now a burning sensation. I heave myself into a crouching position and tug my clothes down. Gritting my teeth, I put my hand beneath myself and then finally start to feel a hot dribble into my palm. Pushing aside how disgusting it is, I hurriedly bring my palm up to my lips and force myself to lap up the small amount of urine I've caught. There's barely any and swallowing it almost makes me retch.

After I'm done I collapse back down. The arm attached to the radiator is numb from being held in one position and I try to shake it around and get the blood flowing but it hurts too much and in the end it's easier to just lie still, and to close my eyes and let myself drift away.

Maybe it's already night. Or maybe it's the next day. I don't know. Lizzie left the light on in the room. I suppose I'm grateful for that because if it was dark, I think I would have lost my mind already. I'm halfway there.

I'm still on the floor, staring into space, occupying a strange hinterland between consciousness and unconsciousness. I can't feel my arm any more – the one attached to the radiator. The cat is meowing intermittently. It comes and nudges my head. I mumble something – totally incoherent.

My eyes flicker open. The cat walks beneath the desk. It crouches down – doing its business. I hear the faint hiss as it pees and my body almost convulses, my mouth trying to make saliva and failing. I haven't drunk anything in over twenty-four hours, maybe more like thirty-six. How many more hours do I have left? I can't imagine going through this for that long. I can't imagine how painful the end will be either.

There's a knock. I startle. My eyes flash open. There's another knock. More of a dull thud. At first I think it's a footstep or someone at the door, but then I realise it's not. It's the cat swiping at the cable that's dangling over the desk. I watch for a few moments and then I push myself to a sitting position.

The cat keeps knocking the cable, swiping at it, and each time it does, it moves fractionally in my direction. I lie down and stretch out my foot once more and this time, I'm able to snag the cable between my toes. I yank. The equipment on the desk moves an inch towards the edge. I keep yanking, ignoring the cat who is trying to swipe the cable and the angry hiss of my skin as my hand rubs against the edge of the radiator pipe. It takes what feels like forever but eventually there's an almighty crash and the sound mixer or whatever it is tumbles to the floor. The cable is within reaching distance. I grab hold of it and pull it towards me.

Somehow this small victory makes me forget the dull ache behind my eyes and the fire shooting up my arm. I grab hold of the sound mixer and smash it repeatedly down over the radiator knob until it breaks apart, revealing its interior of wires and electrical components. I gut it, breaking off a piece of plastic – a needle-like shard – that seems like it might do the trick.

It fits neatly into the hole in the cuffs and within just a few seconds of wriggling it around, the lock springs open. It takes double that time for me to process that I'm free. That it was that easy. I grip my wrist. Because the handcuff was fluffy it didn't cut my wrist, only bruised it slightly, and the skin is unbroken, but I can't feel my arm at all. It hangs uselessly. I rub my wrist and twist it this way and that to get the blood flowing. My fingers are stiff as iron keys and refuse to bend and there's a livid burn running from the inside of my wrist up to my thumb joint. The skin has blistered and bubbled.

The pain is somewhere in the distance, as though my brain has locked it away in another room; something to deal with later. I stagger to my feet and stumble woozily to the door and there's a tiny, hopeful part of me that prays it's open, that she forgot to lock it, but of course that's not true.

I turn around looking for something I could use to bash the door down but the only things are the broken sound mixer and the desk.

What about a window? There must be a window behind one of these panels. I hammer my fists on them. One part sounds more hollow, as though there might be drywall behind it rather than brick, but it's only a guess and when I try to prise my nails under the tile, it refuses to budge.

I drop to my knees by the radiator. If I could turn this damn thing off, that would help at least. I've already tried turning the knob but with just one hand it was impossible. Now I've got two hands I might have a shot at turning it. But it's too hot to touch and my burned hand is still numb and useless. Then I spot the power cord from the sound mixer. Maybe that could do the trick? I wrap it around the radiator knob and twist. Somehow it works. There's a release of pressure – a hiss – and as I twist it faster and faster I can hear the water starting to drain away. The temperature starts to drop. It's another victory, swift on the heels of the last, but it's only temporary because Lizzie will be back soon.

Frustrated, I try the door again, yanking on it as hard as I can and jiggling the handle trying to break it off. I use the same needle-like piece of plastic that I used to jimmy the handcuffs open to try to pick the lock, but it snaps. Shit. My headache is back with a vengeance. The adrenaline rush has seeped away and a wave of exhaustion hits me like a tsunami, totally overwhelming me. I drop to my knees, overcome with despair. What's the point of trying to get out? It's not going to happen. I'm going to die in here.

The cat comes and butts its head against me and I pull it close. The poor thing, trapped in here too. It doesn't deserve this. The cat struggles out of my arms and goes over to scratch uselessly at the door again.

I shake myself out of my half-dream state and throw off my despair. I made it this far. I can't quit now. I need to get out of here. I pick through the remains of the sound mixer one more time, until I find a piece of plastic that I manage to snap into a thinner shard. With that in my hand I approach the door.

Part Four

Lizzie

Sunday, 10 December
Evening

The station is so quiet that for a moment I panic that I've missed the last train and I'll be stuck here all night. I certainly can't afford a taxi. I can only just about scrape together enough cash to buy a single train ticket home, my cards refusing to budge over their overdraft limits.

It's cold and I'm tired and hungry but there's nowhere to shelter. There's just a platform and a ticket machine and a single plastic bench beneath a rain shelter. The next train, which also happens to be the last train, is not for another twenty-eight minutes but it will take me straight to Paddington. I check my phone, which is almost out of battery. I'll be home by one in the morning if I'm lucky. Hopefully the bitch will be dead by then.

I don't want to think too hard about what happens if she isn't. One of my mother's boyfriends killed a rat once by putting it in a bag and drowning it. It thrashed around as though an electric current was being shot through it. It fought tooth and nail to live. I don't think Becca has that in her. I know she doesn't. She's not a fighter or a survivor. Not like me. She doesn't even have the survival instincts of a rat.

I'm not going to suffocate or drown her. I'm going to finish her off with some pills; give her an overdose. I left half my stash of pills in Becca's bathroom cabinet, though. I'm not sure I have enough. I could go up the road to the estate and get some more, but I can't afford to risk it in case the police start asking around. Not that my dealer would ever talk to the police but you never know. I started buying speed from him three years ago after I read that it was a great way to lose weight fast and then I needed the Xanax to come down off the speed. I only bought some a week or so ago; if I went back this soon, he'd find it odd.

Eight will have to be enough and if it's not, too bad.

If I crush them into water, she'd probably be so thirsty she'd down it without even noticing the taste. I could even tell her what I've done. That would be amusing. Then she'd be forced to choose between killing herself from dehydration or killing herself with an overdose. Imagine the torture – that's quite delicious. But unfortunately there's no time for games. I need her out of the house as soon as possible. There's still a chance the police could get a search warrant. I need to get Becca out of there tonight.

I've got a plan to dispose of the body. It requires an animal sacrifice. Chris the cat has volunteered for duty. It's amazing what you can find out on Google. Apparently if you bury a person and then bury an animal on top, the cadaver dogs will sniff out the dead animal and dig that up.

Obviously burying her in the garden is a dumb idea and I'll need to get her in the car somehow, so I'm going to do what I did before, drug her and then move her into the car while she's still conscious. By the time I get to the burial site she'll be dead. Perfect.

I'm going to take her to Romney Marsh, which is a couple of hours drive from here. The ground is boggy so I'll be able to dig, and it's remote too, so I'll be able to find a place off the beaten track. Afterwards I'll come back home and clean the car and the house, top to bottom.

My thoughts turn from Becca's death to James, in prison for life for her murder. What's he doing right now? I wonder. Is he confused about how his button ended up at the crime scene? It was so simple: just a tug of a loose thread and then when his back was turned, I cast his fate with the drop of a button.

I'm sure he did go to see her last night. He went and knocked on the door in his drunken state. He wanted to talk to her but she wasn't home. It did me a huge favour really. I had been wondering how I was going to set him up, beyond the button, but he did it all for me in the end.

I'm feeling a strange sensation in my gut, similar to how you feel after eating something that's off; my guts feel squishy and writhing like fish bait. I wonder if it's regret. I was starting to like James. Not him per se. He's a fat-shaming dickhead who deserves everything that's coming his way. I liked the way it felt when he looked at me, the same way I saw him looking at Becca at the Christmas party when he told her he wanted to fuck her on the desk. I liked knowing I had power over him. Power he doesn't even know I wield. I liked fucking with him.

I had even started to imagine a life with him: where we'd live, what our children would look like, what it would be like to turn up with him to a Christmas party, though of course, as his wife I wouldn't need to work any more. I pictured telling my mum all about him. I imagined her face. Her beautiful disbelief and her jaw-dropping shock when she saw the pictures in *Tatler*. Obviously I'd have to send her a copy as she wouldn't buy a magazine like *Tatler* normally.

I had even started anticipating how I'd feel as I walked down the aisle – filled with pure, dazzling white light – the same way I feel when I fast for a few days or when I take a couple of my magic pills. Everyone would look at me and I'd smile beatifically, radiantly, as James lifted my veil, knowing that I'd won.

One day, when his father died, James would inherit his baronetcy and become a lord. I'd be Lady Elizabeth Wickenden. I imagined it all; images tacked to my mental vision board.

So yes, it was a hard decision to throw James to the wolves like that.

Maddie and Zac would have been far better – ideal suspects really. I tried to steer those stupid cops towards them and it would have probably worked if not for the damn alibi.

Finally the train arrives and I get a seat in the quiet carriage so I can warm up and think about what to do. I'm going to need a lawyer. I'll find one who can work pro bono. Given the status of the case and the publicity, it should be easy. Ophelia, that stuck-up bitch, certainly won't help but she might know someone who can.

By the time the train arrives at Paddington and I get on the tube, I'm almost faint from hunger. I've not eaten since breakfast, apart from an apple and some biscuits that they gave me at the police station. I buy a Big Mac with the last of my change and devour it while I sit on the Circle Line. Halfway through it, I notice a magazine lying face up on the seat opposite. I snatch it up.

The front page is a picture of the bloody seven-figure author PKW reps. The article is all about her unprecedented advance and how she's the next literary sensation. My teeth practically grind each other down to stubs. It doesn't matter, I tell myself. None of this matters.

I throw my half-eaten burger down on the seat next to me and pull out my phone, which has just a few per cent of battery left. I remember what Ophelia said about the media and wonder if the story has been picked up yet. It has. It's splashed over every news site. The header of the *Daily Mail* screams:

EX-MODEL PRESUMED MURDERED

I stab the article and wait for it to load, Becca's face slowly emerging out of the pixels. Ex-model? How ridiculous. Who made up that shit? The police are asking for anyone with any information to come forward but are also quick to mention that arrests have been made. I rapidly scan the article. They describe Becca as single and living alone. It almost makes me laugh out loud, given the lengths Becca went to pretending she was married and had a baby. She'd hate to see how they were describing her as a lonely old spinster. I almost hope she's alive when I get home so I can have the pleasure of rubbing it in her face.

As we pull into Victoria my phone blissfully dies, so I no longer have to stare at her face or read the utter fiction they're writing about her. Thirty minutes later I'm almost home, walking up my street, my eyes fixed on the front door, wondering what lies in wait on the other side.

I hurry past the estate and the gang of boys who catcall me. The guy I normally buy from nods at me, his eyes hooded and gleaming. He thinks he's so hard. All the boys on the estate do.

I laugh as I pass them. They have no idea.

Everything seems quiet. The house is roasting hot – it's like entering a tropical paradise – and I have to strip off my coat and scarf and even my sweater the minute I'm through the door. In the kitchen I turn on all the lights and check the back door and windows are locked. I look around, noticing something strange. Something isn't quite right but I can't figure out what it is.

I stand stock still, studying the room, trying to figure out what it is. It's the cat! That's it! He's not bothering me with his usual medley of meows. I locked him in the room with her. I'll have to tell Tess he ran out into the street and got hit by a car. Or maybe I can tell her he's sick and needs the vet and get her to fork out for treatment, but she might call to check. I'll stick with the hit-and-run story.

I head upstairs, carrying a glass of water. It's time for phase two. Outside the sound-proofed room I press my ear to the door, but I can't hear anything. Not that that means anything: when the door's shut you could be playing music at full volume and no one would hear it. That's what made this room so perfect.

The whole plan came to me quite easily – in the minute while Becca lay on the floor of her living room, unconscious. I knew I couldn't leave her there. If she came around, she'd call the police and I'd be arrested before I made it home. If I killed her, they'd also likely arrest me as Maddie and Zac would identify me. I also knew that I needed to drive straight home as they can always check your phone's GPS records to determine where you are. If I detoured to dump a body, they'd know about it.

I didn't have any other choice but to take her with me. Then I thought of this room and it seemed like the universe had aligned it all perfectly. I could keep her here for a few days, cover my tracks back in Widford by setting up James or the neighbours, and then while the police were investigating I could come back here and dispose of her body elsewhere. The tweets were next-level genius. I sent them from her phone but set them on a timer, and then made sure that I stopped at the pub on the corner of her road so the barman would potentially act as an alibi at exactly the time the tweets went out. I deliberately asked him for the time.

As I walk into my room, I notice my laptop on the bed, just where I left it, buried among the pile of shoes and dresses I was trying on before I left to meet James for that coffee in Soho. It feels like a lifetime ago already. None of those will do for what comes next. I find a pair of old sweats, a T-shirt and a hooded sweater. I stuff Becca's gloves into my pocket and pick up the Burberry scarf I used to gag her. It's a shame I can't keep it but I suppose it would be silly to get caught because I wanted a souvenir.

I memorise the route to Romney Marsh because I won't be able to take my phone, and then clear my computer history. I'll throw the laptop away after tonight. Chuck it in the river, maybe. There's an old paper map in the car that I can use if I get lost. All I need is a shovel.

In the bathroom I tie my hair into a knot and then I take the handful of pills I have left and crush them using the base of the toothbrush charger. Once they're ground fine enough, I sweep them into the glass and give it a stir. The water becomes cloudy, fragments of pills floating on the surface. I wonder if she'll drink it?

Only one way to find out. I unlock the door to the sound-proofed room. I'm not expecting to find her desiccated remains, though that would be nice, but I am hoping she's weak enough that I won't have to get rough with her.

I open the door slowly, apprehensively. The cat flies past the moment I do, and I hear him skitter down the stairs – heading to his water bowl no doubt. Well, I guess I can allow him one last drink. Maybe even one last meal – the final meal of the condemned. Chicken or salmon. Which will it be?

Becca is sitting where I left her, back against the wall, handcuffed to the radiator. Her head is bowed, her legs drawn up to her chest. She doesn't stir or look up when I walk towards her. Is she dead?

I crouch down in front of her and shake her by the shoulder. 'Becca?' I say. 'Wake up. I've brought you some water.'

Suddenly she's wide awake. Her head jerks up. She stares at me and when I hold up the glass I see her eyes, dazed and drooping, track it hungrily. Her lips are cracked and bleeding and she looks drawn, her skin pale. I notice that it's colder in here than the rest of the house. The heating's not on in this room. That's odd. I glance at the radiator – did she manage to turn it off somehow? Damn it.

'Do you want the water or not?' I snap.

She lunges for it suddenly and I pull the glass back, out of reach. It's quite fun really, but there's no time to taunt her with it. I put it back to her lips. 'Here, drink up.'

She opens her mouth and I pour, but the taste must be too bitter because after one swallow she spits out the rest and it dribbles down her chin. Damn. What a waste. She needs to drink it all. I put the glass back against her lips. 'Drink it!' I order.

She glares at me defiantly.

There's a flash of movement and next thing I know she's swatting at me with her free hand. I fall back on my haunches and miss her other fist swinging towards me. The glass I'm holding explodes against my face. I'm drenched in water, and I can feel the sting of a cut and the hot flow of blood dripping down my neck. I'm so shocked I freeze. The bitch! She's on her feet now – how did she get free from the handcuffs? Before I can react she kicks me, sending me sprawling backwards, and then rushes for the door.

I lunge, grabbing for her foot, and yank. She stumbles but manages to steady herself against the desk and then kicks me again – this time in the head – and I let go of her. Once she's free she races out the door. I roll to my feet and stagger after her, blood still pouring down my face, blinding me. I can't let the bitch get away. Shit. Where's she gone?

The hallway is empty. I peer left and right, swiping at my bloody face. Did she go for the stairs or is she hiding in one of the rooms? She's not that fast. She can't have made it downstairs. I would have heard her.

I tiptoe into my bedroom, throwing back the door so it hits the wall. She's not hiding behind it. A noise – a creak – makes me whip my head around. She's run out of Tess's parents' room and is making for the stairs. I start to run after her but then remember the knife beneath my mattress and rush to grab it.

When I come out into the hallway, knife held in front of me, I can hear her downstairs, trying to open the front door. She's tugging on the bolts, hammering with her fists, pulling on the handle, but she won't get out, not without the key in my pocket.

Becca

The damn door is locked. I pound on it with my fists. Shit. I turn around. There must be a back door – another way out. I dart down the hallway, heading for what looks like the kitchen. My leg drags but panic fuels me. I run past the stairs, catching sight of Lizzie stumbling down them, blood veiling her face. She's holding something in her hand. I catch a glimpse of metal. She's got a knife. Oh god.

I run into the kitchen and make straight for what looks like a back door but it's locked. I rattle the knob but it won't give, so I turn and in desperation, hearing her footsteps in the hallway, I look around for somewhere to hide. I notice the knife block on the other side of the room and a door leading somewhere else and I know I haven't time to grab the knife and get through the door so I make a choice and run for the door.

I'm in a living room. There are sofas and a fireplace but nowhere to hide. Fuck. I need to find a way out. I tiptoe over to the far door and peer through the crack in the door. It leads out into the hall. I see Lizzie stagger into the kitchen. She's unsteady on her feet. I wonder if I might be able to fight her if it came down to it. Then I notice the phone on the table by the front door. I rush out of the living room, snatch the phone and make for another door, under the stairs which I'm praying and hoping will be a toilet with a lock.

It is. I slide the bolt across as silently as I can and then fumble with the phone, dialling 999.

As the call connects I cower between the basin and the toilet, staring in terror at the door.

'Emergency. Which service?' a woman asks.

'Please help,' I whisper.

'Do you need fire, police or ambulance?'

'She's going to kill me.'

'You're through to the police. What is the address of your emergency?'

Oh god, what was it? What was it? 35 something. 'Yes . . . it's 35 Leonard Road.'

'35 Leonard Road. I'm sending a car now.'

'She's got a knife,' I whisper, my eyes glued to the door. 'Please hurry.'

'The police are on their way,' she says in a reassuring voice and I start crying because she sounds so near and so comforting and I start to believe I might just make it. I drop the phone to my chest to mute the noise and crane to hear. Is that someone breathing on the other side of the door? Is she out there with her knife?

'Can you get out of the house?' the woman asks.

'No,' I sob.

'Is there somewhere you can hide, somewhere with a door that locks?'

I lower my voice. 'I'm in the toilet . . . Downstairs.'

There's a sudden thud outside in the hallway. Angry footsteps. She's heading this way.

'Please hurry. I can hear her coming.'

The woman's voice stays reassuring. 'Stay on the line with me.'

I can hear Lizzie stop. 'I think she's outside the door . . . I can hear her.'

The door suddenly shakes on its hinges. Lizzie's battering it, trying to break it down.

'Oh god, please, hurry up,' I whisper, sobbing in terror.

The door bursts open.

Lizzie is standing there, blood streaking her face from the cut above her right eye. She's holding the knife in her hand.

I can hear the tinny voice of the operator talking to me on the other end of the phone but I can't answer her. I freeze. This is how it ends.

Lizzie takes a step towards me, bringing the knife up, ready to slash it down. It's either fight or die. I've lived so many lives, escaped death so many times. This isn't how it ends.

I drop the phone. 'No!' I scream and I leap to my feet.

Part Five

I can hear the operator. 'Hello? Are you there?'

'No!' I scream, pushing her off me, watching her body slump motionless to the floor. 'Get off me . . . she's going to kill me!'

Breathing hard, I look down at the body and then, almost wondering how it got there, at the knife in my hand. After a moment I pick up the phone, smearing it with red sticky fingerprints. I press it to my ear, which is wet too. Everything is wet. My clothes are sticking to me. I can smell the iron tang of blood in my hair, on my clothes, saturating the air with heavy droplets as though it might be about to rain blood. The mirror is sprayed with crimson.

I look down at the dead body at my feet, feeling nothing. Is it over?

'Hello? Are you there? Hello?'

'Hello?' I whisper.

'Are you OK? What happened? The police are pulling up outside now.'

'She's dead,' I say. 'I think she might be dead. Oh god. Oh god . . . please . . . oh my god. She's not moving. There's blood. A lot of blood.'

'Is she breathing?' the woman on the other end of the phone asks.

I stare at the matted blonde hair lying in the pool of blood. And I stare at her face. She's slumped against the sink with her face turned to me. Her eyes are open but her lips are turning blue. 'I don't know,' I stammer.

I take a deep breath and then I move. I step over the body. I need to get away from it. From her.

I stumble out into the hallway and then blindly head towards the stairs. Behind me, I'm awfully aware of a blue and red flashing light pulsing through the windows on either side of the front door.

'Can you check for a pulse?' the woman says to me with a very calm and soothing voice.

'I . . . oh god . . . I don't know. Please can you send an ambulance?' I ask as I move up the stairs two at a time, panting. I walk into the sound-proofed room and pull the key to the handcuff out of my pocket and unlock it from the radiator.

'It's on its way,' the woman tells me. 'You need to stay calm. Can you do that for me?'

Even with the shock of what's just happened, with her blood still tacky on my hands, my brain stays calm and cool, giving me instructions for what to do. 'Yes. Yes, I think so,' I say, keeping my mouth as far from the mouthpiece as possible to muffle my voice. 'Oh my god.'

I cross into my bedroom and shove the handcuffs in my underwear drawer. There's a bang on the front door. A furious hammering. It's the police.

'What's your name? Can you give me your name?' the woman asks.

I hurry down the stairs. 'Lizzie,' I say. 'Elizabeth Crowley. She came at me . . . with a knife,' I whisper into the phone. 'She just came out of nowhere.'

I pause on the bottom step and rest the phone on the side table. I put the knife in my left hand and hold my right hand up and then slice it open from the base of the little finger to the right side of my palm as though I'm scoring a joint of meat.

Biting back the scream I pick up the phone in my left hand. The policemen are still hammering away, shouting for me to open the door.

I glance in the downstairs toilet and see Becca slumped against the sink like some ghastly, glass-eyed mannequin. 'I think she's dead . . .' I say into the phone. 'I think I've killed her.'

Partial transcript of police interview with Miss Elizabeth Crowley

DCI Tallack – Monday, 11 December

She was in the house when I got home. She came at me with a knife. I don't know how she got in. She must have found the spare key I keep in the flowerpot. I know it's a stupid place to leave it. She was waiting for me upstairs in my bedroom.

I . . . I'm sorry . . . I don't . . . oh god. I didn't mean to kill her. I'm so sorry. I told you, though . . . I told you she was crazy. You wouldn't listen to me! You thought James had killed her. James . . . Have you let him out? You need to let him go! He's innocent. He didn't do anything. I need to see him.

What do you mean? I don't understand. Detective Tallack, what are you trying to say? She was in my house when I came home. She was waiting for me. She came at me with a knife. She cut me. I ran. I hid in the bathroom downstairs and called the police but she found me and she broke the door down and she came at me . . . Oh god . . . sorry . . . I can't do this right now . . .

I don't know how I got the knife off her. We fought. She was trying to kill me. What was I meant to do? It was either her or me. She told me I ruined her life. I didn't mean to kill her.

What? I don't know why she was barefoot. Maybe she took off her shoes so she'd be quieter sneaking up on me? No. Yes, I suppose I might have gripped her around the wrist. I'm not sure which one. Both maybe. I was trying to stop her stabbing me. The burn? That was probably from when I held her hand against the radiator. That's what made her drop the knife. That's how I got it off her.

Please. Can we do this later? I just . . . I can't . . . I don't want to think about it. Wait? You're not going to arrest me are you? I didn't do anything? She attacked me! I was defending myself. She would have killed me!

I don't understand why I needed to come down to the station. I've told you what happened.

Thank you. No, I'll take a cab. The hospital said they'd call one. I just need to tell them when I'm done with you. We are done, right? I can go home now, can't I? I just want to go home.

How long will it take for them to process it? I guess I could ask my friend Flora if I could stay with her. No. My mother's away.

When can I go back there? I need to get some things and I need to feed the cat. He weed all over the house while I was gone. Oh god, how will I get it all cleaned up? And the blood. All that blood.

I'll have to repaint.

18 months later

'I look in the downstairs toilet and see Becca slumped against the sink like some ghastly, glass-eyed mannequin. "I think she's dead . . ." I say into the phone. "I think I've killed her."'

There's a huge intake of air – a communal gasp that ripples across the room and I look out over a sea of faces, every single one rapt with horror, hanging off my every word, and I close the book. You could hear a pin drop. I look over at James, sitting towards the back. He gives me a tight smile. He's tired. He was up all night with the baby. But even so, he could look a little more happy for my success.

My publicist steps forward and in a loud voice announces that there's time for a few questions before I start signing copies.

A dozen arms dart into the air. I'm used to this part. I have all my answers down pat. I've already had a dozen interviews with journalists ahead of today's launch and, of course, there were the interviews I did after the murder too, several of which were quite lucrative.

I smile benignly at a young, frizzy-haired woman in the second row, sitting beside the po-faced woman they hired to ghost write the book, who frankly did a terrible job – one I had to fix. She looks sour-faced at all the attention I'm getting. I'm sure she's jealous but it is my story, not hers.

'Was it difficult writing about such a traumatic time in your life?' the frizzy-haired woman asks.

I take a deep breath. 'No. It was very cathartic, actually. I felt like reliving it helped me to process it properly, you know?' She nods understandingly, her expression dripping with sympathy. I make a mental note of it so I can borrow it some time.

Someone else puts their hand up. 'Is it true they're going to make a movie about it?'

I nod. 'Yes, it's true. It's very exciting.' I think of the long list of actresses who are vying to play me and I don't even have to pretend to smile.

As I continue to answer questions, my gaze is drawn to the back of the room, to a jowly-faced man standing there in a grubby trench coat like some flasher. I keep my smile plastered on my face and when it comes time to sign books, I sit at the table and make friendly conversation with everyone who's bought a copy. The entire time I'm aware of the man at the back of the room, his presence a black cloud hanging over my special day.

'What's your baby's name?'

I focus on the woman in front of me, whose face is powdered like some extravagant French pastry.

'Lucette,' I tell her, smiling over at James who is busy feeding her a bottle.

'Oh, isn't she a darling,' she coos. 'What a little cherub.'

'Yes,' I murmur, frowning at Lucette as she guzzles her formula, her chubby little fists gripping the bottle like she's terrified someone might be about to take it away from her. Cherubic is one word for it. Her face is like a satellite dish. I might have to cut back her feeds.

James is looking a little pasty these days, and his hair is thinning fast. He isn't going to be one of those men who ages well, after all. Not that it matters. I smile at him. Maybe I'll suggest we book a holiday somewhere nice. The Maldives perhaps. Or the Seychelles again. Or maybe I'll tell him I need space to write my follow-up novel and go alone. Yes, that sounds far more appealing.

One of the last people in line is unexpected, though I did invite her. 'Oh my goodness, Tess!' I say. 'You made it.'

She smiles, a little tersely it seems, and I notice she isn't holding a copy of my book. Did she not buy one? 'Lizzie,' she says by way of greeting.

'How are you?' I ask, moving in for a hug. She stiffens and over her shoulder I notice someone I definitely did not invite. Rob. Her creepy ex-boyfriend. He puts his arm around her waist. Maybe he's not so ex. I wondered why I hadn't heard from her after the initial back and forth about what had happened in her downstairs toilet, and then my moving out. I invited her to both my wedding and the baby's christening but she told me she couldn't make either as she was travelling.

'When did you get back?' I ask her.

'A while ago,' she says.

That's odd, I think to myself. She still hasn't mentioned the book either.

'How's the house?' I ask.

'My parents are having trouble selling it.'

I arrange my face into a look of sympathy, styled on the woman I just saw in the audience. 'I'm sorry.'

She nods. 'I'm back together with Rob.'

'I can see,' I say, turning to Rob who is staring at me stonily and hasn't even said hello. 'Hi, Rob.'

He glowers at me and my hand twitches as I restrain myself from slapping him. How dare he? I suppose he knows that I told Tess he was having an affair. I suppose he told her I made it all up. And I suppose she believes him and that's why they're here, to confront me about it, but I don't have time.

'I must sign some books but it was so lovely to see you,' I say. I turn around but then I pause and turn back to her. 'Oh, I saw your TV show finally got aired. I mean I didn't see it. I read the reviews.'

Tess's face pales. The play she adapted for TV was awful, savaged by the critics. I smile and she takes a step backwards as if I've slapped her, grabbing Rob by the arm, and then without a word she pulls him away, to the door. That's right, I think to myself, you run away, back to your mediocre world of fringe theatre.

I look around the room, which is still full of people – drinking champagne and eating canapés and cake.

'Lizzie,' a voice says behind me.

I turn around. It's the man in the trench coat.

'Detective Tallack,' I say. 'What a pleasant surprise.'

He nods at the stage. 'That was quite the reading. You had everyone hanging on your every word.'

'Thank you,' I say, noting he's holding a copy of the book in his hand. I hope he's bought that copy, not pinched it from the table.

His beady little eyes are burrowing into me but I don't flinch and I don't look away. I'm better at this game than him.

'So what's all this about a movie?' he asks.

'If you want to know who's playing you,' I say, leaning in close and smiling flirtatiously, 'you'll have to wait and see. But I don't think you'll be disappointed. Last year he was voted sexiest man alive. There's a hint for you.' Actually I'm lying. The actor playing him is a well-known character actor with a hooked nose, rubbery lips and a pregnant woman's belly.

Tallack laughs under his breath, his eyes never once leaving my face.

'How's the hand?' he asks.

I show him my palm – the livid pink scar raised up like a thick cord. 'It's better,' I say. 'I still can't grip things properly, though.'

'Probably for the best,' he says.

I narrow my eyes. What's he getting at? I think I should cut this whole conversation short as I'm not liking his tone. 'I have to go,' I tell him.

A sardonic smile brushes his lips. 'Don't want to keep your fans waiting.'

I smile back at him. 'Thanks for coming.'

'I can't wait to read the book,' Tallack calls after me as I walk away. 'I wonder if there's any hints in there about how you pulled it off.'

That stops me in my tracks. I turn to him, keeping my smile fixed in place. 'Pulled what off?'

We stare at each other for a long beat, like two chess players. He's been checkmated but hasn't yet conceded defeat. He will never let it go, but I've won and he knows it. He'll never get his proof. He had so many questions after the event – why was Becca not wearing shoes? Why did the autopsy show she was severely dehydrated at the time of her death? Why does it sound like two people on the 999 call? Obviously I had no idea and my pro bono lawyer, supplied by James's firm, refused to let me answer him.

They had to drop the murder case against James, and because they'd already screwed up the investigation they quickly wrapped up the inquiry into Becca's death, calling it cut and dried. I was the victim who had been failed by the police and Becca was killed in justifiable self-defence. I'd been screaming from the rooftops about Becca being crazy and had warned them that she was faking her death to frame me, so they looked like fools. My lawyer hired a top-notch PR firm to plaster the news with positive stories about me and negative ones about her.

Detective Tallack had doubts but I think he had orders from on high to drop any further investigation. They're lucky that I didn't sue them frankly.

Tallack glowers at me. He doesn't like losing. Neither do I. I learn all the rules and I play to win.

'I'll send you an invite to the premiere,' I tell him and leave without waiting for a reply.

Someone is waving to me from across the room. Flora. She's wearing a fuchsia-pink dress with sparkles all over it. I head over to her.

'Oh Lizzie!' she says, hugging me. 'Congratulations!'

I extricate myself, hoping she hasn't crumpled my dress or got any crumbs on it. 'Thank you,' I say, graciously.

'I heard the book's gone straight to number one!'

I nod again. 'It's all so overwhelming,' I say.

'It's been so long,' she says. 'I'm so happy for you, you know, that everything worked out. I heard about the pay-out from work.'

'Yes,' I tell her, 'they agreed to settle. James was determined they should pay for firing me like that. I mean, it wasn't as much as they gave Becca . . .'

We both fall silent. Flora hurries on. 'I saw James earlier with the baby. She looks like you, doesn't she?'

I frown a little.

'It's just so amazing!' she says, beaming. 'Do you remember when we saw him at the Christmas party for the first time? How we imagined what it would be like to date him? And here you are married to him. And with a baby!'

I murmur something that sounds like agreement. My smile feels frozen, like the Joker's rictus grin.

'I've tried calling a few times,' Flora says. She's still smiling but there's a twinge of sadness in her voice.

'I'm sorry,' I say. 'I've just been so busy, what with the baby and the book.'

'Yes, I guessed as much.' She grins. 'I wanted to tell you that I'm getting married!' She flashes her engagement ring at me and I startle at the sight of it, completely flabbergasted. Flora? Engaged?

'Wow,' I stammer. 'Congratulations. That's fantastic. Who are you marrying?'

'Tim,' she says, beaming ear to ear. 'From IT.'

Tim from IT. Good god. I mean, she's welcome to him, but I thought he was interested in me.

'He's just amazing. The sweetest guy you can imagine.'

'Well, that's wonderful,' I say.

'I'll send you an invite to the wedding. It's in the summer.' She blushes. 'I was hoping you'd be one of my bridesmaids actually. I've chosen the dress already. It's a gorgeous shade of pink.' She chuckles. 'Actually the whole wedding is going to be pink! Tim said that if he could get married in a *Game of Thrones* costume, then I could get married in pink, so that's what we're doing. Everything pink! But not red. We didn't want a red wedding!' She laughs.

'When is it?' I ask.

'June the twenty-second.'

I bite my lip. 'Oh no, we're on holiday then. We're in the South of France. We like to go before the hoards descend.'

Flora's face falls. 'That's a shame,' she says.

I need to get away before she invites me on her pink-themed hen do. I've also spotted Autumn Jones over her shoulder. She's the fashion designer married to the American media mogul who owns the studio that's making the movie of my book. He's very attractive. And very, very rich. *Oligarch* rich. I'm wearing one of Autumn's dresses from her new collection. I just bought it yesterday and I know it looks great. I lost the baby weight within weeks, knowing I had this big launch coming up. I was helped along by a little speed, of course.

When Autumn sees me she steps away from her little knot of friends, holds out her slender arms and holds me by the hands as we air kiss three times, something I make a mental note of. It's a symbol of entry to these upper echelons, like a Masonic handshake. One must know all the rules.

'Darling,' she says to me, 'you look amazing in that dress. What a success today is!'

'Thank you,' I say.

Autumn used to be a model and standing beside her, I come over all funny. My blood starts to run cold but I can feel my face overheating. Beside her, I feel frumpy and unremarkable and the old Lizzie starts to make a reappearance. I hastily shove her back into the darkness where I've long-since banished her.

Autumn returns to the conversation she was having with a man to her left, and I realise no one is looking at me. They're all listening to Autumn who's regaling them with some story about a three-day green juice fast she just did, which sounds about as hilarious as the colonic she's now describing. I'm excluded. It's my party and no one is noticing me. Even James has vanished with the baby. I might as well be invisible.

I drop my glass. Splinters land on Autumn's shoes and champagne splatters her dress. 'I'm so sorry,' I say, aghast. 'Here, let me help.'

I dab at her dress with a napkin. 'No worries,' she tells me with a saccharine smile. 'It'll come out.'

We both bend down to pick up the glass shards at our feet. 'I love your shoes,' she says, nodding at my purple suede platform heels.

'Thanks,' I say. 'I bought them especially. Louboutin. Vintage.'

'They're fab,' she answers. We stand up and she takes two more glasses of champagne from the tray of a passing waiter and hands me one. She chinks her glass against mine. 'To you,' she says.

'To me,' I answer.

The house on Hampstead Heath is almost exactly what I dreamed of. I have a writing room and a gym in the basement and a walk-in wardrobe, and there are marble counter-tops that I love to run my hands over, feeling their cool, hard blankness. The house cost a pretty penny but I persuaded James we could stretch to it if he sold his flat. We had a baby on the way so he couldn't really argue.

There are a group of ladies in North London who lunch. The glitterati who appear in *Tatler* and 'About Town' segments of various papers. I've finally managed to finagle my way into their little gatherings. It took some time: a few donations here and there to charities they support; following them all on Instagram and liking their inane pictures of their children; friendly emails to ask their advice on nannies and schools; casually bumping into them at the right Pilates classes while drinking the right Kombucha and wearing the right lululemon leggings; carefully curating my own Instagram and Facebook with stylish shots of my many #blessings, marrying substance with frippery and cuteness with edginess in just the right way, until finally they sent the formal invitation to become their friend via a Facebook request.

This is only my second lunch with them, these half-dozen women who sit astride the top layers of society. They're royalty, without actually being royalty. They have millions of followers, though I'm catching up fast.

As I walk into the restaurant and see a few people double-take, recognising me from all the press, no doubt, I feel like I've finally arrived. If only my mother could see me now. If only that girl from three years ago with the sweat-stained armpits could see me now. How far I've come. What I've achieved. Who I am now. But, of course, my mother can't see me. I've cut off all contact. I didn't want her to embarrass me.

I smile as I catch my reflection in the gilded mirrors behind the bar. There's no sign of the old me at all. She's gone into hiding. The scar above my eye healed so well that I only needed one cosmetic procedure. Now you can't see it. I look amazing. 'You're everything,' I whisper to myself. I must have said it out loud, though, because a passing waiter gives me a funny look.

Autumn stands up to wave me over and my happiness dulls. Maybe it's her smile. Or how slim she looks, or the fact her hair is the colour of honey and spun gold. Whatever it is, it throws me momentarily off my stride. But I don't let my smile falter. As I sit down opposite her, along the banquette, I make a note to get my highlights redone tomorrow. Maybe I'll find out who did hers.

All the women greet me with enthusiasm. I'm seated next to Cora Webb, who I haven't met before but who I recognise from TV. She's much smaller in real life, with cat-like eyes and a little snub nose. She starts chatting to me instantly, acting as if we're old friends.

'I love your book!' she says. 'I bought it on my Kindle and I've finished it already! My goodness, you poor thing. Everything you've been through.'

I turn to her and she squeezes my arm. There's that sympathy look – the one I'm getting used to seeing but am still not bored of.

'Becca was totally insane!' she says. 'It must have been so terrifying.'

'It was,' I say. I think we could become firm friends, Cora and I.

As everyone starts picking at their salads, I reach across the table for the bottle of water. Cora gasps loudly and puts a hand to her chest like a Victorian lady having a spell.

'Oh my goodness,' she says, her eyes widening with alarm. She's staring at my hand.

I turn it over slowly, so everyone can see the scar across my palm.

'Is that from . . . the fight?' she asks, staring at it as if it's some kind of religious relic.

I nod, stroking a finger up the pink keloid ridge. I can't feel anything. It's numb to the touch. Bowing my head, I pull my hand in closer to my body and lower my eyes.

'I'm so sorry,' Cora whispers and I nod appreciatively in her direction, biting my lip as if I'm reliving the moment. There are condoling murmurs around the table and a few heads shaking in disbelief at all I've suffered. I smile at everyone, blinking away tears. Aren't they all so kind?

After the moment has passed and everyone has returned
to their salads as though they're looking for the elixir of youth
among the lettuce leaves, I draw back my sleeves and pick up
my knife and fork. There's another gasp from Cora, though
this time quieter. 'What happened?' she asks me under her
breath, nodding at the ring of bruises circling my wrist.

'Oh,' I say, quickly pulling my sleeves back down to hide
them. 'Nothing. I just . . . um . . . hurt myself in Pilates.'

Cora exchanges a look with the woman on her other side
who has also been listening. It's an archly knowing look.
They aren't buying my Pilates story. It is rather lame.
Deliberately so.

We keep eating and I mostly listen, gathering snippets of
gossip that I file away for future use. I also make sure to ask
a few questions too. These women love to talk about their
children, their children's nannies, breastfeeding (I agree with
them wholeheartedly that breast is best) and their facialists.
It's quite dull but I suppose necessary.

'Your nanny is a bit gorgeous,' Autumn says to me, across
the table, taking a sip of her sparkling water.

I shrug. Swedish Ursula is fairly attractive, she's right,
though gorgeous is overselling it somewhat. 'She's fantastic
with Lucette,' I say and the other women murmur at my
magnanimity and my trust in my husband. None of them
would trust their husbands with an Ursula.

I'm fairly sure, at this particular moment in time, Ursula is
shagging my husband. She's doing me a favour. The whole
sex thing is so disgusting and frankly, a cheating husband is
also a guilty husband and a guilty husband is a husband who
likes to spend money on his wife. I have photographic
evidence stashed away of the two of them going at it like
they're starring in a shit homemade porn movie, evidence of

which I'll take to my lawyer when I leave James in a year or two, accusing him of both adultery and domestic abuse. I should get the house and a substantial settlement.

He's only laid a finger on me once. He learned the error of his ways. Like most bullies he's a coward at heart. All it took was someone standing up to him and he backed right off. Or maybe he's still a bully and works out his frustration instead on Ursula and his secretary, who he's also having an affair with. I don't really care. It will make it even easier when I go to the police.

'Aren't you worried having the nanny living in, rather than in a place of her own?' Autumn asks. 'I would be if I were you!'

'No,' I say to her. Why would I be worried? Is she suggesting Ursula is better looking than me? That's not the reason James is screwing her. He fucks her because he can't fuck me. I know that Autumn's not taking any chances with Johnny, her husband – the billionaire media mogul who owns a yacht the size of a small country and his own island in the Caribbean. He isn't given a chance to fuck the nannies because she employs only middle-aged Filipinas, a fact I've gathered from stalking Autumn's Facebook page.

When the bill comes, the waiter sets it down in the centre of the table. I'm busy applying lipstick but peek out the corner of my eye as Autumn picks it up and after a few seconds of figuring the bill out in her head, tells everyone it's a hundred pounds each.

I pick up my Chloé handbag – a guilt gift from James – and root around in it for my wallet (my Christmas present to myself), pulling out two crisp fifty-pound notes, as the other women throw down platinum cards and cash like they're poker chips.

Autumn gathers all the money and cards and then frowns. 'We seem to be missing a hundred in cash.'

We all look at each other. After an uncomfortable beat, Cora pipes up. 'Oh, just put the extra on my card. It doesn't matter.'

With the bill settled we get up to leave. I link my arm through Cora's as we walk to the exit. 'Did you see?' I whisper into her ear. 'Autumn didn't pay her share.'

Cora's eyes widen like they do in cartoons and her mouth forms a perfect O as she glances over at Autumn, who hurries over to walk with us.

'Will I see you at dinner Saturday?' she says to me. 'Johnny can't wait to meet you.'

She's invited us to her and her husband's palatial house in Primrose Hill for dinner and drinks this weekend. I smile to myself.

'I can't wait to meet him either.'

Celebrating 8 weeks in the *Sunday Times* bestseller list by sailing around the Caribbean with friends and family. This is the life! **#caribbeansailing #friendswithyachts #whitesandbeach #holiday #yogaondeck #thankgoodnessfornannies #privatechef #yolo #gratitude #blessed #bestfriendsever #friendslikethese**

Acknowledgements

Writing a novel is always an undertaking, not least when you have six weeks in which to do it. I'm grateful above all to my own besthusbandever John, my partner in crime. We've had quite the journey together travelling the world, following our dreams, (re)making our lives over and over, and his support of my chosen career is something I can't adequately express thanks for. Being the partner of a writer isn't fun. It requires a lot of morale boosting and wine pouring and tear wiping and a lot of listening patiently to stories that start 'Imagine if . . .' and end with something about serial killers or the zombie apocalypse. John does it all and more without complaint and has never wavered in his love, or belief in me or us and in extraordinary potential. I love you!

And Alula my darling love, a brilliant writer and creative spirit, there are no words to describe the absolute joy of being your mamma, even when you interrupt me when I'm in the middle of a sentence to ask if I've seen your leotard / book / hairbrush.

I also have to thank my dad and Carol, the best nonno and nonna, for enduring something I could never, something far harder than writing a book: a whole week at Disneyworld with Alula – all so I could work on this book edit. You guys are the best.

My amazing agent Amanda, who I've been with for almost ten years and who has helped me publish a dozen books – I am so grateful that you fell in love with Lila all those years ago and hope our partnership continues until I'm an old lady and it's no longer appropriate for me to write 'erotica' (as my dad puts it), or YA, but I am still going strong in the psychological thriller territory.

Ruth at Hodder, whose editing really was extraordinary and who helped me hone the novel into exactly the shape I didn't even know it needed to be – thank you. It's a gift and you have it and I have loved working with you.

And finally, as I move through life (crossing continents) the thing I always wish I could take with me in my suitcase are the friends I've made along the way. I am far prouder of my friendships than of any book or movie I have written. So thank you, Nichola, Vic, Rachel, Sara, Lauren, Asa, Claire, Clarissa and Becky – the best girlfriends on the planet, who lift me up, inspire me and make me laugh every single day. And not to forget the boys in my life too: Alby, Laurie (I stole your last name for my detective!) and my brother Tom.

With friends like these . . . I am #blessed beyond measure. ;)